This book captured my in
book to put down. Good insight into the civil war era.

Kathryn V Bell—California

Want to go west Lady is the best civil war novel that I have read. Ben has captured the drama, and the tragedy, of the era.

Betty Gard—Oregon

A fascinating book filled with action, romance, and historical facts. So compelling the reader can hardly bear to put it down until the last word has been, devoured.

Sandra Gallagher—New Mexico

A gripping story that puts the reader right there. The characters are so real, I felt they were family and I laughed and cried along with them.

Evelyn Burns—California

This "Endorsement," is not you're usual! It's from the heart of a friend. This story is of a time I should have lived in. It has a strong and true story line. Great clean and entertaining reading. The author has a big heart.

Ann Davidson—New Mexico

A compelling story filled with facts and so real life one almost smells the gun smoke and hears the wagons creak. A must read for both history buffs and romantics.

Irene Steinlage—California

I read the book and it was delightful. I really enjoyed reading about the effect of Civil War on peoples lives instead of the usual war story. Ben could do a sequel to that one. Congratulations on a job well done.

Shirley Knowles—California

Ben Steinlage's portrayal of life during the Civil War, will make readers feel as though they were there living it. Looking forward to its sequel.

Roy Sain—Minnesota

Ben Steinlage has written a well, researched historical novel of the Civil War times. It is, written with insight and empathy for the people caught up in the struggles of the war and aftermath of it.

Roberta McSparrin—Idaho

Want to go West Lady?

Want to go West Lady?

a novel by

Ben Steinlage

TATE PUBLISHING & *Enterprises*

Want to Go West Lady?
Copyright © 2007 by Ben Steinlage All rights reserved.

This title is also available as a Tate Out Loud product. Visit www.tatepublishing.com for more information.

No part of this publication may be reproduced, stored in a retrieval system or transmitted in any way by any means, electronic, mechanical, photocopy, recording or otherwise without the prior permission of the author except as provided by USA copyright law.

This novel is a work of fiction. However, several names, descriptions, entities and incidents included in the story are based on the lives of real people.

The opinions expressed by the author are not necessarily those of Tate Publishing, LLC.

Published by Tate Publishing & Enterprises, LLC
127 E. Trade Center Terrace | Mustang, Oklahoma 73064 USA
1.888.361.9473 | www.tatepublishing.com

Tate Publishing is committed to excellence in the publishing industry. The company reflects the philosophy established by the founders, based on Psalms 68:11,
"The Lord gave the word and great was the company of those who published it."

Book design copyright © 2007 by Tate Publishing, LLC. All rights reserved.
Cover design by Brandon Wood
Interior design by Janae J. Glass

Published in the United States of America

ISBN: 978-1-60247-433-8
07.04.09

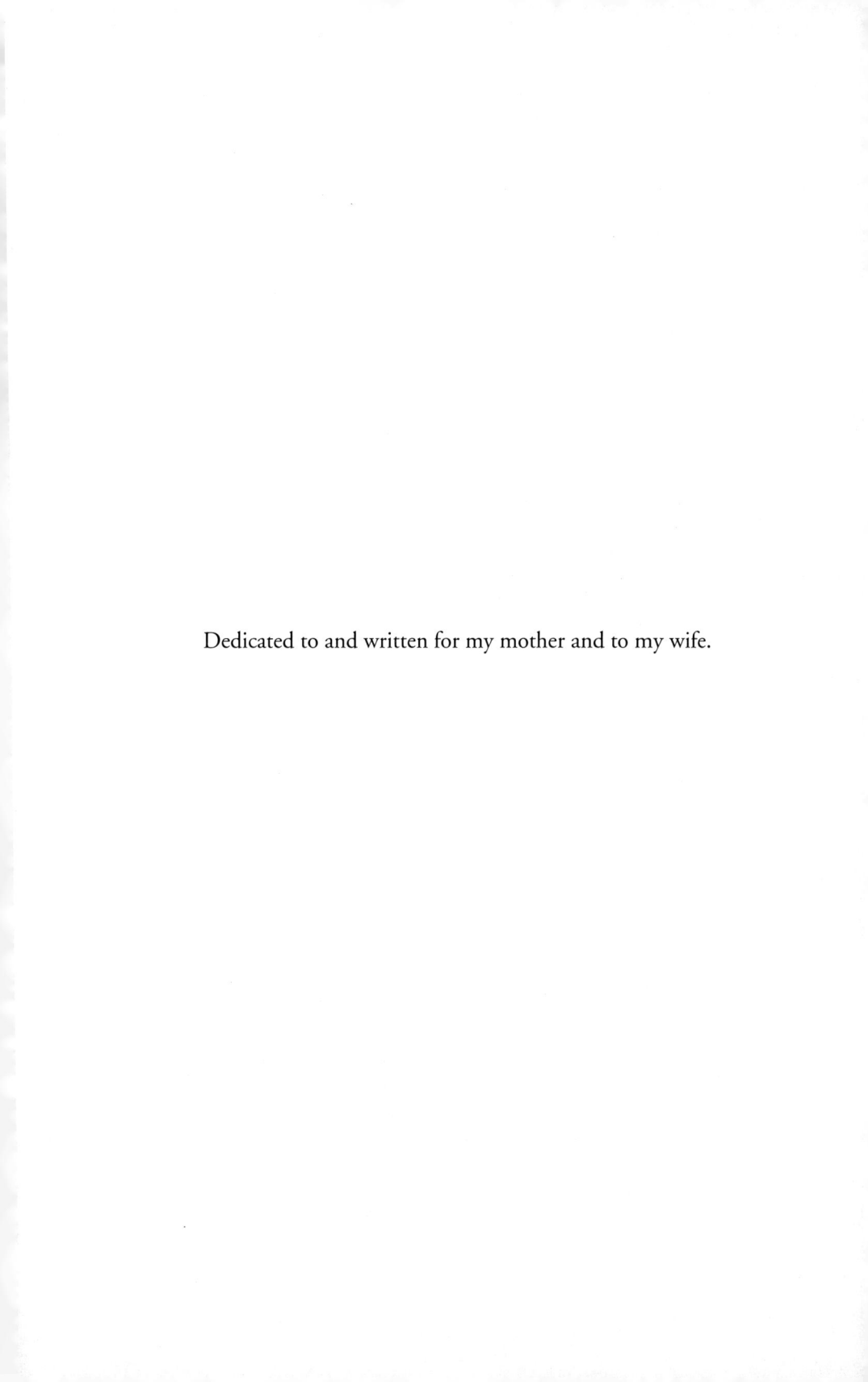

Dedicated to and written for my mother and to my wife.

Introduction

In the late eighteen-nineties and the first of the twentieth century, my great, great-Grandfather was a runner for a San Francisco Newspaper. After working for the paper as a runner for a few years, he decided to become a reporter. After many talks with the Editor, he didn't get far. A reporter for the paper told him to find a good story and write it. If it was good enough the Editor might change his mind. From that day on, he began looking for a subject to write about.

In the first part of 1906, he found his subject. With the interest still being high about the Westward movement, he thought he would write something about it. He decided to write about a couple that had made the move west in a covered wagon. After searching for weeks, he found a couple passing through town and interviewed them. This couple was to be Matt and Ida Duncan.

The one emotion that caught my eye was the openness of Matt and Ida throughout the story, except for the ending.

A few years ago, I found the interview in an old luggage. It turned out that he never wrote his article. However, the couple had an interesting story, and then the earthquake happened. Rather than working at the paper, the newspaper office was destroyed and he went into construction. In the end, he found his calling and the business he started is still owned and ran by the family relatives.

I, on the other hand like him, like to write. In reading the notes on his interview, I fell in love with the couple. With it being nearly a hundred years later, their love for each other has a beautiful ring. I had a problem that I wanted to know the rest of their story. At the same time Matt seemed to be short and to the point, not elaborating on anything. This is what drove me to find a diary to learn what took place. Most of all, I wanted to know what happened to them after my Grandfather interviewed them.

I decided to try to find the surviving relatives of this couple. My hopes were that they might have some information that I might be able to use. After eighteen months on the internet, I tracked down their relatives. Luck was with me, for they had the woman's diary. They were cooperative enough to let me take notes from it. What I found can be read in the last chapter.

Though the story I give you is based on the truth, the names and places have been changed.

From the actual author–Though as the "Introduction" states, the story is based on facts except the "Reporter" want-to-be. To my mother and different relatives, I offer my apologies. In telling the story as simply as I know it, I have tried to put them into a true Civil War era perspective for the reader's sake. I had no wish to make any relative look bad. Still, what I have written are truths as in the way it was back during that era, good or bad. I hope my relatives of this period did not suffer as Ida and Matt did.

Ida (Marsh) Duncan

The "Civil War" was a difficult period for me as it was for everyone of that time. It made me grow up faster than time did. For most, the war came as a shock in 1861. My family began planning for it a few years earlier. Though my Father began talking about secession before I was born, my first memory was the afternoon of September 9, 1859. I can remember that because my birthday was two days later.

That afternoon, we were on the Veranda.

"September 11, 1849," my father said to my mother as she walked out onto the veranda. Then as he sat down a drink for her, he asked her, "Does the date ring a bell for you?"

"Oh Harold…don't be so mean. She knows what day it is," Mama answered, giving me one of her big grins. Patting me on my knee, she told him, "I remember the day well … on that day, ten years ago, our little Ida was born."

I'm the daughter of Harold and Annabelle Marsh. Being their daughter wasn't the easiest person to be. They regularly reminded me of our importance in the county. Many times I wished I were one of the slave kids and had something to do. However, that was not what I was born into. My reaction to having a birthday was "Whoopee." I knew in two days I would be ten years old; I was so excited, and it almost put me to sleep. I wanted to add to their comments, "Yes, on this day little Ida Marsh was born. She had such curly blonde locks everyone just loved her. And that's not to mention my rosy red cheeks everyone had a need to pinch." I had heard that every year since. Now after ten years, I wasn't the normal little girl. I didn't care to have my hair done up in curls but preferred braids. I also preferred getting dirty to staying clean.

In general, everyone thought I looked a lot like Mama. She was a blonde with a thin body. It wasn't that father was heavy but he was taller than Mama and had dark hair. Dressed up, the two of them were a perfect couple. The major difference between them was Father was a loud demanding speaker. In reality, he wasn't so much demanding but taller than most. With his height and position in the area, people didn't bother to argue with him. His way of achieving goals was what I inherited from him.

In later years, I would hear how wonderful I must have had it living on a plantation. Being a plantation owner's daughter was a fascination for people. It was and would have been if it weren't for the war. As with everything, plantation life had its drawbacks. One of the biggest ones was that it didn't prepare me to take care of my loved ones or myself. What it took to live a full life I learned the hard way.

I always found it interesting how some people's understanding of the south was so far from the truth. In learning I was from the south, they would say how sorry they were that we lost everything in the war; everyone lost being Northern or Southern. They would answer, "Yes that's true I guess." Then there were those that would call me a "Rebel." None of them understood what we were fighting for and what it was like living in a battlefield.

They were right about what a plantation looked like. Their visual idea was the only correct assumption. Oh, it was one of those big white houses with a long drive going up to it. The lane going to the house had trees planted every twenty feet for a half-mile, then the house was two stories, with a wrap around veranda and white columns. The windows reached from the floor to the ceiling. To each side of the drive were fields full of cotton. However, in reality, my father said the cotton in our fields was a joke. He had to grow ten acres for every one he used to just to break even. Still we had over five thousand acres. Then further up, closer to the house, we had our horses. Then like most, we had a village for the workers a quarter a mile away.

"Maybe we could have a few kids over the day after tomorrow for a celebration of it…a birthday celebration," Mama suggested.

Mama was born to entertain and it didn't matter what the reason. Father on the other hand was born to fulfill Mama's needs. I didn't understand any of it, but I did enjoy seeing Mama come alive.

"I guess we would have to invite the Buchanan boy…Edgar?" My Father asked with a grin.

Being his only child, he got a kick out of teasing me. He was right, in the sense that Edgar and I had always gotten along. Unfortunately, we didn't see each other that often, but we still kept in touch. We kept in touch by mail, passed along from one slave to another. I always wondered if Mama or Father ever knew about our correspondences. If they had, I'm sure I would have gotten more teasing.

"She's always saying she's going to marry him. I guess we had better invite him and his family…if you think we must," Mama answered giving me and my father a big grin.

I wondered who she was trying to fool; Mrs. Buchanan was her best friend. Not inviting her best friend would have meant not inviting anyone. Then again, it seemed everything in our lives was a set of games. We did things to impress others and then we did things to impress ourselves.

"I guess it's settled then. We'll have a big dinner with our friends," he announced, proud of himself. "Your mother might come up with some games." Then taking a sip of his drink, he suggested, "Us fathers have hunting or riding; your mother and her friends have their food and impressing one another."

"Thanks Hon, you are so complimentary," Mama said in her defense.

"Just like to put everyone into their place," he answered, and then he went on, "the boys will probably want to play that new game… what's it called…? Ah, baseball and you girls can watch."

"Might be better than playing one of those dumb board games," I told him, not thinking him all that funny. Then to get the last laugh I told them both, "Edgar and I can take a walk down to the pond and talk or something."

"That's enough of that idea, Miss Ida," Father told me in a sharp tone of voice.

"Really, Father, we can discuss the number of children we are going to have…where we are going to live," I added to give him a bad time.

"Ida," Father said in a manner that said I might have gone too far.

"I was only kidding," I told him, hoping he would cool off.

"Now, now…enough of that. Let's leave it with me telling the staff about the party, "Mama said, getting up and setting her drink down. Not wanting to put too much stress on an overworked staff, she liked to warn them.

"You are not going to make me dance or any of that stuff are you?" I asked my Father. It didn't matter if it was my birthday or not, any reason was good enough to invite people over.

The day of my birthday, the house was busy getting ready for our company. The windows were all lifted open to their highest positions, so everyone could come in from every direction off the veranda to get something to eat. Then our male slaves, dressed in their little jackets, would be bringing drinks for everyone.

Mama and I had our hair done up into buns and wore our flowery broad brim hats, with ribbons hanging down the back. We wore our long full pleated dresses, looking elegant. Mama's was a solid blue, where mine was white with yellow flowers. I was more than willing to change the dress for pants, then I could chase the boys around and have some fun. In talking to Mama, I was to look like a lady and not worry about playing games or horseback riding.

Most people think of plantation ladies or girls different from others. They think of them as if they pranced around in a frilly dress, broad brim hats with ribbons flowing from them and not wearing anything else. They think we didn't do anything but sit around looking pretty.

Want to Go West Lady?

It wasn't like that, and I was glad for that. Though we had those clothes, I preferred my dirty cotton pants and my old shirt. You were more likely to find me in with the hogs or up a tree than on the Veranda. When I was in the house, it was for schooling, to learn woman things or to eat and sleep.

"We don't have to make a big deal out of it," I told him. I didn't like these affairs, so I would rather keep it small. I knew it was a waste of time to object but I had to try.

"Come over here," he said patting his lap.

"Yes father," I answered, getting off my chair. I thought I was too old to sit in his lap, still it was a longtime habit. Reaching him, I told him, "I think I'm getting a little old for your lap."

"She is a young lady now, Harold," Mama reminded him. She straightened her dress giving us both a smile.

"Yes, I guess she is…I guess it isn't proper for young ladies to sit on their father's laps. I guess it is time for them to find another lap to sit on," he said. He brushed his lap off and looked sad not having me sit on it anymore.

"Oh Father," I answered, feeling a little funny about his comment, perhaps this once.

"Well then, why don't you want a party?" he asked.

"It is so much trouble," I told him looking up into his eyes. I wanted to have everyone over no matter what the occasion. I enjoyed having kids over like myself. I hardly got a chance to see them. Unlike most kids in the city, I didn't have a choice of friends one might like. In addition, as the city kids that went to city schools, I went to school at home. What students there were, learning with me, were slave kids (even then, they were few).

"But you deserve it," my Mama said as she rejoined us. Then as she sat back down, she picked up her drink and took a sip of it. Setting it back down, she told us, "It is all arranged with the staff, so don't worry about it."

"Yes Mama," I answered, not willing to argue with her. Now don't get me wrong, I have nothing against black people. Most of my friends were as black as tar. My two best friends were Sammy and Rachael, both slave children. They were my only reason for not wanting the birthday celebration. My parents wouldn't allow them to attend.

"You work out the details and one of the boys will take the invitations around," father told her with a smile.

"To be honest, I took care of that last week," she told him with a smile.

"I know, Jacob told me. Oh, I heard in town that Jeff Davis and his friends are at it again," my Father told my Mama. Taking a sip of his drink he went on to tell her, "If those old boys do vote for secession, I wonder what it is going to do to our taxes."

"Are the Slave Taxes due next week?" she asked him.

"Yes, and it is more money than I want to give them," he told her.

"The thirty or so you are paying for is better than what it would have been if we still had the three-hundred we used to," she reminded him.

"That's one way of looking at it," he answered and he went into the house. Then coming back out, he asked, "Anyone want anything?"

Mama and I both shook our head no. I looked over at the table next to mama and saw the needle pointing I was suppose to do. I decided to work on it later.

I tried to remember when we had as many slaves as Mama was talking about. I remembered having a lot more than we did then, but not that many. Still, when I was five or six, we had a lot more. The place was a busy place, with this and that being cleaned and polished. The slaves would almost cut each blade one at a time. There were so many, Mama didn't have to worry about me falling, there was someone right there to catch me.

"These drinks sure seem good today," Father said as he came back out onto the veranda. Sitting down, he went on with his frustration of taxes by saying, "If I could, I would make all of our slaves free."

"Why don't you father?" I asked, having never heard him make such a statement, and made me interested.

"I offered freedom to all of our slaves some years ago," he answered and then he went on to add, "with their freedom, I would give them a track of land. All I asked was ten percent of their crops. A good number took me up on the offer; others said they wouldn't know what to do with freedom. It seemed they were happy with their life as it was…not that I understand it or argue; I do understand I am part of making them what they are. People like me have made them slaves and now it is up to me to train them into taking their freedom and make something of themselves. The ones that can't handle it, I owe them everything they need."

I can't say I didn't understand what he was saying, but I did. My father was himself, I think, having problems with freeing the slaves. His parents raised him to believe a man had a right to own slaves. Now he had seen the economic side and other issues on the subject. He found himself caught between doing what was right and making his parents look wrong, and being his own man.

Even at that age, I knew what they were talking about. Eighteen years before my birth, the south decided to succeed from the Union. Virginia's negative vote kept the Southern States from seceding. My father was one of the believers that did not want to secede. He understood the need of the north to control his financial position, though he didn't approve it. They were undercutting the price he was selling the cotton by doing their own fleecing (with the Cotton Gin).

My father understood the fact that it was just business. He didn't understand the feeling the north had about his having free labor. The money it cost him to house, clothe, feed and take care of their health needs was astronomical. Then in the early 1860's, he was giving his workers shares of our land for a portion of their crops.

Most of his financial problems he blamed on himself. Having heard and seen in reading, he knew land suffered for a lack of nutrients, and that by switching out the crops he could bring life back to the soil. When he began to believe it, he didn't have the money to do it. The only thing that kept us alive was his side interest. In the late 1800's, he set up a small manufacturing plant. The plant made shovels, picks, and gold pans. The gold rush in California in the year 1849 made us a comfortable living. As the gold fever died in one area, it picked up elsewhere. He didn't make as much as he did at first, but he made a living.

Another reason he was against the secession was the relatives we had up north. My father and mother had brothers and sisters, as well as aunts and uncles, living from New York to Illinois. If the South, were to secede from the Union, that could mean cutting them off from us. With our family being a close family, it didn't matter what the distance was we were one.

"They don't want to face facts," my Father answered. Lighting his pipe, he went on to tell her, "We have brought all this onto ourselves. Seceding isn't going to solve anything…other than getting loans from France perhaps."

"Have you heard anything from your friend Robert Lee?" she asked him. Robert E. Lee was one of my father's favorite friends, a well-educated, outspoken, and loyal friend. Whenever my father needed advice, he went to him for help.

"He wrote me, and said he was in hopes they would change their minds," he answered her. Then taking a thoughtful puff, he went on to tell her, "On the downside, he said if we did secede, he would have to support it."

"Can I go now," I asked him. I knew where this conversation was going.

"Bet I know where you want to go," he told me, shaking his head. He just didn't understand why I liked going where I did. He went on to tell me, "Be careful in the village."

The village for the workers was probably my most favorite place to go. The music coming from there was always exciting, though my father said the "Black man's" music was sinful. Still, I found it to be exciting because it made me want to dance. Even at that, I didn't like to dance with boys. I could spend hours down there listening to them play. I have to be honest that at night I was a little scared, but not during the day.

Then, in addition, there were the little Mammies that could make anything. They could take bark off a tree and make some of the best meals you could ever eat. I probably learned more there than anywhere else. There wasn't anything those black women couldn't make. Yet, they knew as I did, we were not the same.

My father used to say if I spent too much time in the slave village I would turn black. I would leave the village, and check my skin out for years. When I reached nine or so, I knew he was only kidding. To get even with him, I rolled myself in mud. Once the mud was dry, I went into his study and told him my skin was changing color. He looked at me, and laughed at the sight of me. He suggested that I might want to find a white puddle of mud. Then rolling in it, I might be acceptable to sit at his dinner table.

With my experience in the little slave village, I learned a lot about cooking. To this day, the meals I cook have the flavors I learned there. I wish I could go back and thank them for everything they taught me. More children could learn a lot from those people. If nothing else, how lonely a group of people can be.

"I will," I told him. I thought I might check out the stables first. One of our mares had dropped a colt a few days earlier. My father had told me he could be mine to ride when he was old enough.

"I bet I know where she's going first," my Mama said, watching me head for the steps.

"Checking out your colt first?" My Father asked with a smile of understanding.

"I might look in on the little ugly creature," I answered with a giggle. He knew and recognized my love for horses. Mama didn't share our love of horses, but she didn't disapprove, she just didn't understand it.

As I left them, I wished I could leave and live on my own. From not having any friends, to people that could accept the talk of war, I was tired of it all. I didn't care or understand all the talking about secession or war. In fact, I got tired of hearing about all the problems there were with the crops and all. I didn't care if I had to run away from home or marry Edgar. In fact, I used marrying Edgar as a threat for so long Mama didn't worry about it anymore. In the end, I think the continual threat brought about our marriage years later. Still, that's another story for later.

"My life isn't all bad," I remembered thinking as I got to the stables. I decided I needed to see the colt, for he was cute. At the same time, I was getting tired of the negative side of my life. There were several good events also.

"Good afternoon, Ms. Marsh," a squeaky voice greeted me.

"Good afternoon, Jacob," I replied to a friend of mine. He was the son of our stable tender Samuel. At the time, he had become shy because his voice was changing. Personally, I thought it sounded cute. "How's the little fella?" I asked him as I went into the stable.

"He's bouncing around like a rabbit," he answered, following me to his stall.

"I can hear him," I told him, listening to the commotion in the next stall. "Been working with Jocko."

"A little," he answered with a smile as if he had gotten away with something.

"Come to check on the colt?" Samuel asked with a grin. Then lifting the bar up that held the gate closed, he asked me, "Want to pet him? He may not be ready for riding, but he does like having his nose scratched."

"Can I?" I asked a little too excited. The colt had seen me and jumped back away from me. As I hesitated, I asked him, "Can I feed him some hay or a carrot?"

"Not right now, missies," he answered, and then added, "and he's not big enough to ride either."

"I know that. You think I don't know anything," I told him as I went into the stall and scratched the colt on the forehead.

"I didn't say you didn't know anything, I just wanted to make sure you did the right thing for him," he said giving me a grin.

I didn't stay long, but I did enjoy watching the colt. I did help Jacob give the mare some hay. As the mare ate some hay, the colt went to her and nursed a little. So mother and son were having a snack together. Then from there, I went down to the village.

In the village, I found a female slave of ours called Mary. It was funny how excited she got when I came by to visit. We hugged each other and then she settled back to her wash. I had the feeling she thought of me as her daughter. I sat on a rickety stool under a tree so I could watch and talk to her.

I asked her, "Why don't you talk about your homeland?"

"This is my homeland," she answered, giving me a strange look. Then hanging a dress on a line, she reminded me, "I was born right here, the same as you. My Mammy and Daddy weren't born in this country, but I was."

"Did they tell you about their homeland?" I asked, knowing if she was like the others, she didn't care to talk about the subject.

"Just that they couldn't understand their Chief selling them to the slave trader for two shinny bracelets," she answered as she hung a shirt up.

"Mama says she's from Whales and Father said his Grandfather swam behind a ship from England. Mama also said Father's Grandfather was a wealthy man in England. Wherever they came from doesn't matter. Like you, this is my country," I told her. Then thinking a little bit about her, I wondered if she missed her parents.

As often was the case, we both did our own thing and said nothing. I knew she wanted more out of life, as most of her kind did. At the same time, so did most of my friends, so we shared something. Still, I knew I was free and she wasn't. I decided to break the silence; I found it boring just sitting there.

"You miss them a lot?" I asked her. My father had told me he had to sell them seven years ago when money got tight.

"Yes," she answered. Then to change the subject, she asked me, "Want some sugar candy?"

"Can I," I answered, knowing her sugar candy was the best. I found it hard to think about not having my parents. My parents were my whole life, and to be without them it would be like death.

After getting another load, she told me, "I do hear from them once in awhile. You know, this talk of freedom has me worried."

"How's that?" I asked her and then I added, "Why does it worry you?"

"What would I do? I have everything I need now. What would I do if I were free, other than find my parents, but after that…I don't know," she said. Then looking at me seriously, "It sounds so good, but I'm not for it. Look at your parents…are they free? They have responsibilities, taxes that tie them down to the daily drudgery; so are they free? It's more of a term those fancy people use, with no real meaning. I'm not sure if I want freedom. Your people have been good to us and we owe you a lot. Why leave what I like and love."

Though she made me feel good, she also confused me. What is freedom; do I understand what it means? Is it an empty term as she says it is? Is it something that in reality is controlled by the government? She raised more questions, then she gave me answers. Just hearing that she had heard of the idea of freeing slaves surprised me.

I spent the rest of the afternoon visiting with other friends in the village. I even got into a stick game the kids played. In playing with them, I got so dirty I knew my mama was going to be upset. Still I knew she would understand. When she complained that I wasn't ladylike, I would remind her, "At least I haven't been playing with the pigs."

The weather promised to be perfect for the birthday celebration. Everything was green and the flowers were coming out. It was one of those days you were glad to be alive. The first carriage to pull up to the house was the Merrick's. Everyone got out and we gave them a friendly greeting.

"Haven't seen you for a while," Paula Merrick said, taking my arms and giving me a peck on the cheek.

"It has been awhile," I answered, giving her a peck also.

"Hasn't Paula grown up into a little lady," I could hear Mama tell Mrs. Merrick.

"In no time at all it seems, but Ida has also become a little lady," Mrs. Merrick replied.

Within a few minutes, one family after another, everyone was getting out of their carriages exchanging niceties. It was getting so thick I was surprised no one was getting sick.

"Is Edgar coming?" Paul Bartlett asked as he came up to me with a glass of lemonade in his hand. I noticed he was carrying a stick in his hand.

"I know Mama and Father invited the Buchanan's," I answered.

"Good, I'm hoping he wants to play a game of baseball," he told me.

"You boys always have to be hitting something," I replied.

"You or a ball," he answered with a grin.

"I guess a ball might be more enjoyable," I replied with a smile.

Then looking down the lane, I saw a carriage coming toward the house. I tell Paul, "I think they are about to arrive."

"Good. Maybe we will have enough of us guys to play a game," he said as he turned to watch the carriage pulling up.

"Good morning, Ida, Paul," Edgar said in greeting us. He then walked up to me, took my hand, and kissed it.

"Good morning, Edgar. Want to play some ball?" Paul had asked him.

"Good morning, Edgar, good of you and your family to come," I replied.

"Maybe later, Paul," Edgar answered Paul's question, without taking his eyes off me and grinned.

As with my parents, we all formed our little groups. In these different groups, we did different things. Most of the boys headed for the open field, as the girls mainly talked and walked around. They also wandered to the field to watch the boys.

Though Edgar and I talked to a few other kids, we started out sitting on a step and talked.

"I've got a new horse," Edgar told me.

"What color?" I asked him.

"Chestnut," He answered.

"I have a new colt myself," I told him.

"Let's go and see it," he suggested, with a look of enthusiasm.

"Good," I answered as I got up taking his hand. Then we headed for the stable.

After checking out my colt, we checked out the other horses. When the stable began to fill up with the adults looking at father's racehorses and talking races, we left.

We walked and talked enjoying each other's company. Finally, we found ourselves at the pond where we sat and watched, and talked about what we had been up to lately.

"To get even with my father, I have a question to ask of you," I told him.

"This is your party, ask," he answered.

"If or when we get married, how many children are we going to have?" I had to ask him to irritate father.

"Who said we were going to have children?" he asked.

"Everyone has children when they marry," I told him.

"Why not be different from everyone?" he asked grinning at me.

"Hi, am I interrupting anything?" Sharon asked, as she came up to us.

He loved to tease me and get me mad. I wondered why I was going to marry anyone so mean. In the end, I was glad Mama and Father had held the party. It was good to see the other kids, as well as Edgar.

"No, I think I should go down and play a little baseball any way," Edgar answered.

"That's fine with me," I told him giving him a wink. Then I turned my attention back to Sharon.

We talked for a while about boys and the foreseen war. We finally went down and joined the rest of the kids. By the time we got to the field the game was over. Everyone was sitting on the grass talking about the possibility of war.

"…It is stupid, thinking they can dictate what we can or cannot do," Edgar was telling Samuel, another of one of our friends.

"Then you think we should secede?" Mathew asked.

"Not really. Between the courts and congress, our differences should be able to be resolved," Edgar, answered.

"If we were to end in a war, are we going to fight?" Paul asked.

"You mean are we going to join the army?" Phil asked.

"Yes, stupid, us joining the army," Paul answered.

"But why would we have to go to war? Can't we just be two different countries?" Edward asked.

"First, the north has all the money. Second, the northern pride won't allow them to let us secede. And we wouldn't have enough money to support ourselves," Edgar stated.

"My father says Jeff Davis and his people have deals set up with the French," Paul told them all.

"That all takes time," Edgar pointed out.

This conversation continued for a while. Most of the girls left, finding the conservation boring. They found the discussion boring and unrealistic to think of their friends going to war.

...One year later...

I was amazed in thinking back to it all, but conversations, places and actions were all the same as the year before. Dad offering to invite Edgar and his family over, to me going to the village, it was all the same. My birthday was coming up again, and another celebration was in the making. The only difference was that I didn't sit in his lap and no new colt. I guess there was one other, and that was the growth in the interest in secession.

Last year at my birthday celebration, Edgar and his friends irritated me. It turned out the game of the season was playing war games. With everything being decorated as it was, war games and such didn't seem fitting. One of the boys embarrassed my friend Lori by using her as a place to hide. When another went to grab him, they knocked her off her feet. This little playfulness landed her in some mud.

"It looks like it might get bad," my Father said to Mama. Taking a puff on his pipe, he went on to add, "It looks like this Lincoln fellow is going to win the election."

"What difference does it make? Is he a bad man?" I asked him, looking at Mama for some understanding. I was beginning to realize there was more to life than fun. In fact, through the few kids I did see, it looked like a war might be brewing.

"Give your father a chance to get his thoughts together," Mama said, hoping to let it lay.

"That's all right, she's old enough to understand," he told her looking at me, hoping he hadn't lied.

I didn't say anything, hoping to get a simple answer. It seemed every time I asked him a question, I usually got a lecture. I did as my mother suggested and let him go at his own pace. She was right; in fact, he would get flustered when he felt he was being pushed.

"It's not that he is showing an interest in freeing slaves, as if there are that many slaves left. Like ours, they are all sharecroppers doing whatever they want," he said before he paused to puff on his pipe again.

"Master Marsh, Master Marsh," one of our slaves came up to the veranda yelling.

"What Joseph," Father answered him, not showing any interest in his excided approach.

"The mare is dead," he answered.

"I guess you need to bury her," my Father told him, as if he had expected it. Then as Joseph left he added, "She ate more than she was worth anyway."

"You were telling us about this Lincoln fellow," Mama reminded him.

"Yes…as I was saying, his views on slavery are not a major importance. Still, it might be interesting what he sees for the southern states. This is a major concern, where his opponent is a two-faced politician who might be worse."

"Where does this leave us as far as secession?" Mama, who didn't understand politics or financial conversations, asked.

"If you listen to those yahoos like Davis, we'll be seceding soon," he answered. Then taking another puff as he paused, he added, "With

Want to Go West Lady?

Davis in congress, you would think he could change congress's attitude. They are the ones that get things done, not some dumb President."

"Will seceding lead to war, daddy?" Mama asked him with a tear in her eye. Then as she wiped her eyes, she asked him, "Would you be going also?"

"Someone has to protect our land. It is like Lee said; we can't forget our homes, no matter what we would like."

"But...?" Mama began to ask, but Father interrupted her.

"The land isn't producing anything. The gold mining is almost over, so we are not making anything there. If we let them take the land, what do we have then?" he asked.

From what I heard a few days earlier, my father hadn't sold enough cotton to pay for it. Our meals were getting worse everyday. I had gotten old enough that I could go into our little town and talk to other kids my age. They told me their parents were saying not to worry, it would get better. I had a sickening feeling it was going to get a lot worse. Though it was later proved right, I never would have guessed how bad it would get.

Then at school, I learned Fort Sumter had been attacked by the confederate soldiers. With the Confederate attacking the fort, the north declared war on us. As soon as I got home, I told Father. He sat back in his chair and didn't say anything.

"Something wrong?" Mama asked as she came over to Father's side.

Father didn't say anything, but motioned for me to leave them alone. I left the two of them to talk.

Some time later, it began to get worse, but we didn't know it. Old Jeff Davis and Robert E. Lee came home. There were posters on every tree exclaiming how much better we were going to be. Then the same day, we learned the north was going to take us back; war was at hand.

"Do you have everything?" Mama asked my father, who was wearing his new uniform. He had been commissioned a General in the new army of the "Confederate States of America." Mama found strength and didn't complain but went with what Father said and did. Later I would get to know her, as I never thought I would.

"I think I have everything. With the Indian wars and everything, they won't want to fight for too long. I should be home in a few months," he told her.

Like myself, Mama knew better. We both knew we were in for hard times. We both watched him go down the lane on his horse. I'm not sure if Mama cried because I was to busy crying myself.

In the end, it wasn't long before a general came to the house. Following the general, there was a company of men. The men were on horseback and some in wagons. With their uniforms and flags flying, it was an impressive sight.

"Ma'am," the general said as he came up to our front door in greeting Mama.

"Yes," Mama answered him, looking worried at what he might say.

"The army needs to take your horses. I know you need them, but so do our men," he told her.

"I guess you have to do what you have to do. It would be helpful if you left us one," she told him, sounding as if she might be asking too much.

"Yes Ma'am," he answered. In the end, he took every horse.

It didn't take long for us to realize that without horses, we couldn't harvest the cotton. Though Mama got the sales part of the Plantation down quickly, it wasn't enough. We sold a few bales to Europe but we didn't make enough to live on. One morning Mama met me at the front door.

"It is planting time," she said, hiking up her skirt walking towards the barn.

I had the feeling she meant for me to join her. I stepped in right behind her more out of curiosity than anything else.

"Samuel, where's the seeds at?" Mama asked our favorite slave.

"Next to the barrel of gunpowder," he answered.

Looking around, we couldn't find the seeds or the gunpowder.

"I can't find either one," Mama told him.

"Honest Misses, it was there yesterday," he told us. Then lifting a corner of a blanket, he found the seeds. He had a big smile on his face and said, "Here's the seed."

"Thank you, Samuel," Mama said thanking him. Then as we were leaving, she asked him, "Keep an eye out for the gunpowder. Henry was saying we need some to take out a stump."

"Yes misses," he answered still wearing the same smile.

Later that night, I heard and explosion. I yelled at Mama with a laugh, "*That explosion was probably our gunpowder going off.*"

"What?" she asked.

"*Nothing Mama,*" I replied, not thinking it was worth it. Looking around, I was reminded that most all of the slaves were missing.

Most of our old slaves made it to the Underground Railroad; this was the method most used to make it up north and to freedom. The Underground Railroad was not a railroad in the truest sense. In reality, it was a series of places slaves could hideout and transfer from place to place until they reached freedom. This means of escaping slavery started in 1837. Those that didn't use this method went their own way, joining one or the other army. At least that's what I prayed happened. One such adventuresome slave made it to Deadwood, South Dakota, I learned some years later. A New York writer liked his story so well he wrote about him in the *Dime Novels*. Though he was black, the writer made him out to be a white man.

In losing our slaves it made it difficult for us, since we had never done any farm work ourselves. We learned quickly how much we had depended on them. At the same time, if we were to continue to live, we would have to fend for ourselves. With most all the slaves gone, the vegetables we depended on were not being grown. If we were to eat, we needed to grow our own vegetables. Mama was willing to change her life to get the job done. It wasn't until years later I understood what it must have taken from her. Even then, I didn't understand my mother.

"Yes Mame," Samuel answered, going over to get a bag of seed.

"Ida…take some of these. If you want to eat, you had better give us a hand," Mama said without waiting for me to answer. She grabbed a hoe and headed for some open field.

"Let me help you," Samuel said grabbing the hoe from her. He then led us to the open field and showed us how to plant the seeds.

As we planted the seeds, many thoughts went through my mind. The letters from Father were hard. He told us about his different duties and battle he had been in. However, the worst were the guys I knew that were killed in battle. That was hard for me to accept. Most of my friends were the same age as I was, fourteen to sixteen years old, and now they are dead. I couldn't imagine not seeing them again. Phillip had just begun to carve a Chess set. He didn't know how to play the game, but he was carving it. Lola had dreams of marrying him someday. Like Edgar and I, it was something our parents expected, if we loved each other or not. There were only two things at the time I was happy about: my Father and Edgar having made it through the war, so far. It seemed many families were losing their loved ones. With the army taking horses and food, many died of starvation at home.

Every few months, the two of them would come home for a visit. Each visit, they looked a little more ragged and tired. Still, in talking to them, they saw the end as being near. The battle of Gettysburg proved the north was going to lose. After a few days, they would leave and we wept in a corner and waited. Mama was one that didn't think the war was going to end. She felt neither side was going to give in. She also knew Father wasn't going to make it. Many times, we would pray together on the porch that God would see father home. Then getting up from our knees she would warn me, "We might have to learn to fend for each other." In the end, she was right, and the war went on for four years.

The only good part was an uncle of ours. I remember meeting him once. He told me, "There are two important things in life: enjoy what you do and be a winner." We got letters telling us about his wartime adventures. At first, he was a disgrace to the family. It seemed he didn't have any loyalties to either side: north or south. It was because he felt it was all a joke. It seemed, from what we heard, that he carried a spare uniform in his bedroll. The spare uniform was for the opposing army. Whichever army was winning, he wore that uniform. Then after the end of whatever battle he was in, he would write home. They in turn would write us, giving us his stories. These stories were our entertainment. I guess he enjoyed what he was doing. He felt he was a winner at days end.

A day came when our entertainment wasn't enough. Three uniformed soldiers came to our door. It wasn't uncommon for soldiers of both armies to do this. They came to get a meal. There was something different with these three. The General walked up the steps of the veranda with a purpose.

"Is your mother home?" he asked me when I opened the door.

Having had my sixteenth birthday, I had a feeling what he wanted to tell her. I answered him with a frog in my throat, "I'll get her."

It didn't take long, but I found her. She was fixing supper for the two of us. Sally our cook had taken off with her boyfriend to go north. Mama had to do all the cooking.

"Yes?" Mama asked the general as she reached him.

"Ma'am...I have a message from the battle lines," he said, hesitating a little with each word.

"Your presence tells me I have lost my husband in battle," she answered, not giving him a chance to say anything. As he stuttered, she went on to tell him, "He died early this morning at daybreak."

"But...how?" the General began to ask, but Mama shut the door in his face.

She turned and briefly looked at me, and didn't say a word. Without missing a beat, she walked toward the kitchen. It wasn't until later that night I heard her cry. I have never heard a person cry as she did. The next day she only told me, "Your father died yesterday." After that, we never discussed the subject again. To this day I have wondered how she knew. Was their love that strong that she felt it part as he died.

I was sick for the next three days. I couldn't hold anything down, and I couldn't cry. I realized I never thought of him as my mother's husband, for he was mine. Then it hit me that we both were without the one we loved. To be honest, it scared me because I didn't know what to do. I didn't get over it until I fell into Mama's arms and finally cried. I asked her, "What are we going to do now?"

"Pray," she answered, holding me tighter than I could stand. Still I didn't say anything, for I knew how she felt.

Some time later, Edgar came home and said he was there when Father died. If there was any time I felt close to him, it was then. He had been there when he had taken his last breath. He told me my Father's last words were "Take care of her."

Though it might have been a sick joke on Edgar's part, I knew it wasn't. He felt the same way about my Father as I did. I knew it was an order from my father he couldn't refuse, and I knew I couldn't refuse either. I knew I had a duty also, so on the veranda, I promised myself to Edgar. Once he came home again, I would marry him. Unfortunately, it wasn't the happy occasion most think of in a proposal. Edgar went back to the war, and I hated it more than I thought I ever would. Even then, I didn't know it would get worse.

Making it into town to sell vegetables, I found other kids like myself. All of us were in tattered clothes. No one spoke to each other, knowing we were suffering from similar losses. However, we heard how we were going to come back and win; we all knew differently. I would take a chicken in exchange for my armload of vegetables. It wasn't a fair trade, but I had no choice. Our clothes got more and more tattered; we could hardly stand ourselves. At the same time, our meals got to be fewer and less of a variety. We finally found ourselves eating mainly bread.

The only joy I could find was that Edgar was doing all right. Unfortunately, he lost his father in battle. So in letters, we found in ways we only had each other. It wasn't that I didn't love my mother, for I did. She went into a shell of some kind after the loss of my father. She was there tending the fields but she never talked about anything. I now know she didn't know what to do without my father. After that, the two of us only talked one more time with any meaning.

We had gone without a meal for four days. Every one of our help had moved on. Some of the black men joined one or the other army to stay alive. We heard some found themselves sent out west to fight the Indians. Others made it north but we were never sure, because we never heard from them again. The rest of us existed on nothing. No one had prepared us for what we were to be going through. We only had an occasional bunch of soldiers wanting what we didn't have to offer.

After going without food, my mother came downstairs with a couple of bundles of clothing. I asked her, "What are you doing…going somewhere?"

"Check around and see if I have forgotten anything," she told me curtly. Looking around as if she was looking for something, she turned back to me and told me, "Put together anything you think you have to have. I have packed enough clothes for a week for you already."

"What?" I asked, not understanding at the time what she meant.

"We're going to Richmond," was the only answer I got. She didn't act anything like the mother I had grown to know. She had a determined look about her that scared me.

Now that I think about it, I remember a feeling of bareness about the house as I walked through it. With Mama having told me to get the rest of my belongings, I went to do just that.

I ran around, looking for items I could carry that I might need. The only items I could find were a few pens, ink and paper I could use to write Edgar. With these few items, I added them to what Mama had. I followed her out the front door and down the lane away from the house. Looking back at the house, I wondered if I would ever see it again. In my stomach, I felt I was leaving my father and my life behind. Still again, it wasn't until years later I knew how bad it was.

As we walked, we went through town not saying a word to each other or to anyone else. I found myself thinking about the life we had before war. If we were to believe the northern folks, we had everything.

In years to come, it seems as if we did. On the other hand, we might have had everything, but they weren't the important things in life. We didn't have a feeling of self-worth, or know what love was. Still, in 1863, I didn't understand what we had or had lost. All I knew was that I wanted my father, my horse, and my home.

"Why are we going to Richmond?" I asked Mama.

"To live," she answered short and to the point.

"Where are we going to live?" I asked. "We don't know anyone there, do we?"

"We don't know anyone and I don't know where we are going to live," she answered. Then stopping, she told me, "We can't live at home, because there's no food. All I know is I'm going to have to find work so we can eat."

"What can you do?" I asked.

"I'll find something, and you can learn to do washing and ironing. I don't have any idea right now, Ida," she answered, and then turned to continue our walk.

After two days, we could make out Richmond. I still wondered what my mother had in mind for us, but she wouldn't tell me. With her not wanting to tell me anything, we continued to walk in silence. The rain and crippled soldiers hobbling the same road as we were traveling kept my mind off our problems. Mama kept her thoughts to herself.

We got into Richmond, and Mama kept walking. It appeared that she was looking for some particular place. Knowing she had only been there a few times, I wondered what she was looking for. I tried to think of some relatives she might be trying to find, but I couldn't think of any that lived there. Most of our relatives live up north. The ones living in the south had moved out a year before the war. They had had the brains to get out before they lost everything.

Still, with things as they were, there were flags and people praising the Confederacy throughout Richmond. I wondered even then where their brains were. Where they were getting all of these high hopes they were displaying I didn't know. If any one of them looked at themselves, they would have been scared. Still, they were shouting their praises. In addition, my mother found the place she was hunting for.

"We'll set up housekeeping here," she told me.

I didn't answer, for I couldn't believe what I was hearing. Here in an alley she was pointing to an overhang. The overhang kept the rain from going down a stairwell to the basement of a building. I couldn't even tell what the building held. Still, I stared at the spot thinking she meant for us to go inside and I asked her, "Do we go inside here?"

"No we're sleeping here," she answered, waving her hand across the alley.

I found myself wondering what happened to the advice of my parent's friend General Robert E. Lee. Where could all of these intelligent men have gone wrong? I never held a bad feeling towards the people of the north. I figured they must be having some of the same problems we were. Both sides must be losing their brothers and fathers. It was a case where everyone lost. Again, I didn't understand to what degree.

Now looking back, I feel as if the man upstairs was protecting me. I now know Richmond had more than its share of casualties from the war. Then several months later, Sherman would come through and burn it all down. I missed both events and I can say I'm not unhappy about it. Still, there was one event I wish now I could forget.

Though tired from all the walking we did, my mother told me, "I'll be back later."

"Can I go with you?" I asked her. I had no idea where she was going, but I wanted to be with her.

"I have to go alone," she answered, and she turned and walked away from me.

"You won't be long will you?" I asked her, but she didn't bother to answer.

Eventually, I fell asleep and I didn't wake up until morning. At the time, I didn't have any idea where she went. In fact, being so young I trusted every word she said. Again, it wasn't until later I understood. Still, when I woke the next morning, she was lying next to me fast asleep.

In her arms was more food than I had seen for weeks, if not months.

I began taking the food and stuffing it into my mouth. I didn't have any idea where it came from, nor did I care. To me, food was food, and it was there to be eaten.

"Good morning," Mama said as she rubbed sleep from her eyes.

"Good morning," I answered, feeling stuffed for the first time in more days than I could remember.

She looked down to where the food had been, and asked, "Feeling better?"

"Yes," I answered, and I went on to ask her, "were did you go?"

"Don't worry about it," she answered.

At times during the day and evenings she would be gone. When she was gone, I found several jobs I could do for money and goods. Still, I asked her the same question most nights and got the same answer, "Don't worry about it." Later I was to find out the truth.

Through the final year of the war we kept ourselves alive. As Mama was doing her whatever, I did mine. I brought money and food in by fulfilling the needs of the people in the neighborhood. Sometimes it was only taking care of children. Other times I did cleaning or just took out the trash. There wasn't anything, or almost anything, I wouldn't do. As long as I got something for it, I would do it. Most of the time I did the wash or ironing for people. Ironing was the one chore I hated more than anything else.

During those first few months, Mama and I developed a new relationship. It wasn't that I understood her, for we never talked. Yet, in our own way, we talked even though it was through silence. I learned to care for myself as she cared for the two of us. We learned to work together, but in different ways. This was only a small part of the changes in our lives.

If nothing else, we learned to live without furniture. Even worse, we didn't have a home. We had finally moved from the alley, but it wasn't much better. We finally got a little area in a storeroom off the stairwell where we first slept. It wasn't much, but it was better than nothing was. For as bad as it was, I knew there were other needs that were far more important. The most important being we had each other. Then reoccurring occasionally, I would see a tear from Mama. The tear would remind me that father wasn't with us anymore and he wasn't going to return. I would find myself losing a tear myself, thinking of the changes in our lives. Then after a year, I learned him being gone wasn't as important as staying alive. Somewhere staying alive became the most important game in town. I knew Mama and I were going to win.

When I thought I had learned all there was to learn, I learned something I will take to my grave. It didn't take long to learn possessions were not the greatest losses of the war. The loss of father, brothers, and mothers of course was hard to deal with. The greatest loss was the respect for our fellow man as well as what we once were. There also were cities, homes, and property lost. We, in the end, had lost all of that and some more. My mother had lost the final possession a person could ever lose, and it was for me. It was hours before the war ended; I didn't have an idea where and what she had been up to.

She had come home in the middle of the night. I saw her in the corner of our damp cubbyhole of a place, coughing with a terrible rattle of a sound. I went over and asked her, "Are you all right, Mama?"

"I'll be better once I get some sleep," she answered, coughing again.

"I'm supposed to go over and help Mrs. Warren today," I told her. Then looking at her, I saw black rings around her eyes. Her eyes were bloodshot and sitting deep into her head. Looking at her scared me, for she had never looked like she did that morning.

"I don't have to go," I told her, taking her hand into mine. Her hand felt so cold, I dropped it, but I took it again and patted it.

"No, Mrs. Warren is counting on you. One lesson you have to learn is you have to be both honest and dependable, so be on your way, and be quiet when you come back will you? I have…to get some sleep," she told me.

As she sat there huddled in the corner, I asked her again, "Where have you been going all those times at all hours of the night?" Again, she didn't answer me.

I expected the day to be like so many others. During the day, as I did washing or took care of people, she would sleep it away. However, after Sherman's army made their march through the city, it wasn't the same.

"I'll be back soon," I told Mama.

"Stay out of sight of the soldiers," she warned me.

I only had a block and a half to go to reach Mrs. Warren. With each step, I cried a tear wondering what was wrong with Mama. "Why haven't I seen the changes?" I asked myself. I worried she might die for as bad as she looked.

"Good morning, Ida," Mrs. Warren said greeting me at her front door. Then welcoming me in, she asked, "Something wrong?"

"It's Mama," I explained, going on to tell her about Mama.

"Maybe you should go to her," she said.

"No, she said she needed to get some sleep," I told her.

"Okay, if you say so," she answered, giving me a questioning look.

As we did the wash, she told me, "This war has brought about the worst in people. Fathers killed by their sons. Brothers killing their brothers. I remember getting a letter from Harvey. He said he saw a Yankee out of the corner of his eye. Without thinking, he pulled the trigger and he saw the soldier fall." Wiping a tear from her eye, she went on to add, "Later he went over and checked on the soldier. Looking down at the soldier, he saw it was our only son Gerald. Gerald looked up at him, and told him, "I love you, Father," and then he died. And now Harvey is also dead."

Not being able to control herself, she went into her house crying. As I stood there, I thought how terrible that must have been for her husband. Not having many choices, I finished the wash.

After a short time, she came back and said, "I'm sorry about falling apart."

"No problem…I wouldn't want to be in your position," I answered. As I watched her, I prayed no more of this would happen ever again.

After three or four hours, we completed our tasks and I headed home. Taking the change she gave me, she also gave me a loaf of bread as a bonus. I ran home to check on Mama.

Getting back, I saw Mama still curled up in the corner. She was shaking so hard, I almost felt it across the room. I dropped the loaf of bread Mrs. Warren had given me and ran over to her.

"*Mama, what's wrong?*" I asked her, reaching down to hold her. She felt so hot I almost began to sweat.

"I'm sorry, Ida, but I'm dying," she answered, and with her last breath she added, "Giving what was needed to the men in the army." Though she got the answer out without difficulty, her eyes showed it hurt her.

I asked her, "Whatever you have you been doing that would make you die, you don't need to do it any more Mama. They're coming home." With it out of my mouth, I realized what she had been doing. She had been giving her body to the men for money. I first felt shocked at the thought, but I understood.

As she began to go through another coughing spell, I pulled her to me. I stroked her hair, holding her as close to me as I could. I told her, "Everything will be better since the war is over."

"Not for me. I love you, Ida," she got out with a cough, and her body went limp. I knew Mama had died and something died in me. My thoughts then turned to Mrs. Warren and her losses, knowing we were both losers.

I learned what Mama had given up for me. It was more than I think I could have given up for anyone. For me, she gave up her self-respect, by becoming a prostitute to feed me.

Matt Duncan

I'm a little older than Ida is, having been born in 1847, making me two years older. At same time, I come from Kentucky rather than Virginia. Like Ida, I was born and raised in the country not in the city. Unlike her, I was the second youngest of six boys. There wasn't a quiet moment in our three-room house. At the same time, every day was about the same. If it weren't for boredom, we wouldn't have had a life. We lived day by day; we had enough to eat that day, but no guarantee for the day to come. Other than the war, I never wanted to leave a place so much as home. Thinking back, I think it was an identity problem more than anything else was.

As I said, there were six of us boys. I would like to think we were all hardworking and boys to be proud of. Now thinking back, I can see what we could have done to have been more help to our father. Yet, we were boys and did as boys do. At the time, our ages ranged from Robby, the youngest at 6; I was 13; Mark was 15; Henry was 16; Samuel was 17; and Peter was 18. I find it hard to remember what we looked like. We were all on the thin side, except Robby, who still had a few pounds of baby fat that the rest of us had lost. Mark was the darkest haired one, with the rest of us having sandy colored hair. Samuel and Peter, being the older of us six, had formed some muscle tone. I was the runt of the litter at that age. I didn't begin to grow until I was sixteen. I think it is safe to say we were your average group of kids.

At the start of the Civil War, I see it different from some. As you know, the possible secession and war were subjects everyone was talking about. After the failed vote to secede in 1831, the idea reoccurred as an alternative to any problem with the government. I can remember one day before the war in particular. However, young with many other notions on my mind, most mornings were the same. Still for some reason, one day stands out as the beginning. It started out on a morning in the winter of 1860.

This morning began as every morning had.

"Get your foot out of my face," Henry shouted at Samuel. Of the six of us, these two were always fighting with each other.

Samuel was the biggest irritation among all of us because he was so quiet. He never got into any trouble somehow. Henry, on the other hand, was always getting into trouble. This difference between the two I think is why they both fought so much.

Sleeping together as we did, we always had problems. Then with us being boys, we always fought.

"Both of you shut up," I told them not wanting to be woken right then. As I rolled over, I could hear dad stirring and knew my nights sleep was over with anyway. Knowing what I had to do, I continued to crawl out of my bedroll to feed the chickens.

"Matt you feed..." my father's voice called out from his room, as I was going out the door.

"On my way," I shouted out to him as I left the house.

"...Samuel, you take care of the..." I could hear him continuing to pass out chores.

"You stay out of everything this morning, Robby, and do as Peter tells you." This had been the morning routine since our mother had died. She died in giving birth to Robby six years earlier. Since then, father worked every waking moment, leaving the care of the place to us.

The few times we went to church, everyone would ask when father was going to marry. Peter or Samuel were told of this or that widow that he could marry. They kept reminding us that he was such a good-looking and hard working man. There wasn't a woman alive that wouldn't want him. When they began talking about him, I would leave. One aspect of him I did appreciate was that he wasn't like the father of a friend of mine. His father was also a widower, but he drank heavily. In asking father about that, he said, "Someone needs to raise you six."

"Hurry back with the eggs, I'm hungry," my brother Henry yelled out from the door as I entered the chicken coop.

"Yeah, yeah," I answered under my breath. As dad went to the mill to work, we did the chores around the place. That's not to say Dad didn't do anything. Once he had some supper, he went out and shoed our horse, or other miscellaneous items he could do. He was not the type to sit around and do nothing.

As I said, there were only three rooms to the house (not counting the loft). Mom and Dad built the place about a year before I was born. It was a simple log home built with the help of some of our neighbors. The only major problem with the house was the windows. They only had shutters and heavy material covering them. During the winter, the cold wind would just blow right through. Then dad was finally able to get some glass, and it made a big difference.

"If you don't find any eggs, you might be better off if you don't come back in," I could hear my brother Sam shout out.

"Worry about the milk, and I'll worry about the eggs," I shouted back at him. "If these hens don't lay any eggs, it isn't my fault," I thought. I then told the hens, "You had better have laid some eggs this morning." Shaking my head, thinking of my brothers, I gathered some grain for chickens. Then having fed them, I began cleaning out the mess. The last chore I would do was gathering the eggs.

Once I got back to the house with the eggs, it was my job to do the cooking. After breakfast, most of us went to school. In school, I was the oldest in my class.

Though schooling was important to our father, not all of us had to go. Peter would stay at home and take care of the place and Robby. Being stuck at home as he was, he complained he didn't have a life. He always voiced the fear he was never going to meet anyone and have a family of his own. Schooling was something else that was not available until I was eleven. Therefore, I was the oldest in my class of eight kids. Getting to school meant a ten-mile walk to town. Some of the kids were lucky enough to have a horse to ride; we didn't. We had a horse, but it was lucky to plow the field for us. Even then it wouldn't have been able to carry all of us anyway.

Having helped feed everyone, my mind returned to my schoolwork. At the same time, I thought of what everyone was talking about in our class. We knew Abe Lincoln was born in Hardin County (not far from us) in 1809. At first, knowing he was going to be our next President made us proud. Then his views on freeing slaves scared us. There were rumors the south would secede from the Union. This scared us worse than any snake or anything else. Though not sure how Lincoln was going to take to the secession, we knew it meant war. When we got home, we talked about the problems with the nation. At the same time, what we had to look forward to.

"What do you think Matt?" My father asked me.

After thinking a little, I answered, "Though Lincoln might have the right idea, is it right for him to push it onto us?"

"If it will make for a better country shouldn't he?" Henry asked.

"This is a free country, isn't it?" Peter asked, throwing in his own question on the subject.

"That's my point. No one should be able to tell us what we can or cannot do," I told everyone.

"What difference does it make to us? We don't have any slaves," Sam offered as an idea.

"Whatcha talking about?" Robby asked, pulling on father's sleeve.

"Don't worry about it," father told him, with a pat on his head. There were times when I thought father didn't have a heart. Then times like now, he was warm and understanding.

"We're talking important stuff," Henry told him going on to add, "Why don't you go play with that mutt of yours."

Here again was an example how Henry would play the tough guy. Thinking about it with a houseful of boys it wasn't easy to get attention. I remember a few times I would do or say something, and no one noticed. Then again, we needed father's help but he wasn't there most of the time.

Henry was jealous of Robby because he was the one that had found the mutt. Still the mutt preferred Robby to him. Robby, with his great imagination, named him "Boy." It was good to have the mutt around, with Robby needing a playmate. He didn't have anyone to play with.

In watching the two of them, I always found myself thinking of my dog Digger. Digger was an old hound dog that moved in with us one day. All one summer we were the best of friends. I was closer to him than my brothers; we played, ate, and slept together. Then one morning, I woke and he wasn't lying next to me. In walking around later that afternoon, I found him. It seemed some animal had killed him.

"I want to talk too," Robby told us. Then looking hurt he went to chase his dog outside. "Wait for me, Boy," we hear him yelling as he went down the steps.

"He's going to grow up someday and beat every one of you senseless," father said watching his youngest leaving the house.

"I'll watch and laugh," Peter added with a laugh.

"Now going back to what we were talking about...Lincoln can't do anything on his own, no matter what his opinion is. He would have to get congress to agree to his ideas," our father reminded us.

The conversation went on for an hour or better. When we were through talking, we found that Robby had fallen asleep already. Covering him up, we decided to follow his example. The following spring, all of our lives were to take a change.

All of us boys had other thoughts to keep us busy. Rather than fighting the cold, there was swimming this spring and summer. Then on the other hand, there was the planting and harvesting. Still, the skinny-dipping and chasing the girls around the pond would make up for it all.

Samuel we knew dreamed of his long walks with his young lady. We knew someday soon they would get married. Father kept telling him to hold off as long as he could. Then on the next breath remind him he might have six boys, as he did. By waiting, he might keep it down by one or two.

A few months went by.

"It's happened," father said as he came into the house.

"What's happened?" Peter asked as he got him a cup of coffee.

"Those southern idiots took Fort Sumter," he answered and then went on to add, "Of course, the North has declared war."

I had no idea what or where Fort Sumter was. Still, from the way he referred to the place, I knew it must be important no matter where or what it was. Later I was to learn it wasn't an important fortification. The attack itself became the excuse for a war between the north and the south.

"Are we going to war?" Mark, my next to the oldest brother, asked.

"Are we, father?" I asked, coming over closer to the conversation. I was worried about what it might mean to our family. I didn't think father would be going to war, but Peter and Samuel probably would be.

"It sure looks like it," he answered, as he took his cup from Peter's hand. Sitting down, he ran his fingers through his hair and stared at us boys. Then looking down into his cup, he told us, "I wrote your Aunt Agnes."

"Is she coming to visit?" Robby asked, crawling into father's lap.

Not knowing why he wrote her or what about, none of us said anything. Still, the way he put it, there was something important in the statement. Taking a chair, as a few of my other brothers did, we sat there and waited.

"I asked her if she could come here to take care of you boys for me," he answered finally.

Needing someone to take care of us worried me. Still, if it had to be done, it was better she came to our house than us to hers. We had grown up there and I didn't want to leave. I wasn't too sure I would like to live anywhere but in our house. We had rolling hills covered with trees, with a stream we fish at near the house. To live somewhere else might mean giving up all these advantages. Then there were my friends, though I didn't get to see them often, they still were there for me.

"What do we need her for?" Peter asked, surprised by the request.

"If we go to war, I'll have to join as well as you two," father answered, looking around to see our reaction.

With raised eyebrows, Peter and Samuel nodded their heads in understanding. Though Peter didn't have a girlfriend, Samuel did. I wondered what she was going to say with him leaving. Whatever she felt, I knew it wasn't anything like I was going to.

For the first time in my life, I saw tears in my father's eyes. He was not a man to cry no matter what the pain. On this occasion, I knew he was worried about his sons. He had never gone through something like this and he didn't know what to do. My worst fears hit me in that our family was going to be split apart. At the same time, I might lose the three of them in the war. I began to get mad, for the war was going to break up our family. Even though it wasn't much, it was all we had. Everything my father had worked for might be lost. If it was all lost, what were we going to do? The more I thought about it, I decided to join him and my brothers.

"Then I'm going to join the army also," I told him.

"And do what?" Peter asked. Turning to father, he told him, "And it will go down in history as the baby war."

I jumped out of my chair and hit him. As he defended himself, I jumped on his back and continued to hit him. Then my father's strong fingers dug into me and he pulled me off. Sitting on the floor, I felt bad about attacking Peter. I wasn't mad at him, but at the war taking them away from me.

"Why do you have to fight?" Henry asked, and then went on to add, "We don't have any slaves."

He was right, for we didn't. In fact, we didn't know anyone that did. We knew of people that did at one time or the other, but not anymore. Most of the blacks were sharecroppers growing tobacco or vegetables. The large landowners were breeding horses.

"It isn't that I want to go to war; I have to defend what I believe in," father answered.

Want to Go West Lady?

Going to school the next day, we began seeing posters asking for volunteers. Many of the posters had four or five men reading them. Though we didn't see any of it happening, we heard of fights breaking out between the men reading them. Our little town was split on the issues about which side was right or wrong. I even found myself split on the issues. The main issue of concern was they felt the slaves should be free. As with Lincoln, I didn't remember God saying there should be slaves. In fact, he led Moses and his people to freedom from where they had been slaves. Even if I felt like they did, having someone tell me what I could or could not do, I felt was also wrong.

For the next week, our house was void of any conversation on the subject. In fact, no one seemed too interested in talking about anything. We waited to see what was going to happen. Then everything began to change with the announcement from father.

"Your Aunt Agnes wrote and said she will be here the day after tomorrow."

Everyone sat back without saying anything. I, on the other hand, didn't want to think or talk about it. I ran out the door, sat on a fence rail, and watched the sun go down. Both Henry and Peter called me to supper but I didn't go in. Then father came out and sat beside me. He sat there for a few minutes not saying a word. He reached over and he squeezed my hand. I found myself leaning up against him shaking. No matter how hard I tried, I couldn't stop. All I could think about was Mama was gone, and now father, Samuel and Peter were leaving. It was all coming to an end.

"You miss her don't you?" he asked me quietly.

"Yes," I answered knowing whom he meant.

"Worried…that I won't be coming back?" he asked understanding my greatest fear.

I bit my lip from saying anything. I was going to prove somehow that I was a man. Still, I was shaking and I couldn't stop it.

"You know I have to do this," he said, and then letting me go, he added, "I'll do everything I can to keep myself from getting killed."

"I…know," I got out, with it taking every ounce of energy I had.

"Mr. Jacob…he's putting together a company of volunteers," he began telling me. Then patting me on the head, he explained, "He doesn't think we will be leaving for another week."

"Maybe it will be over by then…then you won't have to go," I said biting my upper lip, knowing it wouldn't happen.

We got off the fence and walked to the house. As we entered, my brothers didn't ask any questions. In silence, we drifted off to sleep in our own thoughts and fears.

The next week went by faster than you can imagine. Each day I felt as if a nail was going through me. Aunt Agnes tried her best to get us to laugh. No matter what she did, we knew the day was coming. Our father tried to paint a picture of how it would be when he came back. He also told us again his vision for the place. In telling us, he told us what we could do when he was gone. He also told us what he wanted us to do. Then he reminded us that Aunt Agnes needed us. Still, we could not find anything to bring up our spirits.

Then one day, Samuel, Peter, and Father took off for town without saying anything to any of us. All of us wanted to go with them, but we were told to stay home and get our chores done. We waited for them to return on the front porch, wondering what was going on. Our greatest fear was that they weren't coming back. Finally, we gave up waiting for them and we went inside.

"I want to play?" Robby asked as we came inside the house.

"Not right now," Henry answered pushing him to one side.

"Be nice…he doesn't understand," I reminded him.

"Where's that dog of yours?" Aunt Agnes asked him.

Robby turned and looked outside. Then turning back to our Aunt for a second and then towards outside, he ran after the dog. For the first time, I smiled and wished I were like him. From that point on we continued to wait for Father, Samuel and Peter.

"What do you guys think?" Father asked coming into the door of the house.

We turned toward his voice and saw the three of them in the doorway. Though our father's uniform was fancier, all three looked sharp. The Gray uniform, with the gold trim, looked sharp. Father was wearing the uniform of a captain; Peter and Samuel wore regular uniforms.

"Don't the three of you look handsome," Aunt Agnes said walking up to them.

"We turned a few heads in town," Peter answered, with father and Samuel grinning from ear to ear.

I turned and walked over to the fireplace and took down a rifle. Without saying anything, I headed for the door.

"Where do you think you're going?" Peter asked me as I was walked past them.

"Let him go," father told him giving me room to pass.

I turned once I got out to the porch and told them, "I'm going to get me a Coon." I spent the rest of the afternoon walking through the woods. I'm not sure, but I think I saw a Coon but I didn't even try to shoot it. I just needed to get out of the house. I didn't like seeing the three of them in their uniforms. It wasn't at all funny to me, because everything was ending. Then with the Coon hunting, father wasn't there to enjoy the hunt with me. Having gotten it out of my system, and tired of walking, I decided to go home.

"Woof, woof," Boy greeted me at the door to the house.

"Get out of here," I told him. I knew he wanted to play; I pushed him to one side. Though I liked him, I wasn't in the mood to play right then.

"If you're not nice to him…he'll bite you," Robby warned me.

"If he's not careful…I might bite him or roast him for supper," I told him with a smile as I tried to hear the conversation that was going on in the house.

"…It won't last long. Neither side has enough money to fight a major war," dad was saying.

"There is talk that we won't get to the lines in time to get any fighting in," Peter added to the conversation.

Then seeing me, dad stood up and asked me, "Get yourself one?"

"Didn't even see any," I answered.

"I guess we had better get going," he said, motioning to my brother to get up and join him.

With that, the three picked up their stuff and threw it over their shoulders. Seeing them head for the door, I felt tears running down my cheeks. Dad came over and walked me to the door.

"You'll see me pretty soon," he assured me.

Dad gave me a hug before he went down the steps. As he waved good-bye, he told us to take care of Aunt Agnes. As Peter and Samuel left, they ruffled up my hair, and laughed at my irritation of their teasing. With that, they walked down the road. We watched them until they were out of sight. As they rounded the last tree, I wondered if we would ever see them again.

The following week after the three marched off was hard not having them around. I guess the four of us boys made it hard on Aunt Agnes. All I could say was her dinners were better than we made. Still to get out of the house, she would walk to town. We offered to go with her, but she always said she liked walking alone. With her gone, I tried to occupy my time doing chores. I kept finding the chores didn't take as much time as I needed to forget. I continued to miss them and thought about them all the time.

One afternoon, Aunt Agnes came back from town. She didn't say anything, but I could see something was wrong. I could see it, even though she wasn't to the house yet. Jumping off the porch, I ran down the path to meet her.

"Something wrong?" I asked before I even reached her.

"What could be wrong," she answered without even stopping. Then stopping she turned and asked me, "Have you got your chores done?"

"Yes," I answered.

"Good," she replied. Without another word, she turned and went to the house.

I stood there and watched, knowing she was lying. Over the next few weeks, I saw a problem coming. Without explanation, Aunt Agnes kept saying I might have to find a job. Then I noticed the meals becoming more and more chicken. I knew where they were coming from because I fed them. I wondered what would happen when we ran out of chicken. About that time Boy rubbed up against my leg.

I looked down at him and told him, "You might be the next entree on the table." I knew he didn't understand, but he did pull away.

Then I knew what I had to do. I decided to join the army as soon as I could. Then with me being gone, Aunt Agnes would have one less mouth to feed. I didn't join right away, for I kept thinking of my brothers. Yet, with each day that passed, I could see the situation getting worse. Then that plan was to go bad also.

"Don't say anything," Henry said in the middle of the night.

"Wh...?" I began to ask, but he put his hand over my mouth to keep me quiet.

"Mark and I are going to join with the army," he told me.

I could see a bedroll hanging from their shoulders. I tried to get up, because if they were going, I was too. Then Mark pushed me down, letting Henry do the talking.

"Matt, someone has to stay with Aunt Agnes and take care of Robby," he said.

"Plus, you're too young and to small to fight in the war," Mark added.

"Don't tell Aunt Agnes until morning," Henry added, and after he gave me a hug, they went out the door.

I waved at them as they left and first thought about Mark's remarks. I didn't understand what he meant, not being old enough. Being fourteen, I should be old enough, I thought. I'm a good marksman; even the best of us boys. I couldn't argue about being short. I was the shortest in my class. Still what difference did it make if I had a rifle in my hand? I found it irritating what he had said. I also missed them and knew it was going to get worse.

I laid there not being able to go to sleep. I was wishing I had left when I did, but I couldn't now because of Robby. The more I thought about them leaving, the madder I got. The madder I got, the less sleepy I felt, and morning finally came.

"Mark, Henry, get down here," Aunt Agnes yelled out. Then with a pause not hearing them, she called out to them again.

"They're not here," Robby told her as he came down from the loft.

"Where are they?" she asked.

"They went to join the army," I answered as I got up from in front of the fireplace.

"*They what?*" she screamed, walking over to me. "Why didn't you say something?"

"Oh well…they're probably to far away for me to catch them," she said sitting down looking defeated.

With it only being the three of us, it was hard. There wasn't any way I could keep up with all the chores. Each day they were gone, I found myself wishing they would be killed. "To leave me with everything wasn't right," I told myself more than once. The only good was that I was able to ride the horse to school. I didn't have a saddle but I still didn't have to walk. Then, too, this meant I got to do more chores.

There was one day after school I stopped to talk to a friend. "Nathan."

"Yeah," he answered as he stopped where I was sitting on the fence in front of the school.

"What do you think of this war? Are you going to join the army?" I asked him. The thought of joining our army was weighing heavy on my mind that day.

"I would like to do something," he answered, looking down at his feet. Then looking back at me, he told me, "Mom just found out that her brother was killed last week. We don't have any idea about dad or my brother."

"We haven't heard anything about my father or brothers," I told him knowing how he felt.

"I'm joining in the morning. What about you two?" one of our older classmates asked as he walked past us?

"I'm thinking about doing just that," I answered to his back.

"He can't make up his mind if he's a Yankee or a Reb," another classmate said with a laugh.

"Real smart. Going off to get yourself killed," Shelly added as she walked past having overheard us talk.

"For a dumb as they are, we wouldn't be losing much," June told her as she turned and gave me a funny look.

"Something wrong in protecting you?" I asked but not getting any answer.

"I know if I could I would join the army…but I'm the only one left to take care of Mama," he told me as he shook his head and hit the rail with his fist. Then looking off away from me, he asked, "*Why*…we didn't do anything. My father and brother are gone; we have no food, horses…Mama's going to die having the baby if she doesn't get more to eat than she does. *I would love to kill them all.*"

"Isn't there someone that can help? Can't we all help one another a little?" I asked not having heard him say anything before.

"Mom and I talked about that last night. You're no better off than we are," he said.

I had to agree with him and I told him so. I found myself getting mad for having asked him anything. We both got down from the fence to go our own way.

Before he got too far, he turned and told me, "I don't know how, but Mama wants to go to her sisters up north."

"Up north?" I asked him, not sure I had heard him correctly.

"We don't have anyone else to turn to," he answered.

"Good luck, if I don't see you before you leave," I told him wishing I could do something to help him. My conversation with him made it a long walk home.

Over the next month or so, I had similar conversation with other friends at school. No one was able to work their land as they had in the past. Even before the war living was rough, now it was even worse. Everyone wanted to leave, but wanted to wait until their loved ones came home. Everyone was upset more about not having any answers, than anything. Everyone was looking forward to the end of the war and the promises of making a living being better. The only news they had were the articles in the newspapers we got occasionally. When the articles announced we had won a battle, everyone would stick out their chest with pride. When we lost, everyone was at each other's throats. I wondered if it was this way all over the country.

Some time later going home from school, I saw a company of Yankees traveling down the road going south. I stopped and wondered how many of them I could take out if I had a rifle. Knowing that was only a dream, I turned the horse toward home. I knew though, I had to warn Aunt Agnes.

Getting home, I ran up the path shouting, "*The Yankees are here.*"

""What…the who are here…in our yard?" Aunt Agnes asked as she turned around from the stove.

"Well, the Yankees are not in our yard, but heading down the road, going south," I told her.

"I have a surprise for you," she said with a smile, pointing towards my father's room.

Turning, I saw Mark walking towards me. His left arm was in a sling and his head was bandaged. He looked as if he needed to say something, but didn't know how to tell me. Rather than opening his mouth, he pulled his arm out of the sling. When it was all the way out, I saw his hand was missing. Then thinking of the Yankees going down the road, I began to worry about Mark standing there. He was in bad enough shape as it was. I turned my attention back to my brother.

"What…" I began to ask him, but he didn't let me finish.

"I got hit by a mortar," he answered but stopping to put his arm into the sling again.

Both of us just stood there, not saying anything. I knew there wasn't anything I could say. I didn't even have any idea what I could say. Then a feeling came over me that brought a smile to my face. I walked over and gave him a hug.

"Better missing a hand than being dead," I told him wondering if I were hurting him. I didn't mean to hurt him, but to express the fact I was glad he was alive.

"Right, one-handed won't be able to do much now," he said with a tear in his eye. Then before it fell, he wiped it away and added, "I still can hug her."

From talking to the guys at school, different guys had talked about coming home wounded. One of the boys had said his uncle got hurt felling trees. His girlfriend wouldn't have anything to do with him. I wondered what Mark's girlfriend was going to say about him missing a hand.

"Why don't you two sit down," Aunt Agnes suggested.

"I'm hungry," Robby said running into the house, then stopped mid sentence when he saw Mark. Running up to him, he gave Mark a hug and told him, "I missed you."

"I wasn't gone that long," Mark answered.

"Long enough," Robby replied as he let him go. He backed away and took a good look at our brother. He saw Mark pull his arm out of the sling again and saw the hand was missing. He was so shocked he fell over backwards.

"Maybe you can be his other hand," Aunt Agnes offered a suggestion.

"Can I really?" Robby asked as he sat up again.

"Why not," Mark answered with a grin. He sat there shaking his head watching our brother. Then back to me he said, "Short war, for me at least."

"What about Henry?" I asked thinking they had been together.

"He was doing fine the last time I saw him. The two of us wish we had stayed here though," he admitted.

"If you were not injured already, I'd injure you myself," Aunt Agnes told him, as she handed him a cup of coffee.

"Did you see father or our other two brothers?" I asked him as I was sitting on the edge of my chair. I saw Aunt Agnes come to a complete stop misstep, as if she was waiting for the answer.

"I heard they had been in a major battle, but I never saw them," he answered as he took a sip from his cup.

"What was it like?" I asked.

"To be honest, I didn't see much action," he told me. Then looking off out the front door, he looked like he was in another world. Then turning back to me, he told me, "I got hit in the first few minutes of the skirmish…it wasn't even a real battle. From what everyone told me later, we won, but I didn't have any part of it."

"Not fair," Robby said hearing what our brother had said.

"What's not fair?" I asked him. From all the talk about war, it became a game to all the kids.

"Not killing anyone and then lose a hand like this," he answered shaking his head in disbelief.

"You can say that again," Mark answered. He didn't look as if he cared if he had killed someone or not. Though he was talking, he seemed to be holding his true thoughts back.

We had supper and discussed how the two of them joined with the army. Then Mark went on with what it took to get home. His making it home was an adventure of its own. In fact, it took a Yankee to get him there. In the end, it didn't take him long to learn he could do something with one hand and a wrist. At the same time, his little lady was glad to see him.

Having Mark home, in one piece or not, got me thinking about joining. He proved he could do a few things and he knew he would be able to do more. With him home, I wasn't needed as badly as I had been. Then one night, I left wanting to leave Aunt Agnes a note, but I couldn't. Having gone to school such a short time, I couldn't write that well yet. Still I did leave a note by the fireplace:

Went to find Dad
Matt

For safety, I left another note in a bottle in the tree in our front yard. This had always been a place for the family to leave notes. If Robby tore the one up, there was this one.

Being in the middle of the night, I wasn't too worried about traveling. I had thought about taking the rifle, but thought Mark might need it. Still, there weren't too many animals for me to worry about. At the same time, I didn't know what I would do if I came on a Yankee. Still, I was intent on finding my father and brothers and was ready to face anything.

As I walked down the road, I heard a rustle in the brush. I must have jumped back three feet. Then hearing a horse neighing, I was worried a Yankee was nearby. I dove into a bush hoping not to be seen or found. I began to realize how scared I was. Then thinking the noise was from a nearby farm, I ventured onto the road again. With each step afterwards, I waited to see if I could hear something. It took me awhile to gain my confidence to carry on.

When I left, I thought enough to grab a few loafs of bread. By morning, I was so tired I got off the road and slept against a tree. A couple of times, a horse going by or a dog woke me up. It took me three days before I found a company of our army. With every step getting there, I would look at one hand or the other, wondering which one I would lose. Then feeling my chest, I wondered if I would end up dead. I finally decided that I didn't care; I was going to join the army ahead of me. As I looked at them marching along the road, I wondered how Mark, Robby, and Aunt Agnes were doing. I felt bad about leaving them, but I knew my father and brothers needed me.

Taking a breath, I headed for the army marching in front of me. I was glad that I had finally found them. It was a good, because I was out of bread and I was hungry. The bad issue was that they were on the move. Not knowing what to do, I just followed them.

"What are you doing?" A soldier asked me from behind me.

"I..." I began to answer, but another voice interrupted me.

"What's going on here, Sergeant?" the voice asked.

"Found us a straggler, Captain," the first soldier answered.

"What's your name, kid?" The Captain asked, as he motioned the other soldier off.

"Matt Duncan, sir," I answered, as I stood shaking. I think I was shaking because of his attitude or that this was making it final.

"What do you think you're doing?" he asked.

"I want to join the army," I answered shaking.

"Something wrong?" he asked. "You're shaking pretty bad."

"Hungry, sir," I answered him, not wanting to tell him I was scared. I also didn't want to tell him I didn't come to fight but to find my father and brothers.

"We can take care of that," he answered with a smile and looked over toward a wagon sitting not far from us.

"Then follow me," he told me, leading me over to a wagon.

"Yes sir," a soldier said greeting him. As he answered the captain, he gave me a wink.

"Our new drummer boy Matt is hungry," he answered giving me a pat on the back as he walked off.

"Well Matt, I don't have that much but it's better than nothing," the soldier told me. As he dug some food out, he introduced himself. "My name is Private Dick Anderson."

"Glad to meet you, Dick," I replied, waiting for him to hand me some food.

Turning back to me, he handed me some bread and jerky. I took his offering and told him, "Thanks."

He watched me, as other soldiers did walking by. One asked, "Who's the kid?"

"Our new drummer boy," Dick answered, giving him a grin.

"Are you dumb or just acting that way?" the soldier asked me.

"What?" I asked him, not understanding what he meant.

"Nobody would join this army if we were winning or losing," he told me as he stared down at me as I ate. He gave me the look as if he wanted the rest of the story.

"I'm out to find my father and brothers," I confessed to him, wondering if he was going to tell the Captain or not.

"There are plenty of them around here take your pick," he answered with a chuckle at himself for being so funny. He went on to ask me, "We have thin ones, we have fat ones, in fact, we have fathers in many shapes sizes and descriptions. What would you like?"

"Mine, that's good enough," I answered, with a grin.

"What's their group?" he asked me.

"What?" I asked, not understanding what he was asking me.

"The group they're in, or don't you know," he answered.

"Kentucky's 5th battalion. My one brother, I'm not sure," I told him. I realized that I hadn't asked Mark what outfit he and Henry had joined. I wondered how I was going to find Henry. I began to pray that I would be able to write Mark someday and find out which outfit Henry was in.

"Never seen any of them, but I heard they were at Gettysburg. They did a right fine job whipping them Yankees," he said with a big smile.

"I wish you luck," he told me shaking his head. As he pulled some food out for himself, he muttered to himself, "I might like to have them together...but I sure wouldn't join either...not in any man's army."

"Feeling better kid?" The Captains voice asked coming around the wagon.

"Yes sir," I answered jumping up to my feet.

"Now that you have some food in you, you had better make it back home. This isn't a war for kids," he told me.

"I'm fifteen, sir," I told him, hoping it would make a difference.

"I've already seen enough of you kids, I don't think I want to see another," he said shaking his head.

"Then I'll go at it alone. I'm going to find my father and brothers one way or the other," I told him getting mad.

"Get out the drum," he told Private Anderson. Then turning back to me, he warned me, "You might want to keep the harness on at all times. We don't have enough uniforms to outfit everyone. Still, you will want our boys to recognize you from the Yankees. The Brass emblem on the drum harness will do that."

"Thank you, sir," I told him as I watched Private Dick pull out a drum.

"Do you know how to play a drum?" Private Dick asked me as the captain walked away shaking his head again.

"I can learn," I answered as I took the drumsticks and the drum. Then sitting down, I tapped out a couple of quiet beats. Dick took the drumsticks from me as I asked him, "What's his name?"

"Captain O'Leary," he answered. "Let me show you how to hold the drumsticks."

For the next half hour or so, I played with the drum. I finally sat there wondering again what I was doing there. All the soldiers around me looked tired and beat up. Still, they were in a good mood, which made me feel better. A few came by and strummed their fingers on the drum giving me a big grin.

One soldier stopped and asked, "Do you know the beats we need to hear?" With that, he walked off to join a group of other soldiers not faraway.

I guess the soldiers question left me with a dumb look on my face. For Dick told me, "The drum isn't for marching in parades as much as letting the men know what to do next. Depending on what's going on, we use bugles and other times the drum, most times the drum. Don't worry, I'll teach it all to you. You will become the most important person in the company."

I had a feeling I was in for a heck of an education. I also had the feeling what I was going to learn might keep me from getting killed. This thought made me ask myself, "And how many of my family are dead already?" With the thought going through my head, I heard a shot ring out, and the bullet hit the wagon. Then for the first time I wondered if I was going to die soon.

Ida alone in Richmond

I felt lost sitting in the ruins of the building I was in. In the time frame of a week, my life as well as the Confederacy was a total loss. General Lee had left Richmond on April 2, 1865, and then a week later, he surrendered at Appomattox on April 7, 1865. Still the greatest loss was not the war but my mother dying the same day.

"Can I be of some help," a voice above my head offered.

Opening my eyes, I saw a pair of boots in front of me. Then lifting my head, I saw a white bearded man looking down at me. He looked as if he was in his mid to late sixties. He looked like he was in good shape for his age, but was carrying a few pounds more than he should. His eyes being dark said trust me, I care. Having the feeling I did, I decided it was safe to talk to him.

I told him, "I don't know if there is anyone that can help me. My father died on a battlefield. My Mama died a little while ago in the cubbyhole back there. My home, if it wasn't burned down, was ten miles north of here. I have no idea who in my life is alive or dead. Everyone around here is in the same condition as I am, or worse. Then, for I don't know how long, I haven't had a decent meal."

"Can't promise to solve all of your problems, but we can take care of some of them. I'm Reverend Paul Moore," he told me, with his hand out to help me up.

"Thanks Reverend," I answered, taking his hand letting him help me up. Thinking of what Mama had gone through, I wondered if he would say a prayer for her.

"What may I call you, young lady?" he asked.

"Ida Marsh," I answered him, brushing off some of the dirt from my dress. I felt funny being so dirty in the presence of a Minister of the Lord.

"There are so many like you, Ida. Now where are your folks?" He asked me, as he looked around to see if there was anyone near.

"Right around here," I told him, letting him follow me. As we entered the cubbyhole room, mother could be plainly seen. She was lying there with some papers covering her. I had covered her in hopes of keeping flies and animals away. As we walked up to her, I saw one of her hands sticking out. I knelt down and stroked it before I put it back under the newspaper.

Touching her cold body flooded me with so many memories and shattered dreams. Our place, father, my colt, Edgar, my friends and my whole life was gone. Overwhelmed, I fell on top of her still body and broke into tears. I found myself asking her, "What am I going to do without you, Mama? What am I going to do?"

"I'll have her taken care of," the Reverend said from behind me, sounding understanding.

"I want her to know I love her. She gave me everything and more," I told him through my tears. I found myself thinking how much I must have meant to Mama and the sacrifices she had made for me. I wanted to tell him how I felt about her, but I couldn't put it into words. At the same time, I didn't want to make her look worse than she really was. I decided the truth was between Mama, God, and me.

"She knows," he told me giving me a pat on my shoulder.

"But she didn't deserve to die like this…a dirty dress, torn to shreds…holes in her shoes…her hair a total mess," I tried to explain to him. Then reaching down to touch her again, I told him, "We have such a beautiful place north of here. That's where she belongs."

"Maybe we can find someone that can take her home where she belongs," he offered, reaching down to help me up again.

"She would like that," I told him standing up again, looking into his eyes. I saw a tear in them, and I felt as if someone cared.

"Is your mother around?" A man asked as he walked past us.

"No," I answered, not thinking it was important to tell him she had died. Watching the man walk down the street, I wonder why no one cared that Mama was dead.

"Marge is waiting for me. She should be able to get you something to eat and some clean clothes," he told me, then he stopped midstep. Turning to me, he asked, "Would you like me to say a prayer for her?"

"If you would," I answered, feeling a little better. Mama wasn't religious, but she did believe in God.

"The least I can do," he answered, as he took out his bible. Opening the bible up, he began, "In the name of the Father…"

I tried to listen to his prayer, but my mind was on why this had to happen. If we had stayed at home, she would be alive yet. If this war just hadn't happened, everything would be so different. Then I heard him finish his prayer.

"…I pray that you will help her daughter who is left alone in this world in trying times. I ask you to give her some guidance along her way. Amen," he said, ending the prayer.

"Marge is your wife?" I asked as he put his hand on my back, guiding me along.

"Yes," he answered. As we reached the end of the block, I turned and looked back at the alley entrance. I prayed Mama would be all right.

We walked another eight blocks before the Reverend stopped. Looking up at what was a church, we continued walking. Looking down at me, he said, "We'll rebuild it someday.

"Everything is such a mess," I said commenting on everything I could see.

At the end of the block, we stopped and he told me, "This is home."

"Oh," I answered, looking back to where Mama was lying. Then for some reason, I felt a chill go up my spine. I didn't understand, for it was warm today. Then a feeling that I wasn't alone came over me. It was the same feeling I would get when Mama tucked me into bed. I knew Mama was with me and I felt better.

"Afternoon Reverend," a man said in greeting as he walked up to us.

I noticed the man had a piece of cloth covering his mouth and nose. I realized from having talked to a few people why he was covering them. I learned that people working with dead bodies did that to protect themselves. At the same time, it decreased the smell of the decaying bodies they were working around. Then taking a breath, I could smell decaying flesh. The odor almost made me sick. I wondered why I hadn't noticed it before. Then it hit me that Mama had taken my mind off my surroundings.

Then looking at him again, I saw a man in his mid-forties and that he hadn't taken care of himself very good. I noticed he was also partially bald, but the hair he had was as black as black could be. Other than that, he was a normal fellow, like I had seen hundreds of times.

"Good afternoon Brother Morgan. I would like to introduce you to Ida Marsh," the Reverend replied, introducing me.

"Nice to meet you," I replied, as I tried to smile, as Mama taught me to.

"I know how busy you are…" the Reverend began to tell him, but pausing for a moment.

"I can't wait to hear the other half," Brother Morgan said with hesitation.

"Would you pick Ida's mother's body up and take her to their home?" The Reverend asked him.

Looking down at me with a frown, then with a grin and a shrug, he answered, "I guess I can. Where is home?"

"Ten miles north," I answered him. In answering, I felt almost happy for a second. It seemed something was going to work out for once today. "Mama's going to go home to rest forever," I said to myself.

"Let me get her something to eat first," the Reverend told him.

"I have to harness the horse and get the wagon out anyway," Brother Morgan, answered still shaking his head.

"That worked out better than I expected. We'll get you something to eat and then you'll be on your way," the reverend told me with a broad grin, guiding me up a set of steps.

"You're going home," I said under my breath to Mama.

"You found another one, I see. What's your name, young lady?" A woman asked with an understanding grin. She waited for us holding the door open at the top of the steps.

She also looked as if she was in her mid-sixties like her husband. Her height was in the neighborhood of five foot two or three. She had a full head of white hair, but done neatly. She wasn't real heavy, but she wasn't small either. Still, I found her to be a caring person.

"Marge, I would like to introduce you to Miss Ida Marsh," the Reverend told her, pushing me into the house.

As I entered, I saw a few other children filling up the Parlor. Looking back at the Reverend, I got the idea he was trying to help everyone. Then turning back to his wife, I told her, "It's nice to meet you."

"Her mother just died this morning," the Reverend told his wife as he took his coat off.

"That's a shame. Sit down and I'll get you something hot to drink. Tea maybe?" she asked me.

"That would be wonderful. I haven't had any tea for years," I answered.

"Brother Morgan is going to pick her up and take them home," the Reverend told her adding, "Have we anything to put into her stomach? She hasn't..." Their voices trailed off as they left me standing in the parlor.

"You too?" A kid asked leaning up against the wall opposite to me.

"Yes...I guess I'm not alone," I answered, not knowing what else to say.

"I think that's safe to say," another kid added.

"Where's your mother?" a girl asked. I wasn't sure, but I thought her name was Betty.

"She died in my...arms," I answered.

"I'm sorry. I lost my mother last night when a wall collapsed on her," she told me, looking worse than I think I did.

"That's terrible," I answered, feeling shocked at the thought of it happening.

Over the next few minutes, we discussed our losses. As it turned out, not everyone in the room was an orphan. When the Yankees began burning Richmond, some became separated from their families. Yet, some of these had their homes but no food. A couple wore bandages from falling walls nearly killing them. The saddest were the stories of the dead just stacked up in the center of town. Then the hundreds or thousands of soldiers lying around waiting for a doctor to help them. These twelve kids were perfect examples of the disaster of the war. Though the conversation didn't lessen my losses, I didn't feel so alone.

"Not much, but it should fill you up a little," Marge told me, suggesting for me to sit at the dining table.

"I can't remember when last I saw this much. Thank you," I answered, forgetting my problems for the moment.

"And here is your tea," the Reverend added setting it down in front of me.

"The two of you are so kind," I told them both as I took my first bite of roast beef.

"It's time like this we have to pull together," Marge said watching me.

"We wish we could do more. However, you had better get to eating. Brother Morgan should be here any minute," the Reverend reminded me.

"Yes, then I can take Mama home," I answered under my breath as I took another bite. Every bit was like a touch of heaven. The different flavors running across my tongue were such a thrill. I didn't care how long it took; I wasn't going to leave a crumb on the plate.

"Do you have any people you can go to?" Marge asked me.

"Up north somewhere…I don't know where though," I answered, as I took my last bite. Wiping my mouth off I added, "Maybe once I get home I will find some addresses or something…if there's anything left of the place."

"I wouldn't hold my breath on that one," the voice of Brother Morgan said behind me and then added, "I'm ready whenever you are, Missy."

"This is kind of you," Marge told him. Then turning to me, she told me, "Before you leave, I have another dress for you."

"It's either doing this or listen to one of the Reverends sermons, Ma'am," he answered with a laugh.

"God may forgive you, brother. I won't, so you will get two sermons when you get back; the first on respect for the clergy," the Reverend told him with a smile, "I do appreciate everything you are doing."

"Can't help it, she reminds me of my little girl," he answered, and then he turned and headed for the front door. Before leaving, he told me, "I'll be outside when you are ready."

After he left, Marge told me, "He lost his little girl to the fever some months back. Since his loss, he has vowed to help all the kids in trouble."

"That's sad; I guess there are many of us that have lost someone," I answered, getting up from the table. I thanked the Reverend's wife for the dress and changed into it. Then after giving my thanks to the Reverend and his wife again, I went out to join Brother Morgan.

"Coming over to play," a little girl named Susan cried out from across the street.

"I sure could use your help," her mother Beatrice said as we went by.

"I don't think so. We're taking Mama home," I answered them, pointing to Mama on the back of the wagon.

"I'm sorry," Beatrice said seeing Mama on the back and then she went on to add, "Good luck."

"You too," I replied with a wave.

I told him to head towards Ashland, and then when we were close, I would give him better directions. As we made our way, memories of Mama and I walking down this same road came back to me. Thinking about it, I remembered as we walked, we really didn't talk much about what we were going to do in Richmond. Nor did Mama say anything about what she was going to do. I just figured we would get a house and everything would be as it had been. I never gave it any thought as to what Mama would do to earn money. I found myself also remembering, not once did she complain about anything. I found myself feeling bad knowing what Mama had to do to keep me alive. I also wondered if it had been worth it.

I then tried to think of more pleasant memories of home, such as my little colt and our slaves in the village. I wondered if Mary ever found her parents when she headed north. I said a silent pray that Samuel and Rachael were all right. Then a vision of Edgar came to my mind. I felt a tear running down my cheek in fear he didn't make it home. I found myself surprised with my thoughts about him. I decided I would check his place out first.

I found my thoughts replaced by father going to war, then seeing both the Confederate and Yankee soldiers marching past our place and the few times they would come up to the house. Both sides, it seemed, never had enough food or clothes. I remembered the soldiers from both armies held the same expression: worn, tired, and beaten. I asked, "Is it worth it?"

"A good question," Brother Morgan answered and then added, "I doubt anyone will ever figure it out. Father killing son, brother killing brother...just didn't make any sense. There had to be a better way of solving our differences"

"I pray there will never be another war," I told him, as I looked back at Mama. If the war had never happened, she would be alive. I prayed I would never have kids and have to live with them as she did me.

"You're not alone," he answered.

Thankfully, Brother Morgan had brought along a blanket for Mama. Now no one could see how bad she looked now. Where she had what men called a nice shape, she had lost weight in the past year. Her auburn hair had gotten to be such a mess, she probably would have looked better if it was shaved off. Then as my clothes had been, hers were also dirty and full of holes. We had gone through all the clothes we had brought with us. "I'll miss you, Mama," I whispered as I looked at her.

As we traveled, I saw one home after another burned to the ground. I felt sorry for them as we passed by. From their actions, it seemed they had hope of rebuilding their past. The people I saw were going through the rubble and ashes trying to find what was left. As we went past one home, a woman was jumping up and down with joy. It appeared she had found a spoon, for she was waving it at a man nearby.

Seeing them, I remember I hadn't gone back for our belongings in our little cubbyhole of a place. I start to touch Brother Morgan's sleeve to ask him to turn around. As I touched the sleeve, I decided it was not worth it. What few items there were weren't worth going after.

"Yes?" He asked me having felt me touch his sleeve.

"Nothing. It wasn't anything important," I answered as I looked at what was left of the city.

"Okay," he said understanding. Then watching me look around, he told me, "This is nothing compared to the other side of the city."

"Worse than this?" I responded finding it hard to believe. Thankfully, most of the buildings in our area were brick and stone. Still, cannon fire ruined a good part of them. The buildings made of wood were burned to the ground, with soldiers cheering as they were burning. Yet, with the rubble around, it was a mess. The area was bad enough that the birds haven't returned.

With it only having been a few days ago, I remembered only to well the Yankees coming through. Mama and I hid, being afraid that they might kill us. In the basement corner, we still could hear the screams and the destruction. A soldier had come into the basement and we were even more scared. Then someone outside yelled for him, and he left without finding us. When we walked outside, we weren't prepared for what we saw. We couldn't recognize anything of the area. People lined the street crying and holding each other. Then for the next few days, everyone would run when they heard footsteps. Everyone was scared that it wasn't over. Then we got word the Yankees had left and we began trying to put everything back together.

"Oh yes, much worse than you see here. They were warming up when they hit here. Their main goal was the warehouse area and business district," he told me looking sad.

"Why?" I asked him for a better understanding. When the Yankees came through, Mama tried to explain, but it didn't make any sense.

"They wanted to take our supplies and ruin the supply lines going to our army. If the army couldn't get the supplies they needed, they wouldn't be able to fight," he explained.

"We're not part of the war…I don't understand why they had to kill the women and children," I tried to explain I didn't understand the widespread destruction they did.

"I know. I don't understand why they had to do what they did," he admitted. Then after taking a breath, he told me, "At least it's over."

"Hi Brother Morgan," a man in the street shouted out.

"Hi Bill…Ethel," Brother Morgan returns with a half wave.

"Not another one?" Ethel asked looking sad.

"Afraid so," he answered as we continued down the street.

"Isn't ever going to end. Every day," I could hear her say behind us.

Alongside the road were, worn out soldiers, trying to take naps. Most of them bandaged up pretty good. The injured soldiers were also covered with blood. The saddest, were the ones with their arms and legs amputated. I wondered if they had any idea what they were going home to. Then I wondered if it was worth the effort. The ones not injured were riding horses. They appeared to be determined to get home, for none said anything as they passed us.

One of our soldiers went by on horseback. I saw he was about the same age as I was. That by itself wasn't too major of an incident. It was his slowing his horse, and looking back at us. I got the feeling he was crying and I wondered why. I couldn't see any wounds and it didn't make any sense. I would have thought he would be happy to have it ended.

Looking at the soldiers made me wonder if it was worth going home myself. Then looking back at Mama, I was reminded the real reason I was going. Yes, I was taking her home, no matter what was there or not.

Want to Go West Lady?

At a fork in the road, I had Brother Morgan to go right. From the fork, I could see our home. What I saw took my breath away; there wasn't much left of it. The house was nothing but rubble. The columns looked like broken teeth sticking up in the air. The stable wasn't much more than a pile of ash, with a few pieces of burned wood sticking up.

"Not much left of the place," Brother Morgan said as he turned into the drive. Then snapping the reins, he asked, "Where to from here?"

I directed him to the cemetery, and he went on. I wished I had an instrument of some kind to welcome Mama home. If the people were still in the village, they would give her a great send off. As it was, the place was dead silent. I decided it was fitting, Mama, Brother Morgan, myself, and God. How much more did we need. It was far better than just the cubbyhole and newspapers.

Once we reached the cemetery, Brother Morgan began digging her grave. I went out into the field and found some flowers. I felt Mama should have some flowers of some kind on her grave. I picked and picked flowers until her grave was, dug.

"I'm sorry misses, she deserves better, I know. A proper box and friends around, but there's no time for that," Brother Morgan told me, with a tear in his eye.

"Her only true friend died in battle," I got out through my tears.

"Hopefully," I thought, "they are together again."

He didn't say anything as he began to pull Mama off the wagon.

"Let me help?" A familiar voice asked.

I turned and saw Jacob coming around a tombstone. I guess I was so shocked, my mouth gapped open. I had to look at him twice though to be sure. This Jacob wasn't that much taller than the one I knew years ago. Yet, he had grown some muscles and his hair was a little bushier than I remembered. Though I would never have told him, but he had grown a few lines in his face. I had the feeling he had been working where it took some muscles, for as good a shape as he appeared to be in. Then I noticed he had stubble on his chin. The idea that he had to shave made me want to laugh.

"Miss Ida, flies might fly in if you don't shut your mouth. Your Mama?" He asked, as he helped take her off the wagon.

"Yes," I answered with a tear, thinking she had made it home. Now one of Mama's favorite boys was helping to bury her.

"They brought your Papa home a few years ago, and I buried him over there," he told me solemnly, as the two of them took care lifting Mamma from the wagon and laid her to rest into the ground.

It wasn't just the fact father made it home that shocked me, but where he was buried. Brother Morgan had picked out a spot full of weeds, and that made me feel bad. Still, it was next to the spot Jacob was pointing too. It turns out that Father and Mama were buried next to each other. They were going to be together at last, forever now.

From his pocket, Jacob pulled a flute out and played a short tune. Brother Morgan said a few words, and they began to cover Mama over with dirt.

As they worked, I touched the dirt that covered father. Softly I told him, "I wish I had been here father, but we didn't know. At least I brought Mama home to you." I sat there watching the two men cover Mama. I turned back to father's grave and told him, "Don't hold it against her father. She did it to feed me." I knew he would be shocked but he would understand.

"Well missy, I had better get going. Are you going to be coming with me?" Brother Morgan asked me.

"No, I'm going to stay here," I told him looking down at Mama's grave.

"Where are you going to stay? You have some friends or relatives in the area,"

"I'll find a place. I belong here," I answered, wiping another tear from my cheek.

"It's up to you, but I have to get going," he told me. Then he turned to Jacob, "I didn't get your name. Nevertheless, thanks for your help, and you take care of yourself, Missy."

"I will," I assured him, wondering what I was going to do next.

"The least I could do for the Lady," Jacob told him. He turned and looked at me with a grin, and told me, "It's hard to think of you as a lady, but that's what you have become."

As he talked, I noticed his "Slave Tag," was still hanging from his neck. Without looking at it, I knew his number was 106789D. I remember a few days before Father went to war he paid his "Slave Tax." He was irritated that he needed to register Jimmy's newborn son. "He can't even feed himself and I have to pay a tax on him," Father said as he left for town.

As Brother Morgan got into the wagon and drove away, I asked Jacob, "I thought you went north?" While I waited for his answer, I wondered what he meant I had become a lady.

"I did Miss Ida, then I got to missing home. No work up there, so I figured I would rather take my chances and starve at home. Having come to that conclusion, I came back," he answered with a smile. Then seeing the many questions in my eyes, he added, "Remember my working with Jocko."

Jocko had been our blacksmith, and Jacob kept pestering him to teach him what to do. Every minute he had between chores he was stoking the pit or doing something. The memory brought a smile to my face, and I nodded my remembering.

"What he taught me got me a job. I'm not making much, but enough with my misses doing wash, we can buy food and live in a little shack," he told me.

"Oh, where did you get a job at?" I asked, not being able to think of a place that could be hiring people.

For a long time he didn't say anything but look back towards the village and then back at me. The taking a deep breath, he told me, "You people had all left. With all of you gone, Mr. Smiley took over your daddy's place. He isn't doing much, but it's enough for me to live on."

"The place isn't going to do father any good now. And I don't know what to do with it," I assured him. Then what he had told me hit me that he had said his misses. I went on to ask him, "You said your misses."

"Yes, and we have us a little boy now," he told me with the biggest smile you could ever ask to see.

"I'll be. Congratulations," I replied, amazed at how things can change in such a short time. I remembered father taking me out to the fields.

"Just plain old dirt. Nothing pretty about it, wouldn't you agree?" Father asked me.

"Yes father, it is ugly," I answered wondering where he was going with this. I was a little afraid I was about to get one of his lectures.

"You wait. One of these nights, you'll go to bed and it will still be ugly, then the next morning, there will be touches of green everywhere. God gives life to everything, no matter what happens to us. Things will change and it will be new and beautiful again."

A few weeks later, I went to bed and the fields were brown with dirt. The next morning, new plants were growing all over the field. Each day, the field was prettier than the day before. Maybe life can come back to the place once the house is rebuilt and people are living here again.

"How is it that you are here this afternoon?" I asked him.

"As with my parents, I owe your Mama a lot," he told me. Then looking down at her grave, he went on to add, "She sat with my Mama for days, putting cold rags on her forehead and gave her medicine when she had the fever. If it wasn't for her, Mama would not have made it."

"I never knew she did anything like that," I answered, amazed what I didn't know about Mama. It was a rare occasion she ever went any further than the veranda. Let alone leaving the veranda, she actually helped out a Slave family. I found myself missing her even more. I wished she had told me some of the actions she had done.

With a laugh he went on to tell me, "My pappy said the master wasn't too happy with the idea. He was afraid what people might say about her doing such a thing. Then he agreed someone should do it, and told her to go ahead." Then with a smile, he added, "Both of them helped everyone in one way or the other. That's why I had to come back. I owed them, so I have been coming up here every night for better than two years."

I was tired of crying, but I found myself crying again. Hearing new things about my father and mama made me feel proud. I reached out, took his hand, and kissed it. In letting it go, I told him, "Thank you for being here. I'm sure they both appreciate it also."

"Do you want to stay with us? It's not as fine as the house was but we have room," he offered, and then went on to add, "You must be hungry."

"Thank you, but I think I will stay here. I have to think everything over, but I will be seeing you soon," I told him as he got up to leave.

"If you need anything, let us know. I had better get going, or my misses will get worried," he told me with a smile. Then as he left, he added, "I sorry about you losing them."

"Thank you Jacob," I answered as I began walking with him. As I left, I turned and whispered softly to them, "I'll be back."

"Thanks for everything and I'll be around to meet your Misses and your son," I told him giving him a hug.

"I sure hope all of those that wanted freedom think all of this was worth it," he said as I let him go. Then looking around, he shook his head and added, "Most of us were free and those that stayed with the Master were happy, as they were."

I reached up into his shirt and pulled out his tag. I told him, "I see you're still wearing it yet."

"It's part of my identity I never want to forget what once was that I will always miss. I don't ever want to forget the ones I loved. The Master and his wife, you, Jocko, Mary and the rest of them," he answered and then he turned and walked towards home.

Him mentioning Jocko and Mary got me to wondering where they were. I had fond memories of the two of them. They were a couple that wasn't black or white; they were friends. I prayed they were doing okay and happy with their life. I hoped Mary had found her parents.

Watching him walk away, I was proud of who I was. I was even more proud of my parents. The conversations of slavery my parents talked about came back to me. The Northerners just don't understand the slaves were part of our family. Maybe they were jealous of what they thought was free labor.

With dusk coming, I wondered where I was going to stay. I realized that sentiment might have driven me too far. I couldn't sleep out here in the open, so I wondered what I was going to do. As I sat down in the dirt, I wondered where I was going. A bird flew over chirping as he found a tree branch. I wondered if his nest had room for one more. I shook my head and laughed at the idea.

I looked up at the house, and I could see where my room once was. Now there was nothing but air and rubble under it. I laughed at the thought of finding information on my relatives. I wasn't going to be finding anything in that rubble. Then a voice told me, "Root Cellar." I looked around and I saw no one. I realized it must been my imagination, but it did sound like a voice.

Then it came to me what the "Root Cellar" meant to me. I remembered my father's worries of the coming war. He was afraid; the Yankees would take everything we had. To rest his fears, he had a false wall built in the "Root Cellar." He had told Mama if anything didn't seem right to put everything in it. The first time we saw Yankee soldiers I remember that Mama ran into the house. After a short time, she returned with a smile on her face. I wondered if Mama had hidden something of use for me. Then it dawned on me I could also sleep in the cellar. Then I remembered they use to use straw to cover the vegetables with to keep them longer. I figured I might sleep on the straw and be better choice than sleeping outside.

The next morning, I found myself with more sore muscles than I knew anyone could have. Still it was wonderful to have spent the night at home. Stepping outside, I found a surprise for me. Jacob must have figured out where I was staying. He had left me some food to eat. Thanks to Jacob, hunting for something to eat was not a concern right then. My first chore then would be to find out, if anything, what Mama had hidden away.

Going back into the root cellar, I looked at the back wall. The wall was solid brick and I couldn't see a broken joint. Then looking at the sidewalls, I saw they were dirt. "With the back wall being brick, I had the idea it might be a false," I thought. Another thought came to mind, "If that was true, how did Mama hide anything and get back to me so fast." I pushed and hammered, and nothing happened. I ran my finger across the joints, and they were solid. I finally gave up and decided to go into the village and check out the plant and Jacob.

As I began the walk, Edgar came to mind. I decided the first place I was gong to stop was at his parents' home. Though they lived as far out of town the other way as our place, it would be worth it. The village wasn't very large anyway. At least a few years ago, there were only a few hundred living there. Now if it were the size of Richmond, then I would have a problem.

As I walked down the main road going through the village, I passed father's building. From the building, Jacob's voice rang out, "Miss Ida."

I turned, and went back to the building. I told him, "I was going to stop by and thank you for the food you left."

"I didn't want you to starve. It's one thing to let you sleep in the Root Cellar, but another to let you starve. Where were you going?" he asked me. Then stopping me he asked, "Mr. Buchanan's place?"

"Uh oh, I didn't think to ask you if their place was like ours, demolished," I told him wondering why I hadn't thought about it.

"As flat as flat can be," he answered. He went on to tell me, "They died of a broken heart, seeing all of their horses taken away, as well as the paintings and whatever else worth having. Then the Yankees loaded up two of them cannons and blew the house down."

Later I was to learn the Buchanan's were inside the house when the Yankees turned their cannons on it. Everyone inside the house died. The Yankees never gave them any warnings.

"You raise an interesting question. Why Mama didn't take some of our belongings to Richmond? Our life might have been a lot better," I asked myself as well as him.

"I hope you are not going to try to take the business back?" Mr. Smiley asked as he walked up looking scared.

"No, I don't want it. As long as people like yourself and Jacob are getting some good out of it, it's yours," I assured him, still thinking of the stuff father and mama had in the house. Then thinking back to the day we left, I vaguely remember the inside of the house looked bare. I knew mama must have hidden all away.

"Good," Mr. Smiley said sounding hesitant but added, "Thanks." Without another word, he turned around and went back to work. Then for the first time since last night, I remembered where I had heard his name. He was father's lead man, making him the perfect one to take over the business.

"I saw the Yankees take everything out of the house," Jacob told me. Then he went on to add, "The only items they brought out were tables and chairs, everything made of wood, which they put into the stables and burned. They didn't take anything that I saw with them, unless it was real small."

"That proves it. Mama hid everything before we left. But why didn't she take it with us?" I asked again.

"Afraid someone might steal it," he suggested.

"Might be, but it would have been nice to have had some of it," I told him. Then looking around, I commented, "Not in as bad of shape as it might have been."

"Nothing worth taking," he answered, giving me a big smile.

"True. So Edgar hasn't been back?" I asked him hoping he had seen him or heard something.

"No, not that I know of," he answered, as he turned to look back at the shop. From the way he looked, I knew he worried about his job.

"I had better let you get back to work. I will see you later," I told him. As he walked back into the shop, he pointed at a house next to it. I realized it must be his place. As I walked by it, I knew it was better than where I had been living. At the same time, it was better than the houses in the old slave village.

I walked by the school and many other places. Everyone was sorry to hear Mama had died. They all asked what she died of, and I had to be honest. The first was I didn't know, but I thought it was loneliness. In reality, she probably caught something from a soldier and that killed her. I don't know for she never complained. In reality, we didn't talk as we use to. That one lack of communication, made it hard for me to accept her death. I had so much to say to her, but she died so soon. The biggest emotion was that I loved her and I was sorry for everything. It wasn't that I could do anything about the war, but I was the cause of her doing what she did.

Other wise, I heard the problems the rest of the area had with the war. I also heard who was injured, mutilated, and killed. No one though had heard anything about Edgar. I found myself accepting the idea he had died like so many others, with having talked to almost everyone.

I learned there was a camp just before the Buchanan place, on the other side of town. It was a temporary hospital. With the Reverend and his wife being so kind in getting Mama and I here, I needed to pay his kindness back. The only way I knew how to do that was to help others. What better way but to help at the hospital camp. I decided that in the morning I would make my way out there.

Somehow, the day went by without me realizing it. Rather than going home, I went to Jacobs's place to meet the Misses and his son. I didn't stay long, but we had an enjoyable time chatting. His wife was quite a bit like he is, genial and friendly, showing interest in what you have to say. After a quick bite and a cup of tea, I decided to leave. His wife Molly insisted that I take a blanket and I couldn't refuse. I prayed it might help me sleep better than the night before. With that, I went back to the home place. I still wanted to look at the back wall again.

"I'm opening you one way or the other," I said to the root cellar, as I stood in front of it. Before I went inside, I looked at the outside a lot closer. I looked as if the roof went further than it seemed to on the inside. It made me think there was a whole room behind the wall. I decided whatever there was, I was going to find it.

I went inside, and looked at the wall again. I looked at each brick one at a time. More times than not, I lost track of where I was. I finally touched each brick one at a time. Then halfway down, I found a brick turned end for end. The one end was sticking out, about the same distance as the width of my finger. I tried pushing on it and nothing happened. Out of frustration, I kicked the wall. Then taking a deep breath, I tried pushing the brick.

As I pushed, the brick went inward. Then as it stopped, I heard a clicking sound and the wall swung open a few inches. With the door to the cellar open, I was able to see inside the cavity behind the wall. As I had guessed, there was a whole room full of the items from our house. Rummaging around I even found Mama's jewelry. Looking at it I began to come up with and idea. Then I noticed some of her clothes. I wondered if they might fit me, for I didn't have anything to wear but what was on my back.

Not having any other clothes and no bath for as long as I could remember, I came up with an answer. I was going to solve the problem in the morning. With there being a pond not far from the house, I was going to bathe there. At the same time, wash my dirty clothes. Though the idea was sound, I worried about my clothes dissolving and someone seeing me. Still, I had to do something. Now with Mama's clothes, I had a change. The one problem with them was in what shape they were in. I was afraid they might be full of holes having been stored for so long.

Before I could grab anything, I heard footsteps outside. I quickly closed the wall before anyone saw what was behind it.

"Ida, are you in there," a familiar voice rang out not to faraway.

I screamed out with joy, "*Edgar*, you're alive." I didn't wait for a reply, I ran out of the cellar to greet him.

"Well hello, hello, hello. Haven't you grown up," he replied as I ran towards him.

Not stopping me, I realized there was a two-year difference in our ages. The last time he saw me, I was twelve years old. Four years had gone by since then, so there might be a change or two. Looking down at myself, I brushed off the dirt on my dress. I was glad the Reverend and his wife had given me this dress. I would have hated for him to have seen me in my torn dress.

With that thought, I jumped into his arms and gave him a kiss.

"Well that's a first," he said as he let me go.

I laughed, knowing he meant it was the first time we had ever kissed. Then stepping back, I looked at him again. Every part of me felt a whole lot different about him than I had ever before. I wondered if Mama felt this way about Father. Then I remembered watching Mama look at Father and she would have this funny smile on her face.

Stepping back again, I looked at him closer. He now supported a nice head of blonde hair. He was also wearing a beard, which I found strange thinking of him having to shave. It wasn't as full as some men were, but they are older than he is, I realized. In looking at it, it did give him an air that was nice. At the same time, his body had filled out. The last time I had seen him he was skin and bones. Now he stood straight and was muscular. It was the sparkle in his blue eyes I found to be intriguing.

Matt and the battlefields

The first night with the company of soldiers was a little exciting. With the sound of gunfire, I knew we were under attack. I rolled onto my side and crawled under the wagon. Lying there waiting for more gunfire, I wondered if it was the best place to hide. Then a roar of laughter rang out through the camp.

"Hey stupid, hasn't anyone taught you how to clean a rifle," I heard one soldier ask someone.

Though hesitant in coming out into the open, I got the message. Either someone had made a mistake doing something, or it was a joke. If it was a joke, I was for shooting whoever it was. The shot aged me by a good ten years. Right then I wasn't ready to die. As I lay there, I thought how my father yelled at us in the way to handle a gun. He yelled so much about being safe, I could recite his speech in my sleep.

It turned out one of the soldiers made a little mistake cleaning his rifle. He forgot it had a load of gunpowder in it. In pulling the trigger, he shot the ramrod across the camp. We found it stuck in the side of the wagon. Pulling it out, Dick and I had a good laugh.

For the longest time, the accident was the subject of many jokes. The Yankees were even made part of the joke. One or another of us would shout out, "Watch out for flying Ramrods," or we would tell them, "We'll get you with a bullet or a Ramrod be sure of that." In the end, the joke took our mind off the battle for a second or two giving us a chance to laugh. With the beautiful countryside covered with blood, laughter was not something we got to do often.

Want to Go West Lady?

It wasn't often we had something to laugh at. From the start, I worked on the drumbeats I needed to play during a battle. I was scared thinking if I made a mistake, no matter how small, someone in our company could lose their life. Everything Private Dick told me became gospel. I didn't take long for me to wonder if I had done the right thing in joining this outfit.

"Duncan, front and center," our Captain cried out clearly wanting me.

His voice was the kind that sent shivers up my spine. It was about like having a mountain lion roar right behind you. A couple of men not including Private Dick warned me that he was a rough officer to serve under. With him calling me, it had me a little worried.

"Yes sir," I answered as I ran up to him. Once I reached him, he seemed to be relaxed and he had a grin on his face. Then seeing me, he began to frown, and I got worried again.

"Tomorrow we will more than likely engage the enemy again. I don't…" he started telling me, but stopped for some reason.

"Yes sir, you were about to say?" I asked, wondering what he was trying to tell me. Though I was looking for father and my brother, I knew I was going to be going into battle. Being of the mind where I wasn't sure if I was for or against the confederacy made it harder to kill someone. Yet, that's what war was about, and I wasn't leaving.

"I was going to say, I want you to stay off the battlefield. Anytime we are under fire, I want you to find a tree, gopher hole or anything to get out of the line of fire. As I said last night, I'm tired seeing you kids getting killed," he told me looking concerned.

"Yes sir…but the drum, don't you need someone to beat out the commands?" I asked him, having been told of its importance. I could understand and appreciated his feelings; I didn't want to die. At the same time, if the drum needed to be beaten, why not let me. Why have men die, only because they don't know what's going on.

"It can be heard for miles. It doesn't matter where you might be," he answered giving me a pat on the head like a kid.

It only took us minutes to start my first march. By the time the sun was straight up overhead, we hadn't stopped for a rest. Though I was in the wagon with Private Dick, I was tired of bouncing around. Later I got use to it, and could go all day on that wagon. That first day I was tired as I knew the infantry were even more tired than I was.

I had been watching them all day, and felt sorry for them. In their long johns and the wool uniforms, they were sweating to death. However, some were luckier than others were, for not everyone had uniforms. Still, the march was taking its toll on them. Some it seemed didn't even have any shoes. One soldier in particular, I remember seeing him rubbing his feet as he walked. He made it hard for Dick to keep the wagon going.

"*Get out of my way*," Private Dick shouted at him.

"Sorry Private, it's not easy walking with blisters," he answered as he stepped to one side, letting us by.

"If you stray too far behind, no one's going to go back to get you, unless it's a Yankee company," Private Dick warned him with a hardy laugh.

"Be right back," I told him as I jumped off the wagon. Running back to the soldier, I told him as I sat on the ground, "Hey soldier, here, take my shoes."

"Really? You're not serious are you?" He asked looking shocked but happy at the thought.

"I'm riding the wagon, so I don't need them," I assured him. I prayed it was the right action to take. I felt a little funny with my toe's sticking out as they were.

"Thanks a lot," he replied with a big grin.

I ran back to catch up with the wagon. With each step, I knew the soldier was going to appreciate my shoes.

"Relieve yourself?" Private Dick asked as I climbed up to where he was.

"In a manner of speaking," I answered, as I raised up a foot to rub it. I wondered what he was going to say when he saw what I had done.

"Don't know what I'm going to do with you," he said with a smile and then added, "If he gets himself killed, there goes your boots, and getting new ones might take an act of God. That's why he didn't have any on his feet."

"They were getting worn anyway. I have been thinking about getting new ones," I answered as I started to rub the second foot.

"Right. But remember what I told you," he said.

We finally stopped, and Private Dick began to pass around some hardtack. It was as nasty in taste as the food Robby would make. Still, when you are hungry, you will eat anything. I found myself praying with the first bite for a piece of chicken. I don't think I got to the second bite and we were back fighting again.

Gunfire was coming from both sides of us. Every man and animal seemed to be grabbing a rifle or pistol returning fire. I dove under the wagon, not knowing any other place to hide. The infantry mounted and tried to go around the backside of the enemy. As all of this was going on, I saw some of our men fall. Blood was flowing and I was getting sick.

"*Get into the wagon!*" Private Dick ordered me. It was obvious he meant right then and not later. His command also told me something was up and I was supposed to be part of it.

With a little hesitation, I jumped over the back of the wagon. As I cleared it, a bullet passed over my head. I barely got the drum over the wagon's gate without it strangling me. Once in the wagon, I grabbed a bag of flour and held onto it with all my life. I didn't know what it was going to do for me, but I wasn't letting it go. Mind you, this all happened in the blink of an eye. There was only time enough to do, and get scared later.

Peeking out of the end of the wagon, a spectacular sight was before me. I could see hundreds of muzzle fire crisscrossing the road. For as beautiful as it was, it was even more deadly. I quickly got my head down out of sight. As soon as I heard the first shot, I began hearing the screams of pain and the dying men ahead of us.

"*I've been hit*," a voice cried out, giving me an indication what was going on.

"*Shut up…Or I'll shoot you myself…I can't concentrate*," an unsympathetic voice replied.

"*Drum out the order to advance,*" the Captain shouted out to me as he passed the wagon.

"*Where are you worthless Yankees…? Show yourselves,*" another voice yelled out to the attackers.

In between the conversation, there were many more moans. From the way they sounded, I knew most of them weren't going to make it. I had no idea what I could do. I was afraid; I might be moaning shortly myself. I asked myself, "Don't they know the captain doesn't want me killed? In fact he wants me out of the line of fire." I wondered if I yelled those thoughts to the enemy if it would do me any good.

Without answering the Captain, I began to beat the drum. I wondered where we were advancing to, but that was only a passing thought. My main attention was the drum and the bullets coming through the canvas of the wagon.

"*I think he is taking us to the clearing ahead…Hopefully it will draw the enemy out where we can see them,*" Private Dick told me as we made it out of there.

"*My leg…My leg,*" another soldier cried out. With all the gunfire, his plea was barely heard.

If what my father told me was right, a miniball going through a leg or arm will take it off. I wondered if the soldier's leg got a direct hit or was it grazed. If he was lucky it was just grazed and he had a chance. The problem then would be if he didn't bleed to death. However, if it was a direct hit, he might bleed to death anyway. Later I would be told most deaths on the battlefield were from bleeding to death.

I looked over the boxes and saw the clearing he was talking about. In reality, it wasn't an open space. Covered with boulders, the infantry could hide behind them. At the same time, anyone coming out of the woods would be seen. With the enemy having the advantage of being in the forest, it made it hard for our guys to move. It seemed we were caught in the crossfire and we might not get out of.

"*Johnny's been hit,*" another voice cried out.

"*I'll make you Yankees pay for killing my brother,*" another voice answered. The gunfire seemed to increase for a second or two.

"*Johnny's not the only one hit…His entire squad is gone,*" another voice confirmed.

I can't describe the sounds that floated through the countryside, the noise from the muzzles, bullets flying by and men in agony. Other than a deer or a raccoon, I had never seen death. It's something a person can't put to words. It seemed so pointless. All we were doing was traveling down the road. In doing so, many men lost their lives. *Why?*

"*That's enough,*" Private Dick told me.

I hadn't stopped from the time the Captain had told me what to drum out. I noticed my wrists were a little sore, but not as bad as my back. Playing a drum on your back was not the most comfortable position to do it. Having stopped, I felt a need to see what was going on. I looked out the back of the wagon again back toward where they were. The entire area was so full of smoke; I couldn't see what was happening.

"*Are you all right back there?*" He asked as he got out of the wagon and began shooting.

"I'm all right," I yelled back to him. As I answered, I ran my hands over my body.

"*Then you might want to get out of there,*" he suggested.

Looking up at the canvas over me, I had a feeling it might be better outside. Because I didn't bother to argue or answer, I joined him. After the first couple of bullets bouncing off our boulder, I began looking for a better place to hide. Looking around, I couldn't see anywhere that was better. Then I heard shots fired from inside the woods and I prayed it was the Calvary.

The shots from the woods toward us stopped. It seemed my guess was right, and the Calvary was coming to the rescue. It didn't take long a couple of dozen Yankees marched out of the woods with their hands up. My first battle had ended.

"Now we have to feed the bastards as well as find a regiment to drop them off at," a soldier told another as they passed us.

The second one offered a suggestion, "We could kill them where they stand"

"Sounds like a good idea to me," the first answered going on to add, "and if they capture you, they would do the same to you."

"Your wife would miss me," the second one replied and the two broke out into laughter.

"They make a good point," Private Dick told me, as he was getting up. Then as he was brushing himself off, he added, "What's the difference...you kill them in battle or you kill them when they surrender. Either way, they're dead."

"Then who buries them?" I asked him.

"Good point. It might be better to let them walk a ways," he answered with a laugh.

"I'll be right back," Private Dick said as he walked away.

"He's deserting," one of the soldiers said with a laugh.

Later, I was to learn deserting was a common event. It was understandable why they deserted. Most of the time, food was short, no uniforms, no boots and there was a chance of dying on the battlefields. What most deserters didn't realize was that most were shot when another outfit found them. There were a few times a prisoner or deserter was offered a chance to serve the Union Army out west fighting Indians, but this wasn't often. In the end your choice was, did you get shot by a Yankee or by your own.

"And give up this beautiful job," I replied, laughing with him. Then getting control of myself, I added, "How could anyone leave such wonderful meals and the chance to travel like this."

"You have something there. Meals of beans and hardtack, how much more could a person ask for? In fact, what I have eaten is better than my mother use to fix," the soldier answered laughing. He got up and headed toward the main body of soldiers. As he walked he was whistling a song I didn't recognize but it was fitting for the area.

A few minutes later, I saw Private Dick coming towards me. He had a funny look on his face and his hands were behind his back. I had a funny feeling he was about to play a practical joke on me. With all the dead around, I almost was looking forward to whatever he was going to pull on me. The bit of laughter I just had didn't last long enough.

"Got something for you," he said as he got close to me.

"A snake?" I asked him grinning.

"Hadn't thought of that," he answered as he held out a pair of boots to me.

"For me?" I asked, not sure he was serious.

"Officer's boots too," he told me and then went on to add, "Get them on so we can leave."

"But if these belong…" I began to comment with him interrupting me.

"He's not going to need them anymore," he told me.

I knew then he had taken them from a dead officer. Putting my first toe into one boot, I had a funny feeling. The idea of the boots having belonged to some else was bad enough. Boots off a dead man was something different. Yet, I did need something on my feet. Without worrying anymore about it, I put them on. Once on, I strutted around like an officer wearing a grin.

"It's going to take a lot more than boots to make you an officer," he said as he got up into the wagon.

"Thanks," I told him as I got up into the wagon.

"*Mount up*," the Captain shouted out the order, after we had buried the dead. Then coming back to us, he looked inside the wagon and checked on me, "I see you survived." A few minutes later, he shouted out, "*Forward.*"

"Yes sir," I answered with a grin.

"Good. Private Dick, you know the routine," he said as he continued ahead of us. Then faintly, I could hear him shout out, "Move them out."

"What did he mean, you know the routine?" I asked Private Dick.

"We're to follow the prisoners, and make sure none of them get free," he answered as he snapped the reins.

"Have any escaped before?" I asked. I couldn't see anyone dumb enough to try with someone right behind them.

"One tried," he answered, as he looked over at me with a grin.

"What did you do…shoot him?" I asked, not sure if I wanted to hear his answer. As we were talking, I watched the prisoners ahead of us. If I didn't know any better, I would have sworn some were neighbors of ours. With living so close to the Kentucky border and not having any slaves, people were divided about which side they supported. In looking at them, I saw what looked like a common problem with both sides. They all look as underfed and tired as our men were. I wondered if we really had beaten them, or if they were just tired of fighting. If nothing else, I thought, they have a better chance of making it home now.

"Came close…I placed the shot about two inch's from his one foot," he answered.

"Then what happened?" I asked having a feeling it might be one of his jokes. I was beginning to learn people joke more when they're under tension. I wondered if dad and my brothers were trying to make jokes.

"He stopped dead in his track until I tied him to the others again," he told me as he snapped the reins again. Not getting the response he wanted he shouted out, "Let's get this parade moving.

In thinking about being in this war, I decided I would never marry. Why make a wife a widow and leave your kids fatherless. It just didn't make any sense to me. Then looking back at the prisoners, my thoughts went to them. I knew people would feel sorry for them for the way we were treating them. We were making them walk rather than moving them by wagon. People have a way of forgetting this was war. The average soldiers in the Infantry of both armies walked. What's the problem with prisoners walking?

As we progressed, I learned the company was part of a Battalion ahead of us. With any luck, we should be catching up with them the following day. Then the prisoners would be transferred to a train, and we would be on our way.

Seeing a piece of paper flying around behind us, I picked it up. Looking at it, I asked him, "What's this?"

"A manifest document," he answered, and then seeing my confused look, he went on to explain, "It's a list of the items that came in our last shipment of supplies."

"Manifest…" I repeated, as I looked down the list. I saw a few words I recognized but most of them I didn't know.

"Can you read?" Private Dick asked.

"A little," I answered being as honest as I could.

"I guess we have something to keep ourselves busy doing," he told me as he snapped the reins again.

"What?" I asked him, not understanding what he was talking about.

"You are going to learn to read and write, even if it kills me to teach you," he told me.

I wondered if picking up that piece of paper was a wise action. Years later, I would appreciate the work he put into teaching me. At the time, it did keep down the boredom and thoughts of being hungry. With the idea fresh in his head, we started right then. I would point at a word and repeat it. Then he would have me spell it out for him five times. After an hour or so, he would ask me to spell the same word. Learning as I was, I would never be able to use the words in a sentence. Still, it was a beginning, which he added to later.

When we caught up with the Battalion I was amazed at all the men also with them, and the number of wagons and cannons. I couldn't believe there was any way we couldn't win every battle we got into. I was to learn how dumb my thinking was. Especially when two armies the same size meet in the middle of a field and fight it out.

Still it was impressive, and I felt safe after the skirmish I had been in a few days earlier. We camped in the middle of a field, next to a small town. The only purpose of the town was to be a place to put a train station. It was here supplies could be received and prisoners shipped back to a prison camp.

The encampment was in an open field not far from the town. As far as I could see, there were tents and more tents. Without seeing the insides of them, I knew there were beds. Every bone and muscle in my body cried out to be in one of them. I was so tired of the supply wagon and feeling every rut in the roads.

As I was beginning to learn, every good thing had a bad side. As we pulled into our spot, we passed a tent I wished I could have missed. The canvas of the tent was splattered with blood.

"Looks like the surgeons are busy enough," Private Dick said as we passed it.

As if someone had staged it, there was a moan. With another moan, we heard a scream.

"I wouldn't want to be that guy," Private Dick said shaking his head. Then seeing my questioning look, he added, "He probably just lost an arm or leg."

"Ouch," I replied trying not to think what it must be like.

"With all the body parts stacked up in back there, I wonder how many will survive," I said feeling sick to my stomach again. I wondered if I would ever get used to the sight of so much blood. Then on closer inspection, I saw two or three dozen wounded men waiting for their turn. Most of them were moaning so loud I wanted to cry.

"Their odds are not too good," he answered shaking his head in disgust.

"A shame," I answered quietly. I did finally learn not to accept what I saw, but to expect it. Death, wounds and mayhem were a big part of war. There's no way you can fight a war without having all of these happen as a result.

Once we left the camp, everything got boring no matter what I learned from Private Dick. We would either be starving or getting bored. The boredom was broken up with raiding Yankee supply lines, towns, or homes along our march. In raiding different homes, we took the food and horses that were left. There were reports of raping the women, but I never saw any of it. Still I felt a nasty taste in my mouth and a fear for my home.

As we moved around, I learned a lot about the war. It seemed we had just taken control of New Mexico. Not having any idea where the state was, Private Dick drew a map in the dirt. From the way it looked the, majority of the states across the country were a part of the Confederacy.

The first major battle I was at was Shiloh. It was in the first part of April 1862. We were spotted a mile from the Northern troops. I was also told we were near Corinth road. In reality, I didn't care where we were. Later, I was to learn the camp we had overrun was General Grant's camp at Pittsburg landing. We overtook the Yankee camp and rest of the day was our victory. There again, with all the gunfire, I couldn't hear anything and didn't care. I did as the Captain said and tried to stay out of the line of fire.

Somehow, the screaming of the dying and wounded soldiers was louder than the cannons. Even through the trees I could see the fire escaping the muzzles of the rifles. The noise from gunfire of the pistols and rifles filled in the voids of the screams and the cannons. That first skirmish had introduced me to death but I doubt anyone gets where it doesn't bother them. We sat there not being able to help or do anything, but listen. I didn't know what I would do if I could, so I sat there and got sick. One of my worst fears was that one of those screams was one of my brothers' or my father's. The only thing I could be thankful for was that I wasn't one of them.

That night, fighting halted. As with the other soldiers, we went out to pick up the wounded and the dead. One of the strangest events was to be in the battlefield and bump shoulders with the enemy. If I had had a pistol or rifle, I would have shot him. Then in mentioning what had happened, I was told truce time was recognized by both sides. It amazed me that in battle there was a civil side to it. That's the time when you go after the dead and wounded; no matter which army you belong to.

First light in the morning, everything started to go wrong. We were badly, disorganized, but General Beauregard pulled us together. At first, we thought we had control of everything. Then mid-afternoon fresh troops of Yankees swiftly overran us. The general called out for us to retreat.

In the end, I don't know who won and who lost, as far as the North or the South goes. I know from the reports there were almost 24,000 men killed.

The rest of our company got, transferred to another battalion, I found myself in another major battle. In the end of August, of 1863, we fought the second battle of Manassas. Here was a deciding victory for us. We had crushed the Yankees left flank and then drove them back to "Bull Run."

The one notice I should note was the change in me. I had done as the Captain told me to do, by staying out of the line of fire. That didn't mean a stray bullet didn't come our way, for they did. As our troops were turning the Yankees back, events were going to change.

From the battle lines, I could make out orders that were shouted out to the troops. I could also hear complaints and observations from the men on both sides. One such comment got me a little more than worried.

"*Got any ammo…I'm out,*" a soldier shouted out to another soldier.

"*Get it out of the wagon…And while you're at it get me some also,*" the second soldier told the first.

Having heard the same request I had, Private Dick jumped in back with me. He began pulling out ball, powder and wades from cases. As I watched him, I knew why the captain told me to find a tree to hide behind. I wondered why I had never looked at the cases to see what was in them.

"Need some ammo," a soldier said from the front of the wagon.

"Got it for you…just enough for you to take all the Yankees to their graves," Private Dick told the soldier.

"Thanks," the soldier told him as he took everything and made it back through the trees.

I noticed the soldier wasn't any older than I was. It worried me if he was going to make it to his next birthday. Maybe the Captain should have told him to stay behind a tree. As I watched him, I looked for a better place to hide than where I was. If a stray bullet were to hit one of these cases, the wagon would go up. I didn't want to go up with the wagon, in one piece or many pieces.

Through the trees, I saw a Yankee attack one of our guys. The Yankee must have run out of ammo himself, for he was running straight for our guy not shooting. He lowered his rifle, and on the end of it, there was a bayonet. I had seen a few of them before, and I knew it was three-sided. The Yankee stabbed our guy in the stomach. With one swift move, he threw him to one side. The sight made me sick to my stomach and I lost everything in it. I found I was getting tired of war.

Out of the corner of my eye, I saw movement coming our way. The movement was five Yankees headed in our direction shooting at anything they could see to shoot at. Our wagon was big enough for them to see and they shot at us. Private Dick and I dove off the wagon, to get out of the line of fire. Once on the ground, I looked over at him and he wasn't moving. I crawled over to make sure if he was all right or dead. Not wanting to be heard, I reached out and touched him. He was still warm of course, but I knew he was dead. I grabbed his pistol and Kepi cap, about the same time a Yankee came toward me on his horse. Without thinking, I pulled the trigger. As he fell off his horse, I thought about his wife, kids, and his parents. I felt as if my heart stopped, but I know it didn't. I did feel that I had lost a part of myself. As I cried, I had a new feeling go through me.

I got up and grabbed his horse about the same time as his body hit the ground. I mounted and I went after the other four Yankees. When I got back to the supply wagon, I couldn't tell anyone what happened. In the back of my mind, I knew those Yankees were not going home under their own power. I found myself feeling cold about the whole affair.

I was shocked when I got back to the supply wagon. They greeted me with a round of applause. A couple of the company had seen what had gone on. They ended up telling me what I had done and they thought it was good. From that point on, there was a new respect for me. Still the Captain when he heard about it said I was to stay out of battles. He did let me keep Private Dick's pistol, holster and cap.

Later that evening, the captain came by the wagon. He found me brushing down the horse I had taken. He walked over to me and gave me a smile. He didn't say anything for a long time. Finally, after taking care of the horse, he began talking to me.

"You were forced to become a soldier today…the hard way," he began watching my reaction.

"Yes sir. They killed a friend of mine," I answered not knowing what else to tell him. I didn't want to be a soldier anymore but I didn't feel like sitting in a wagon either.

"You have outgrown the wagon I think," he said as he began walking around in circles. He seemed to have come to a conclusion he didn't like. He stopped and turned to me, and he went on to ask, "You don't really want to sit in the wagon anymore?"

"Not now. I just realized I have been sitting on a powder keg," I answered with a grin. I tried my best to take the grin off my face, but I couldn't.

"I guess I can find someone to take Private Dick's place," he told me and then he added, "You have to find another drummer boy."

"Yes sir," I answered, not sure if I won or not. Still, I knew I would rather be on the lines getting killed than in the wagon.

I knew where the feeling came from. Seeing a friend killed before my eyes was more than I could handle. This feeling took a long time to work itself out of my system. After the battle, I would see more wounded and dead, which helped. By the time I got to Richmond, I was my old self again.

Looking back on it, I think the only one that won was the "Grim Reaper." Still General Lee chased the retreating Yankees, putting a good end to the battle. In the newspapers it was listed as being a "Decisive battle of the Northern Virginia Campaign."

Our company escorted many convoys. Though there were a few skirmishes, we never again had to fight in a major battle. I couldn't have been any happier. I didn't want to do what I had to do at Shiloh. I even got to know a few women in a few towns and had some fun. Now I didn't do anything a mother would be embarrassed about what we did together, but I enjoyed their company. Though at first I was shy, my Kepi cap, drum harness and pistol brought them to me. I wondered how many of the girls back home would think I was something special.

Though with some thought, I couldn't think of any that I would care if they felt that way.

One afternoon, I found us back with General Robert E. Lee. Though I can't be for sure I ever saw him. I did hear plenty about him and his dedication to winning the war not for his beliefs but for the south. He had to be the most respected person I had ever heard anyone talk about, other than God. The main concern in us joining his troops was the possible chance of a battle.

Like so many soldiers I got to know, we preferred the stories that were sent back from the lines. The most enjoyable were the ones about "Morgan and his Raiders. Though most of us knew that most of the stories were fabrications, they still were good listening. My favorite stories were his raids into Ohio. He ended doing more damage to the North than most of our Generals had. The biggest laugh was he was told not to go. He went on his own, and did so much more than planned. Then he got himself killed and we all grieved for him.

The closest we came to a battle was when we were chased out of Richmond. Our company was sent back to Richmond to clean up the area after the Sherman raid. Lee went onto Gettysburg to take Grant on. Everyone knew this was going to be the battle of battles. The first battle at Gettysburg had been a victory for us. Everyone expected it to be the same again. I had my doubts, knowing how tired and underfed our troops were.

The day before we got the news about the surrender at Gettysburg, a wagon brought a load of wounded men to Richmond. Since Lee had left, the wounded were brought to us. I was about to do some reconnaissance around the city, when I was awestruck by the wagon. Something told me to wait and watch the wagon. One by one, a man was pulled off the wagon. Once off the wagon, the soldiers were laid out in the street. I don't have any idea how many more were in the wagon, but I had a funny gut feeling I knew one of them on the ground.

I dropped the rifle I had and ran to the soldier. The closer I got, the sicker I became. I had by then seen more dead and wounded than anyone should ever see. Still this soldier was different. This soldier was my brother and he was badly hurt.

I looked down at him, and I saw a hole in his stomach big enough for my fist to fit into it. He was a mess, from riding in what everyone called "The Meat Wagon." He was one mass of blood from head to toe. His stomach wound was gapping open, with the edges pure black. I wanted to scream but I couldn't get enough air to let go.

I picked his head up and cried out, "Peter, what's happened to you."

"Leave him to die. There are others that could use your help," a soldier said passing by.

"*Shut up*. This is my brother," I cried out, feeling Peter trying to get his breath.

"Matt…is that you Matt?" He asked, sounding as if it was taking all the energy he had. Getting a breath, he told me, "I can't see you. There's too much blood in my eyes."

"Yes Peter, it's me. Don't talk, save your energy," I told him realizing it wasn't going to do any good. Still hoping, I prayed he would make it. After more than two years, I had finally found my oldest brother. I had to ask him one question.

"Where's Father?" I asked him.

"Didn't you get my…?" he asked, stopping to cough. Then taking a breath, blood ran out of his mouth. Yet, he had enough energy to add, "I sent you…a letter…didn't you get it…?"

As I wiped the blood from his eyes I told him, "No." Then I remembered Aunt Agnes going after the mail. When she got back, she was silent the rest of the night.

"Can I help you, soldier?" A woman asked as she walking up to me.

I didn't bother to answer, but shook my head. I didn't know for sure, but when I looked up at her she seemed to understand. She left, after giving us the sign of the cross.

"He…died…" he began telling me, but needing to cough, he coughed up more blood. I wiped the blood from his mouth and he went on to tell me, "In the first battle...just before Samuel was killed." With another cough, he died in my hands.

As I laid his head down, I gave him a kiss on his forehead. I looked in his open eyes and told him, "You almost made it. I'll miss you, brother." I sat there for a while not being able to move.

"We'll take care of him," a surgeon told me, as he stood over me. He then went on to ask me, "Unless you want to take him home with you?"

"I would like to, but I don't have any way to get him there," I answered, wishing I could. He deserved more than they would do for him.

"You might as well go on home. There is no more Confederacies, so you're not obligated to stay," he told me, with a smile.

I gave Peter a pat on his hand, and left him there with the surgeon. I knew I couldn't do anything for him. I couldn't even turn back knowing what seeing him would do to me.

I went and got my horse and bedroll to head for home. As I got to the edge of the city, a Yankee greeted me. He had me sign a peace of paper that I have no idea what it was. Then he told me the surrender agreement said I could keep my horse and clothes but nothing else. I didn't argue, but handed my rifle and pistol to him. I found out later he took more than he should, but I didn't care.

I had my brother die in my arms and learned of another brother and my father's death. No, it was time to go home, and, hopefully, Henry would be there waiting with Mark, Robby and Aunt Agnes. In leaving Richmond, I didn't even say good-bye. Just outside Richmond, I came across a dead soldier. Beside him, I found a rifle and a pistol in his holster. Knowing he wasn't going to need them, I took them with me.

As I rode out of Richmond, I remember passing a wagon. There was a man with a bandanna around his face, I believe. Beside him was a girl about my age. If memory serves me right, she was wearing a tattered blue dress. The one item making them stand out was their cargo. Having seen as many dead bodies as I had, I knew what it was. Thinking of my father and brothers, I felt sorry for the man and the girl. Looking back at them as I passed them, I found myself thinking how many paid the price for this war. Seeing her eyes were red, I knew she had been crying. I figured they were carrying her father or brother home. With having watched Peter die and hearing about dad, I felt sorry for all of us.

Thinking of the dead person on the wagon, I remembered how close I came to being dead. In one of our skirmishes, I was almost killed. Going through a grove of trees, five Yankees appeared. I turned my horse to make a retreat as they began firing at me. As I made my horse turn sharply around a tree, my drum harness got caught on a branch. As I was pulled backward, a bullet nicked the buckle. Hanging on, I managed to break free and got out of there. If it hadn't been for the harness, the bullet would have gotten me.

The rest of my trip home I don't remember stopping. I know I must have for I had too many miles to have traveled in one leg. Still, my focus was on getting home. I could imagine Henry, Mark, Robby, and Aunt Agnes standing in the front of the house. Then riding up to them and them welcoming me home. Then if I got there fast enough, I might be able to welcome home Henry when he got home. With these thoughts, I raced home, trying to forget everything I had experienced of the past few years.

I finally reached a piece of land I recognized. I remember Dad and I taking my mutt through the woods looking for raccoons. I brought my horse to a halt, and looked at the woods and remembered. There to the west I knew was a small pond. At the time Dad and I were there last, the pond was full of lilly pads. Dad had gotten ahead of me, and I tried to catch up to him. In rounding around the pond, I slipped and went in. Dad laughed so hard, I thought he was going to cry. "Yes, the area has some fond memories," I found myself saying aloud.

Wiping a tear from my cheek, I took one last look and headed home. I knew I only had another two miles to go. I reached down and gave my horse a pat, feeling good. When I pulled my hand up, it was wet. Looking down at him, I could see his coat was soaked with sweat. I knew I had been riding him harder than I should have.

"I'll let you have a good cool down walk and brush you real good," I promised him. If my father saw what I had put this horse through, he would have had my hide. Right then though, that was the least of my concerns; I wanted to be home. The idea of a home cooked meal and being able to relax sounded like heaven. I knew I would have to take over for Mark, but that was all right. In fact, I might have to hire myself out and that was fine with me. The main thing was to be home and not on a battlefield.

As I pulled around the bend, I saw the house and felt excitement fill me. Visions of a decent meal and a homemade pie sent pangs of delight through my stomach. The main driving force was to see everyone, and make sure they were all right. As I got closer, I saw that it looked deserted and my heart almost stopped. My mind couldn't handle the thought, so I spurred my horse on. Reaching the yard, I saw it was nothing but weeds. The weeds were growing though the porch, giving me more of a feeling that it was empty. My heart jumped into my throat for I was scared. "Where could they have gone?" I asked myself.

I jumped off my horse, dropping the reins saying to my horse, "Be right back." I looked around, and everything looked as I had left it. The rolling hills, the trees, and the stream I knew was behind them were the same. It was the house and it being deserted that caught my attention. I knew I didn't have to go inside to find out they all had left.

I walked into the house and there wasn't anything in it. For as small as the place was, it didn't take long to realize no one was living there. I stepped back out onto the porch and stared at nothing. Then I realized my horse had wondered off. Thankfully, he hadn't gone too far, having found some grass to munch on. Still, I walked over to him picking up the reins and walked him to the barn. With a glance around, I saw everything was gone there also. Knowing what I needed to do, I reached into my bag and brought out a brush. The next few minutes I thought about what I was going to do next, as I brushed my horse.

After brushing him, I began to mount him again. Then bringing my leg down, I knew we both needed a rest. I got back off and took his saddle off. Opening the corral that wasn't in bad shape, I let him go. I knew I might have been able to go on, but he couldn't. As he drank the water I had gotten him, he relaxed, and I did the same.

Lying against the barn wall, I couldn't figure out what happened. It didn't make any sense, with the house being in the same condition as I had left it. I wondered if they ran out of food or if the Yankees chased them out. With the latter being the best possible answer, I began to get mad. I found myself so mad I couldn't relax enough to sleep. I decided to let my horse relax where he was. While he was relaxing, I would walk into town. I hoped someone there could give me some answers.

If it weren't for no one being at the house, the walk into town would have been fun. There were so many memories I could have enjoyed, but I wasn't in the mood. Each step was driven into the ground with determination of getting answers. I needed to know what happened to my brothers and Aunt Agnes. They must have talked to someone and told them what they were planning. I also needed to know where I was to go and what I was going to do.

With that thought, I wondered if I should clean up the place. I had a rifle, pistol, saddle and a few other items I might be able to sell to buy some seed. Then if I were to get a job, I might be able to get it going again.

If it all worked out, Henry would find something to come home to. Then the fear that he wasn't coming home hit me. If Robby, Mark, and Aunt Agnes weren't going to be there, why stay. In the back of my mind, a little voice said, "It's your dad's place." I found myself answering, "Without them, who cares."

Once in town, I was shocked by what I found. Most of the homes were empty, and the school looked as if it wasn't being used. Ex-slaves occupied the houses and there was no sign of anyone I knew. Still, I walked around and found one old man I did know. For a second, I felt a ray of joy seeing someone I knew.

He was as shocked seeing me, as I was in seeing him. Our conversation covered the war and everyone's losses. He told me everyone in town had to move, for lack of horses and seed to plant. Everyone had gone in different directions and he figured my family did the same. He hadn't seen them go, but that was his best guess. He did remember something bad happening out at our place, but he couldn't remember what it was.

As I walked back to the house, I laughed thinking to myself, something bad happening at our place, right. Our place wasn't a plantation, so a Northern army wouldn't even stop here. I guess he was right, my dad killed as well as two brothers and a brother losing a hand; yes, something bad had happened.

Then walking up to the house, I saw the tree in the front of it. I remembered leaving my note in it. Maybe someone left me a note. I looked up and saw the bottle resting in the crotch of the tree. Taking it down, I saw there were several pages in it. "Not my note," I told myself adding, "Mine wasn't even a full page." Thanks to Private Dick, I could now fill a few pages, I thought as I pulled the pages out. Opening the pages, I got a bad feeling, knowing something must have happened. I read:

> Dear Matt,
> Knowing what I know, you are the only one in the family (except Peter maybe) that could be reading this letter.

A tear welled up in my eyes thinking of Peter dying in my arms. At the same time, the way he started the letter, Samuel and Henry were also dead. Wiping my eyes, I began to read again:

> When you left, Aunt Agnes felt as if she had let father down, with having Henry and I leaving and me coming back with a missing hand. Then you taking off like you did. Then we heard that Dad had died in his first battle. That piece news was more than she could handle. She was almost completely bedridden for the next three months. The news of Henry dying was the final straw of her letting father down. She died the next day.

My eyes filled up again and I dropped the letter to the ground. I found myself sitting there not knowing how or when I had sat down. My only thought I could think about was the loss of dad, my three brothers and Aunt Agnes. I found myself not caring what the rest of the letter said. I wished there was someone that I could turn to. On the battlefields, I felt alone, but nothing like I did right then. Then it hit me that I might be alone, but I still had two brothers. They might not be with me, but they were out there somewhere. I knew Mark must have left the note to let me know where to find him. Being upset enough, I read still further:

> Robby and I tried to keep everything going for the next six months, waiting for you to return. You never returned and we had nothing to eat to speak of. I tried to get work, but no one wanted a one-handed man and Robby is too young. It got to the point, even Boy ran off to find something better for himself. This was the last straw with Robby crying all the time.
>
> With the few jewels Aunt Agnes had and a few items here I have sold we are on our way. Before Aunt Agnes died, she told me where Uncle Phil lived out west. We are going to try to make it, and see if he can help us. I hope that Julie will join us, since we have fallen in love.
>
> With the way you left, I felt you didn't and don't care about us. I wish you luck with your life.
>
> Don't bother trying to find us,
>
> Mark

"*I didn't care!*" I screamed, mad at what he wrote. It's because I cared that I went to find father and the rest of my brothers. I now know how dumb that was; I learned there wasn't anything I could do to help them. Was me joining any worse than Henry taking off to do the same thing? Nothing was working and I knew it. The only ones I knew that might help were dad and my brothers. All I tried to do was to get help.

Sitting there, I knew he had a point. Even if I had found them, what could I have done? They couldn't have left the war and come home with me, no matter what I wanted. Though back then I didn't know what I did, sitting there looking at the words he had written. "I pray you will forgive me," I said to myself as I looked up into the sky. As I thought everything over, I carefully folded the letter up and put it into my pocket.

Being hungry and tired, I didn't have any idea what to do. I thought about checking with friends around where we lived, but I didn't care to see them. I doubted they knew anything and their life probably was as bad as mine was. "Why bother going to see them," I asked myself. No money, just the clothes on my back, a pistol, and a rifle is all I had. These few items were all that I had to show for my efforts.

Looking around, I asked myself, "Why did I leave? I didn't bring them home. What I fought for…is now empty and my brother is mad at me. Why." Of course, I didn't come up with any worthwhile answers. I did what I thought was right at the time. Then the important question came to mind, "What do I do now."

Ida starts a new life

The second morning was one of the best days of my life right then. I went to the Root Cellar and found some of Mama's clothes would fit. The big problem was most of them were formal wear. Still, some I could wear around here without people laughing. However, although that was fine, my bath I took in the pond was the most satisfying.

I would have preferred my old bathtub to bathe in. Still, the old pond was better than just washing off with a wet rag. I have to admit I didn't just undress and jump into the pond. You never know who is around or what might be in the pond. Standing on the edge, I looked around and made sure no one was there to watch me. Seeing no one, I almost took all of my clothes off, but I didn't. I decided to wear my undergarments going in and then take them off. I would then wash them and put them back on while I was in the pond.

Getting out with everything wet, I got a revelation of how my body had changed. As I had in seeing Edgar yesterday, I had also changed. Looking at my reflection in the water, I was surprised at what I saw. My hair wasn't quite as blond as it once was and that was a surprise. The biggest shock was my body. I had curves that I should be covering better than what I had been.

It sounded funny when I thought about it, for who else should know their body but themselves. Then I knew why I didn't know what my full body looked like. For the past few years I had not seen a full mirror. The only reflections of myself were in small windows. I knew

I had grown breasts, and that I had passed into womanhood. What I didn't know was how it looked put together. I wouldn't have said I was beautiful or anything, but I was a woman. I found myself staring at a wet headed woman. No, not a young lady, but a full-grown woman.

While I looked at myself, I came up with a thought that I knew made me blush. I could feel it creeping up from my neck to my eyebrows. I got to wondering if Edgar's reaction to my changes were like mine to his. Almost before the thought went through my head, I looked away. I found myself feeling embarrassed thinking what he might have thought about me. I put my old clothes on, and headed for the Root Cellar. In the back of my mind, a theme rang out saying, "You're a woman now."

Having put Edgar out of my mind, I went through Mama's dresses. Many of the dresses and undergarments were for parties. Though she had more everyday type clothes than I thought she did, there weren't many. I did find some simple dresses I could use. After much thought, I found one I liked and put it on. The feeling of being clean and wearing something that wasn't torn was great. I felt so good, I forgot about the bad happenings for a short time. I got to wondering if Edgar would like it on me.

I looked at the rest of the stuff to see what I could use. I knew I had no need for them or the jewelry she had stashed away. There were some of our paintings up against the back wall behind the clothes. I thought for my new life style they were a little much. Still, I doubted I would get rid of all of them. Then for whatever reason, Mama had stashed some pots and pans. Then to one side were a couple of boxes of stuff I didn't go through.

Stepping outside, I enjoyed the moment looking out over the landscape. Then sucking in some fresh cool air, I knew I had to get going. Though there wasn't anyone pushing me to a deadline, the day was wasting away. The trouble was what I would do next. Then feeling a hunger pain, I knew I needed to take care of that need first. Though I could do without a meal or two, I couldn't forever. At the same time, I needed a place to call home. The root cellar wasn't somewhere I could turn it into anything.

Thinking of the root cellar, as I looked back at it, I wondered if it had flowers painted on the wall if it would look any better. "Who cares about the looks? It's too small," I reminded myself. The only real advantage of it was the temperature stayed constant year-round. The constant temperature and a roof over my head were the only two good advantages about the place, if you didn't count the contents. With that, I turned back to the landscape and enjoyed it.

A couple of birds flew over and landed in a tree not far from me. Their chirping took my mind off my problems for a minute. At the same time, I looked around and realized how pretty the countryside was. I found looking around it was far better than Richmond. Though I knew I had problems as everyone else, I couldn't see them like in Richmond. That one fact made me glad I had come back to stay.

On one hand everything was moving so fast, my head was spinning. I found out my mother had gone beyond what anyone should have to do. Then she dies in my arms the same day the war ended. I go back home, and find nothing was left of it. Jacob, an ex-slave friend, came to my aid and at the same time he tells me my Father had been buried here while Mama and I were gone. The list just kept going on and on. The two events saving me was the stash my mother left behind and Edgar showing up.

With two thirds of my life gone forever, I knew I couldn't just sit around and die. I had to be strong and make everything work, but I wasn't sure how. I knew I had to begin one-step at a time. Though Mama's stash gave me some interesting possibilities, there were more pressing matters. Was I going to stay here around the old place or move on? Moving on sounded like a good idea, but where would I go? Other than Richmond, I had never been anywhere else. With the choice having been made for me, I decided I would start where I was.

With that, some of the basic needs came into play, a place to sleep and food. The Root Cellar might work temporarily but it wasn't going to make it long-term. I decided the old place wasn't going to work for me. Even if I could rebuild it or something else in its place, there were too many memories. I had to start new, even if it was around a corner. This decision brought me to the slave village and the sharecroppers' homes.

I began to go to town, and found the same thoughts going through my head, as the main house area. I froze putting my thoughts together about where the sharecroppers' homes were. A couple of the houses were closer to town than the main house of the village. "Maybe I should look at one of them first," I thought.

"Don't we look nice this morning," Edgar's voice said from behind me.

I turned and prayed I wasn't blushing and answered, "Thanks and a good morning to you also." He wore a grin from ear to ear. I wanted to give him a kiss and hug him, but he was too dirty. I told myself, "Later, when he's a little cleaner." Still, it was comfortable just to be near him.

"What are you doing?" He asked as he came over to me.

"Trying to decide where I'm going to live," I told him as I sat on a stump looking around. I knew I wanted to live in the area, but that also depended on him. I didn't understand why I felt that way, but I did. If he told me he was going somewhere else, I knew I would try to go with him.

"Here, or are you thinking of going somewhere else?" he asked me. Then looking around and turned back to me, and he asked, "I don't know of any vacant homes here in town, at least a livable vacant home."

"Yes, here, or at least in this area," I answered, as I looked around. A house in town was my first thought also, but I liked where we lived before. My next thought was the houses in the slave village but I didn't care for that idea either. I then remembered where the sharecroppers' homes were. Then looking back at him, I asked him, "What are your plans?"

"Not having any family, I can do anything I want," he said as he sat on the ground in front of me. Then getting comfortable, he added, "I haven't made up my mind yet. I thought I would talk to you first."

"To me…first?" I questioned him thinking there was more to it than that. An interesting situation; I'm waiting to find out what he was going to do and he's waiting to find out what I'm going to do. If one of us doesn't decide soon, winter is going to be on us.

There was a long silence, and much staring at each other before he answered. He looked up to the sky and told me, "I'm not me, at least not the one I used to know. Since I lived here last, I have seen men die. I have seen them maimed, I have killed men." He stopped having a problem getting his feelings out. Then looking up at me, he added, "I don't know if I'm strong enough to go out alone. I need someone I can talk to. Someone I can do for. Right now I need someone that knows the true me and not what I was forced to become."

"A friend?" I asked, hoping that he wanted more of me.

"As a start," he answered, with a big smile. Then taking a breath, he went on to tell me, "I do owe you an apology."

"For what?" I asked.

"I meant to write you, but I didn't and I'm sorry. I can tell you that you were always on my mind," he answered.

"I forgive you and I understand, and they wouldn't have gotten to me anyway. At the same time, I meant to write you also, though with me, I didn't know how to address my letters," I told him.

"That's my fault also, but I'm here now," he admitted giving me a grin.

I took his hand and reminded him, "If we start over here, there will be five of us—Jacob, his wife Molly and son—not just the two of us."

"I have some good news," he began telling me, as he rubbed my knuckles sounding cheerful. He told me, "Mr. Smiley is going to let me do odd jobs around the plant beginning tomorrow. I won't make much but it will be better than nothing. He's also going to let me stay in the back storage area. Not that it's that comfortable, but it's a roof over my head."

"It's a start," I told him, feeling good that something was working out. Standing up, I went on to tell him, "Now to find me a place to stay."

"The space isn't that big, but…no, that wouldn't work. Jacob said you could stay at their place. There isn't much room but it's got to be better than the cellar," he reminded me.

"No, they don't have room for themselves let alone me," I told him. As an explanation I went on to tell him, "I need my own space, anyway. I was thinking of taking over one of the sharecroppers' homes." In the back of my mind, I thought it interesting, the idea of me sharing a space with him.

"Hadn't thought about them. You know, that's not a bad idea," he said giving me a smile as he got up. Looking around, he asked, "Which direction?"

"Not that far," I answered, and I felt a grin coming on as he took my hand.

"You know, to my way of thinking, those Yankees should rebuild all the homes they destroyed," he told me looking mad. Giving my hand a light squeeze, he added, "Isn't it enough that we lost our families."

"I agree with you, but there's not much of a chance of them rebuilding," I told him. "The Yankees had grown up with my father. He used to say, what you break you fix."

"You're right, but they should. We didn't burn their homes and cities down," he added.

The conversation went back to the different sharecropper homes there were and where they all were. Most were to the east and south, with one being on the north. We decided to look at the one on the north side. He agreed with my way of thinking; it was would make it closer to town; this would be an advantage for me. At the same time, there was enough land to farm. As we walked to the place, we danced like two school kids. We may have lost a lot over the years, but we were moving on.

I told him I was also going to see if I could help at the hospital tent. Edgar was against the idea, but I explained my thinking. Let alone wanting to help those that needed it, there was another reason. I was in hopes that I might get something to eat every day. This would help until I got something going. I also said I would be looking into doing wash, or any other job I could get. I even was thinking about taking the school over. Taking the school over was an idea he liked. There again, I wouldn't make any money, but I was sure the parents would contribute a chicken or some beef occasionally.

I told him, "We do what we must to live."

"I understand. Working for Smiley isn't something I'm looking forward to either," he said. He then added, "Though once orders begin to come in, then I will be able to do something I enjoy. It's the odd jobs that are going to bore me."

Though I had known him all of my life, I realized there was a part of him I didn't know. I didn't know that he could work with his hands for an example. I found it a little exciting thinking of him building something. My excitement led me to thinking he might be able to help me, once I decided on what I was going to do.

"You never know, you might like the work once you learn a little more about it," I offered him as a thought to think over. Then as we continued, I told him, "Maybe between the four of us, we can plant some crops and make some money that way." He knew I meant Jacob and his wife as well and the two of us.

"I think I might, but I'm not sure. I do know it's time to give it up for the day. What we have to do will take too long to start now. Tell me, do you want to do something?" He asked.

"As I said, I was thinking about checking out a place to live in, such as one of the sharecroppers' homes," I told him.

"Sorry, my mind slipped for a minute. Mind if I join you?" he asked. "I would appreciate it, kind sir, I just might need you advice," I answered with a grin. I had thought about seeing a few different people. I was in hopes they might have something for me to do for some food. Still, being alone with Edgar seemed like more fun, and it would get one item done. If it led to me having a home, rather than a cellar, it would be worth it. Before we left, I told him, "You might want to wash your face off."

"Too good to be seen with a working man?" he asked with a grin.

"I don't want to be mistaken for walking with a dirt ball," I answered him giving him a grin back. As he walked over to a bucket of water,

I noticed his beard was gone. I asked him, "What happened to your beard?"

"I wasn't sure if I needed it anymore," he answered as he scrubbed his face. Wiping his face off on his sleeve, he took my hand and we were on our way.

The walk to look at the houses was filled with conversations of our past. One or the other of us would point out a spot where something had happened. Though they were memories of a past life, bringing up sad memories, we still laughed at each other. I found myself wishing we could have a picnic.

"Oh Jacob said to have you come over for dinner," he told me.

"Do they have enough for me also?" I asked him. In talking to Jacob, it sounded as if they were just getting by. With Edgar working he at least could contribute some to the fund.

"They'll just add some water and make enough," he answered, as he joined me in some laughter.

Once we got to the little house, I remembered how small they were. In fact, from memory I remembered the ones in the slave village were even smaller. Where the ones in the village were only one room, this one had at least two rooms. Stepping into the place was a little difficult. The door was half off its hinges. Edgar was able to lift it out of the way so we could go in. Once inside, I almost turned around and left. Edgar held me back and we looked at the other room.

Rather than the big windows that opened so you could walk through them in the summer, like in our old place, there were only two small ones. Rather than having a finished look, this house was made of slab wood, chinked with mud. Looking around, the inside as the outside, you saw the natural wood. In fact, from the inside, you could see through the walls in places. Some of the mud was missing between the wood slabs.

"It's a mess, I agree. Still, some of this furniture can be made usable. In fact, we might find more in the other houses, a bed maybe," he reminded me. Then seeing I wasn't running away from him, he added, "A good sweeping and some paint will do wonders."

"True, I guess," I agreed with him, cringing a little. I found it hard to think that this was going to be my home. Then thinking about the hole Mama and I lived in Richmond, I knew this was better.

I also knew some of my problem was in the way I was raised. I never had to keep house or worry about making repairs to one. A house to me was something that was always there. The same went with the furniture and everything else in my life for that matter. I knew I was in for an education to say the least.

"Before we do too much, let me check out something," he told me as he went out the door. Then a short time later, he came back inside and told me, "No problem."

"What do you mean no problem?" I asked, not understanding what he was talking about.

"The well…" he started out to tell me, and then going on to add, "I thought I had better check to see if it was dry or not."

"Thanks," I told him, and then added, "I would never have thought about checking the well. I knew there was a reason for bringing you along."

"See, having a man around isn't all that bad," he added with a smile.

"Let me think about that for a moment or two," I answered giving him a wink. I didn't want to say too much, in fear of how I felt. I then went on to comment as I looked around the place, "This is a real mess."

"It looks worse than it actually is," he added as he picked up a few pieces of wood. Then looking at them, he broke some of them and laid them down by the fireplace. Then looking back at me, he explained, "Firewood for cooking and heating this winter."

"Thanks for giving me more to worry about," I answered, and then added, "if I make it that long." We both laughed and it didn't seem so bad looking at it.

Then following his example, I began to help clean the place up. As I picked up a piece of wood, I asked him, "Why did you come back here?"

Want to Go West Lady?

Hesitating, he stopped and turned to me. Empting his arms, he answered, "I knew mom and father were gone, Mr. Smiley, wrote me." He stopped to wipe a tear from his eyes, brought his shoulders back, and went on to tell me, "I also knew the place had been destroyed. Without help to rebuild it, I knew there was no reason for coming back."

"As I asked, why did you come back?" I asked again. I reminded him, "I know you said you needed someone to talk too but…" I let him go ahead with his answer. I wasn't sure how he felt. When he told me he needed someone that knew him, but that could mean anyone we grew up with. Yet, when I offered him my friendship, he answered, "For a start." If there was more, I needed to hear it

"I thought about going to my uncle's place, he owns shipping lines. I heard he had helped running supplies for the Confederacy. I suppose he still has his ships, but I never liked him."

"So…?" I asked getting irritated not getting his answer.

"The idea of traveling by ship around the Cape, taking goods to San Francisco, losing my lunch over the side, doesn't sound like it's for to me," he added, still not answering my question.

"*Edgar*," I shouted at him and then in a quieter voice told him, "You haven't answered my question." Then as he was getting himself together, I told him, "He might have a job on shore."

"*All right*, if you must know, I came back hunting for you," he told me looking down at his feet, showing embarrassment. Then looking up at me, he went on to tell me, "I needed to know if you and your mother were all right. I also needed someone that I knew." Then with a grin, he added, "About my Uncle, he has a bad attitude and I couldn't work for him."

"Any plans now that you're not going to be a sailor, now that you have found me?" I asked him.

"Just taking it one day at a time," he answered as he went back to picking stuff up.

We didn't talk much more that afternoon. We worked on cleaning the house up until we got tired of it. At one point Edgar got, tired of it very soon.

"*Ouch*…ouch…get out of here quick," he shouted at me running for the front door.

"Why?" I asked a little concerned at what he was yelling about.

"I broke a wasp's nest," he told me as he checked out a couple of bites he had gotten.

"Oh," I responded as I broke into laughter.

"Dang it, it's not funny. They hurt," he answered as he began to laugh. Then looking at me, he told me, "It's time for a break anyway."

I grabbed some water and made some a paste of mud. Mary had told me, one time in the Slave Village, mud on wasp bites helps heal them. Going over to him, I said, "Here, let me put some mud on them, it'll make it better."

"Thanks, I hadn't thought about mud," he answered looking uncomfortable.

Once I got all the bites dabbed, he looked funny and I broke out into laughter.

"What's so funny?" he asked.

"You," I answered and I knew it wasn't nice to laugh, but it felt good.

"I'm glad I'm so entertaining," he answered as he moved his arm breaking the mud. Then looking at the mud on his arm, he began to laugh also. Getting control of himself, he admitted, "I guess I do look funny. Think it's time to get back to work."

I leaned over and gave him a kiss. The poor guy was trying so hard, I felt he needed some reward.

"What was that for?" he asked.

"You earned it," I answered.

"Maybe I had better get busy, so I can earn another one," he told me with a smile.

"We'll see about that," I answered, not making any promises.

"Are you coming?" He asked as he began to go to the house.

"Maybe we should let them clear out of there and use the time to get some stuff out of the root cellar anyway," I suggested, hoping the wasps had cleared out by the time we got back.

With it being light enough, we moved some of my belongings from the root cellar into the part of the house that was cleared out. Not having any use for Mama's petticoats and fancy dresses, I left them where they were. Though touching them brought a tear to my eyes thinking of her.

"At least there were no more wasps in there," he said looking around. Then coming over closer to me he saw I was crying. He was thoughtful and gave me a squeeze telling me, "She was a wonderful woman."

I wanted to tell him the story about our lives in Richmond, but the time wasn't right. There was so much I wanted to tell him but I couldn't. At the same time, I wanted to ask him a few questions. Still, in looking up at him, I was glad there was someone that cared about me. Burying my head into his chest, I let the tears flow. He didn't let loose or say anything. After a few minutes, I got myself together and picked up the rest of the items I felt I was going to need. The most important items were a couple of lanterns so I could see at night. With the place being as dark as it was, I needed them the most. I also took a couple of my father's favorite books someone had put down there. I thought it might be enjoyable to read some of them, though I wondered if I would have time. To my surprise with the pots and pans, I found utensils and dishes as well. I figured I would get them the next day. Looking around, I didn't see any furniture, and, of course, the little hideaway wasn't large enough to hold any, but it would have been helpful. I found myself remembering the piano and my bed. Mama would have been happy to hear I was missing the piano. She had fought me for years to get me to play it. She was always saying, "A fine young refined lady should be able to play the piano."

"Your father had a great idea when he built this hiding place," he told me as he looked around it. Then he went on to add, "If my father had done the same, I don't know what I would do with their stuff."

It only took another day to clean out the rest of the house. Edgar had all the usable wood stacked up. His thoughts were he could make some furniture out of the wood. However, as we had talked earlier, we might find some in the other houses. If we were that lucky, he wouldn't have to make any.

Then one afternoon, I heard a wagon coming into the yard. Walking outside, I saw Edgar driving it and it was full of furniture.

"Mr. Smiley let me use the wagon and team," he said as he got off the wagon. Then seeing where my eyes were, he told me, "I made the rounds of the other houses and found a few things. I'm sure you might need a few more things but at least this is a start."

I walked over without saying anything and broke into tears. As I cried, I felt his arms go around me giving me a squeeze.

"I know it's not what you're used to, but they're not that bad," he told me.

I gave him a slap and told him, "I crying because of you being so thoughtful and having something to sit on."

"If you notice, there is a bed, two tables and some chairs. The bed is a present from Mr. Smiley. It was his mother's and she died not long ago, so they don't have any use for it now," he told me as he released me.

"It's all so wonderful, I'll have to thank him," I answered him as I gave him a kiss.

"I knew someday I would get another one of those," he said as I slapped him. Then grabbing a chair, he told me, "We had better get this stuff into the house before it begins to rain."

"Yes sir," I answered grabbing a chair myself.

After bringing everything in, I made us something to eat. While cooking, he undid the harnesses on the horses. Once I was done, we sat down and ate. After we were finished with supper, we took two chairs outside and talked. With it being late, he agreed to spend the night.

"You can share the bed with me," I offered.

"Someday maybe, when it's right," he answered me looking as if this was the right time.

"I wished I knew what love is, then I might know how to describe my feelings for you…but thank you," I told him as I went to bed, leaving him to sleep on the floor.

The next morning, I got up and he was gone. I hadn't heard him leave or drive off with the wagon. I figured it was the bed I had slept on. It had been years since I had slept on one. For the next few hours, I marveled at my home. Then a week later, Edgar and Jacob brought the wagon back. They had made me a couple of cupboards. The only thing I needed then was some paint and a sofa. With these two items, my home would be a comfortable home.

In days to come, we would go out to Edgar's place. We weren't sure what we would find; with the Yankees burning the place. As we walked up to the site of the house, we weren't sure if we were at it or not. With their home not having a foundation, being built all of wood, there was nothing but ashes left. All the salvageable there might have been carted off. Weeds had overtaken the rest of the place. Edgar did find a doorknob; he could take as a memory, a sad memento of one's home.

The next day, I got up and went to the hospital tent to see what I could do. As I walked by the manufacturing building, both Jacob and Edgar came out to talk to me.

"Going to see what you can do up there?" Edgar asked.

"Not much else I can do," I answered.

"My Misses found some good seed you can plant," Jacob told me excitedly.

"It shouldn't take too long to plant a few acres," Edgar said looking happy with the find.

"Sounds like we might have a future after all," I told them both, trying to grin. As I left them, I wanted to laugh but I didn't want to hurt their feelings. They hadn't thought about the time between the planting and harvesting. I was going to need something to live on. I also told Jacob, "Give your Misses my thanks. With a little luck, we might get a good crop."

"That I'll do," Jacob answered with a big smile.

Letting them go back to work, I made it to the hospital tent area. It wasn't just a tent, but a series of tents. All the tents were nestled among some trees. If it weren't for their purpose, it would have been a beautiful setting. Still looking at them, it was another reminder of what the country had just gone through. Four years of death and destructions, was it worth it? Letting my thoughts go, I made my way to the first tent.

Looking around, I didn't see too many soldiers waiting for a doctor's help. There were a few with rags tied around their heads, legs and arms, but not many. There were a few hobbling around on crutches, but even they were few. I had a feeling I wasn't going to be needed much. As I got to the first tent, I felt as if it was where surgery was preformed. No one was in it, so I headed for the next one. Not far from the tent, I saw a clearing that stopped me in my tracks. The sticks sticking up told me the story. The clearing was where they had buried all the soldiers that didn't make it. Standing there I noticed something else, the stench. It was the same stench, I remembered in the meat cutting room out by the stable. I knew what the smell was, and I didn't want to think about it. I found myself wanting to put a rag over my nose, but I didn't have one. Swallowing hard, I continued to the tent.

"Good morning, young lady," a soldier greeted me as he came out of a tent with a big smile. Then not waiting for a reply, he asked, "Looking for someone? You can always take me home with you."

"And do what with you?" I asked him, not thinking about his condition. In looking at him, I saw he was missing one leg. The other leg had a bandaged foot. Then looking at the rest of him, I could see he had suffered even more wounds. Then seeing the look on his face, I told him, "Sorry, I didn't mean it the way it sounded."

"I know. Still you are right; I'm not much good for anything the way I am."

"Where did you get wounded at?" I asked him as I sat on a stump.

"Every battle I fought in," he answered with a grin.

"I'm Ida Marsh," I told him as I extended my hand as a greeting. I then went on to add, "They came close to doing you in, it looks like."

"They darn near did. Billy Ward, ma'am," he replied.

"May I help you?" A voice asked behind me.

In turning around, I saw a man covered in blood. It was obvious he was a surgeon.

"*Hey boys… There's a pretty young thing out here,*" a soldier announced when he saw me.

"*Where,*" a voice could be heard answering from inside a tent.

"*She's not going to want anything to do with you,*" another answered.

"You have stirred up some interest," the surgeon said with a smile. Then he went on to ask again, "can I help you, are you trying to find someone in particular?"

"No, I'm not trying to find someone, but was wondering if I could be of some help?" I asked him. Standing there, I watched men wander around the camp, seeming, to be lost.

"Well as you might have guessed we are about done here," he told me. The way he said it, I had the feeling I wasn't needed. Then looking at the men watching us, he shook his head and grinned. Then looking back at me, he said, "Maybe…you seem to have raised their moral a little. And they need something for as much as they have gone through. I will hardly be able to give you anything to eat."

"I understand," I told him giving Billy and the others a grin. Looking back at the surgeon, I told him, "I'm Ida Marsh and my parents use to have a plantation on the other side of town."

"Not much left I suspect," he said and then went on to add, "most call me Andy or Captain. It used to be Captain Andrew Morrow."

Andy took me around showing me the tents and the goings on of the camp. Inside the tents, he introduced me to his patients. In each tent, I got cheers and applause. In the neighboring tents, there were cries for him to bring me to them. Though the men were in bad shape, they were in good sprits. Some didn't even move, and he told me they were dying.

Once outside, he asked me, "You still want to help?"

I answered yes and worked with him for the next three weeks. I mainly helped the soldiers write letters, and washing and feeding them. The work itself wasn't hard, but the grief was hard to take sometimes. Some looked as if they were going to make it. More than I would like to remember died in my arms. Some were considerate and died before I got back in the morning. Still, I think I did some good, and I'm glad I did it. If the need were ever to come up again, I would do it again.

There was one day I try not to think about, but it was part of it all.

The stench was so bad the soldiers began to complain, so a few of us went behind the surgeon's tent to see what we could do. We found a pile of body parts rotting away. In the pile, there were arms and legs sticking up here and there, with fingers, hands, feet, and every other part of the body. At first, we turned around, and we all lost our meals. Once we tied bandannas around our mouth and noses, we went back to the pile. It took us all afternoon, but we got it all buried. We did our best to bury the blood soaked ground also, but we couldn't get rid of the stench. I will never get the feeling of the blood and rotting flesh from my skin. Then again, it was something that had to be done.

In the twilight of the moon over those few weeks, the three of us planted the seeds. One morning on my way to the hospital camp, I looked at the field. If what I saw was right, our rows were not very straight. Maybe, I thought, if we had had a horse they would have been better. At the same time, did straight lines mean a better crop? I didn't think so. However bad the rows were, the seeds were planted, and that was what was important.

"Same idea I had," Edgar's voice said coming up next to me. With his arm around me, he went on to add, "Our first crop."

"That it is, and I'm feeling proud of it," I answered giving him a hug. Then letting him go, I asked him, "Shouldn't you be working?"

"Jacob is stoking up the furnace. I thought I would check out our crop and walk you to town."

"You don't think I can make it on my own?" I asked kidding him. At the same time, I looped my arm into his.

"Probably, unless you got lost or some rich guy came by," he answered as he stepped back, knowing I might try to hit him.

"Then let's get going and keep me from getting lost or carried away. Next year let's try to do our planting in daylight," I suggested.

"Might be a good idea," he said with a smile. Then he went on to add, "Even dividing the sale of the crop by three, we still should make a few dollars."

"My only problem is accepting corn in the fields rather than cotton," I told him looking back at the fields. I could hear Father saying someone said he should rotate the crops. If the plantation owners had rotated their crops, the soil wouldn't have been as bad as it was. Well Father, we have planted a different crop. Now if we only would get some rain.

The two of us walked in silence for a while. I was in deep thought wondering if the crop was going to be good or not. Though the seeds looked fine, we didn't have any idea if they were or not. We knew they were corn, but we didn't know where they had come from. Now it was time to wait and see what happened.

As we did the planting, there were many times I found myself being thankful for Jacob's wife. If it wasn't for Jacob's wife, I would have been dead from starvation. They didn't have much to live off either, still she cooked for us. Most nights it would be some pan fried bread and beans. Occasionally, I would find a piece of pork in the beans and thought I was in heaven. Other nights, I prayed a fly would land in the beans to add some flavor. Still it was good to have something in my stomach.

As we ate one night, Edgar came up with an idea, "Why don't you teach? I remember you having that idea not long ago, I think it might be a good idea."

"What?" I asked him not sure what I heard.

"These kids around here need to learn how to read. I'm sure their parents would agree and be willing to contribute a chicken or a piece of beef once in a while."

"The schoolhouse is just sitting there doing nothing," Jacob added, sounding as if he thought it was a good idea also.

"Yes I know, but I have never been a teacher before," I replied.

"And what have you done before? Wash clothes and take care of people," Edgar reminded me.

"I'll think about it," I told the two. I knew I was a good reader and my math was acceptable. Between the two I could teach the kids something. Another problem would be getting supplies to teach them with.

With the soldiers from the hospital camp and the camp gone, the idea wasn't that bad. Between Edgar working at the factory and me fixing up the house, we were both busy. Still I talked to a few of the families around, and they thought opening the school was a good idea. The day after the house was where I didn't get sick entering it, I opened the school for the first day. About the same time, our area had a new group of visitors; we would later call them "carpetbaggers."

When these men came into town, they were just men from the north. They seemed to be honest and wanting to help us. They were offering to buy land we wanted to sell or anything else we had. I didn't learn until some years later what they were. Every one of us was so poor, we would have sold our skins for blankets. Meeting one, I got to thinking about Mama's stuff in the root cellar. Later I learned that they were giving people two cents on the dollar for anything they bought from us. Then whenever possible, they would just take possession of anything they could.

"What do you think of me selling Mama's stuff?" I asked Edgar one night when he came over.

"Might help keep you going until the crops come in," he answered as he took a sip of water.

We decided we would go through her stuff and see what I could find to sell. The next day after school, I began to pull stuff out, one piece after another. It was one of the hardest chores I think I had ever done, other than having Mama die in my arms.

"Finding anything?" Jacob asked as he walked into the house with Edgar.

"A few items," I answered moving some of the stuff out of their way.

The next day, I took Mama's fancy dresses and some of her jewelry in. It didn't take long for one of them to find me. Before I could say anything, he began asking me what I had for sale.

"What's you got there young lady?" One of them asked me.

"Clothes and jewelry," I answered, laying everything on the ground for him to see.

"How much do you want for them?" He went on to ask me without even looking at them.

I didn't have any idea what they were worth. Mary or someone would take the cloth Mama bought and sew it into a dress. Even the cost of the cloth, I didn't have any idea what she or Father had paid for it. Down deep in my stomach, I knew I was going to be taken. I guess the look on my face answered the question for him, because he made me an offer.

"Now if you had some land, I could offer you some big money. Still, I can give you five honest Northern dollars for all of it," he offered.

Thinking about the price of meat and everything, five dollars sounded good. I took it reluctantly, thinking about his saying he could give me big money for land. I had all the land of Father's that wasn't doing me any good. Maybe, I thought, I should sell him the plantation. It was something to think about and talk it over with Edgar. At least I thought I might get enough to make it until the crops came in. Then in the back of my mind, I wondered how well I was going to do with teaching. With what the different families gave me, maybe I wouldn't have to sell any of the land. I just didn't know what to do, so I prayed Edgar would know.

Taking the money from the man, I asked him, "How much would you give me for two thousand acres?"

"Maybe three hundred," he answered looking at me with interest. Then before I said anything, he asked, "You have the deed for the land?"

As I was about to answer, a raindrop hit my nose. I answered him by telling him, "Yes, for now though, I think I had better make it home before I drown."

"Sounds like a good idea, little lady. If you decide you want to sell that land of yours, come find me," he answered as he began to pick up Mama's stuff."

"*I will*," I shouted back to him as the first clap of thunder hit. In the back of my mind, I was thinking of selling the land, but right then I was thinking of the rain. With the corn needing to have been planted a few weeks earlier, I prayed the rain would make up for it going in late. Five lives were depending on the outcome of this coming crop.

The first time I had a chance to talk to Edgar I asked him, "What do you think about me selling the main part of the place?"

"One of them made an offer?" he asked.

"I was offered three hundred," I answered him. As he took the information in, I saw mixed emotions across his face.

"I have an idea what the place is worth. It is worth a lot more than he is offering," he finally answered, stopping mid sentence. Then taking a breath, he added, "Still as money is right now, I doubt if you could get a fair price for it. At the same time, a horse and wagon would help in bringing in the crop and taking it to market."

"Do you think I should sell then?" I asked, not sure what he was saying. I wondered if he was just thinking it through.

"I'm not sure," he answered looking irritated. He went on to add, "I asked about selling father's place the other day. He said I had to have the deed."

"I was told the same thing. I found father's deed the other day," I said as I sat down.

"If I had a deed, I would sell our place. I know I wouldn't be able to get the price of six-thousand dollars, which my father said the place was worth. Still, I would be willing to take whatever I could get. However, I don't have the deed, with it having gone up in smoke with Mother and Father. Even then I would have had a problem, because someone has settled on the place," he told me.

"*They can't do that.* It's your place," I answered, both excited and mad. At the same time, I got to thinking about our two places. If his place was worth six thousand, Mama and Father's should be worth a lot more.

"What do I do, shoot them?" He asked, shrugging his shoulders. With that, he sat back in his chair and added, "Enough shooting has been done in the past few years."

"It's an idea, but I don't think I'll get that drastic," I answered and

Want to Go West Lady?

then I went on to comment, "if our places are worth that much, three hundred is nothing."

"True, but something is better than nothing," he reminded me.

Though everyone in town was disappointed with me selling, I did. Everyone understood, but they hated to see the varmints stealing the place from me. Still, I had forty acres, which was more than we could handle by ourselves. From the sale of the rest of Mama's paintings and most of her clothes, I made enough money to live a while. Edgar was able to get us a horse and wagon, leaving me with some money for the future.

What I didn't tell everyone was what I had gotten for the place. Originally I had been offered three hundred dollars for it. Then after talking to Edgar, I knew what the true value was, so I held out for six hundred. I still didn't get what it was worth, but the knowledge helped me bargain for more.

"Have you heard the news?" Edgar asked me one afternoon.

"What news?" I asked him, trying to get some chores done.

"Lincoln was assassinated a few days ago," he told me.

"What? Someone killed him?" I asked sitting down to hear everything.

"They're saying it was a Confederate plot. He was killed while he was at a theater, with his wife by some actor named John Wilkes Booth," he said.

"For what reason? The war is over, we have lost our loved ones, our lives, everything we hold dear. How was killing him going to make anything better? I'm not even sure I can blame the war on him. He only voiced his views on slavery prior to winning the election. He never presented anything I know of to congress. We never gave him a chance, and to kill him," I answered, wondering what was wrong with people.

"I agree. I think the reason he wrote the Emancipation Proclamation so late into the war was to justify the war. I know it didn't start the war. In fact I would support shooting "Good old Jeff Davis" and the rest of the politicians," Edgar told me. Then sitting down himself, he went on to add, "Just like the war, pull a gun out and begin firing. Don't sit down and talk it over, shoot someone that solves everything."

"I think animals are smarter than we are," I said as I got up trying to think what I was doing. Then thinking about the war, I added, "If the reported is right, six hundred thousand men were killed between the two sides during the war. As if the six hundred thousand men weren't enough, now we have to kill another one."

"How did it go today?" He asked, changing the subject.

"Pretty good, other than the Paterson boy Billy and Lucy getting into it," I answered.

"Maybe you should solve their issue like the politicians do, give them guns," he suggested with a smile.

I didn't give him a verbal answer, but I threw a towel at him. I found it sad that he was right in his assessment of our politicians; act first think later. Now with the papers saying a Confederate sympathizer killed Lincoln, all southerners are going to pay the price.

For the next few months, I spent most of my time worrying about my class. All I had was eighteen students, but that was more than enough for me. Having no experience in teaching, I had to learn as much as my students. I have to admit I was scared in the beginning, but it faded. Even though I made many mistakes, there were those rewarding moments. Not least to say, some of those moments were when I was given a sack of flour or a chicken. Still seeing a student read an entire page without help was rewarding. Everything had begun to come together finally. I found myself glad I took the chore of teaching on. My most rewarding moment was when a student and mother would greet me as teacher. I found myself feeling worth something for the first time in my life.

My free time I spent in fixing up the house. Some of the parents gave me a few items to make the place more like home. Mr. Smiley even gave me a few buckets of whitewash to paint the house. There was just enough to paint both the inside and outside. The difference it made could not be put into words. I felt like I finally had a place to call home. I did give Edgar a bad time, in telling him I needed a white picket fence to dress up the yard.

All he did was to make a face at me, and then he told me, "I'll be bringing you a sofa tomorrow."

"All right," I answered, forgetting the paint job and all.

"The Williams are moving and they don't have room for theirs," he told me with one of his smiles.

"Thank them for me, if you would," I answered, not believing my luck.

"I had better go back and check what Jacob has going in the furnace," he said as he gave me a kiss good-bye.

Having the house finished, it gave me some time to relax a little. The rest of my time, I spent walking with Edgar. On our walks, we both voiced our hopes and dreams for the future. Then if we weren't walking, we were weeding our field. Jacob and his family would come over and help us.

One night after working at Smiley's, he came over and asked me, "You know the stables of your father's?"

"Yes," I answered, wondering where he was going with the thought, and then it hit me. I asked him, "Jacob and I could take the wood from the stable and make you a barn."

"The guy that bought it said he didn't need a stable that big. If I were to tear down enough for a barn, he can have the rest," he answered.

"Talk to him first," I suggested.

"Maybe I should, but if he wants me to pay for the lumber?" he asked.

"Remind him the damage the weather can do if the place isn't fixed," I suggested.

"Anyway, I'll see what I can do," he told me.

"Thank you for thinking of a barn. A barn will come in handy in time," I told him giving him a kiss.

Five weeks later, I had a barn off to one side of the house. Looking around the place, it looked like someone lived there. I was happy to have Edgar and Jacob around to take care of me.

It wasn't long, and our crop of corn was ready for picking. Edgar and Jacob had to continue with their jobs, but I closed the school for the harvest season. In the end, I picked most of the crop by myself with some help from Jacob's wife. However, in the end, I was sore but I still felt happy about something working outright. I kept some of the crop and canned it for our own use. Julie was a great help in teaching me how to can vegetables.

Edgar and Mr. Smiley put our crops together and took it to market. Getting back after a long day in Richmond, they were mad as hornets. They figured they only got a third of what the crop was worth.

"With our jobs, we have enough to buy seed for next year and live on," I assured Edgar when he showed me the money he was paid.

"But it's not fair," he answered, looking defeated. Then taking a cup of coffee from me, he added, "If we had any sense, we would go out west."

"And do what?" I asked, surprised to hear this new idea from him. A couple of my students told me their parents were thinking about moving also. It seemed the west was the place of choice for everyone.

"I don't know, but getting away from this mess would be a blessing," he answered. The job at Smiley's and helping me was beginning to get to him. I could see it in his face and the way he carried himself. It might not have been so hard on him if we could see an end to it.

The idea of going west became a reoccurring idea. Occasionally, I worried that if I went to town, I would learn he had left. Still, I understood what he was saying. In the papers, as well as people coming through town, no one gave us any respect. It was as if the war had turned us into trash. With all the changes from before the war, it was easy to see why he wanted to move.

Still everything got a little better, or at least that's what we told each other. A minister moved in, and everyone had something to be thankful for. Mr. Smiley was even getting decent orders, so he was also doing better.

With winter coming, we stayed inside most of the time. Edgar and Jacob had tilled the stalks into the ground, so there wasn't anything to do until spring. With this being the case, we waited for spring to arrive. With the teaching and working at the factory, Edgar and I didn't suffer from boredom.

Christmas will always be a special day for me. Though it's a special day for most, it was even more special for me. I had invited Jacob and his family as with Edgar to dinner. So looking out one of my windows I wasn't surprised to see them coming to the house. I was a little surprised to see Edgar carrying a small package in his hands. We had all agreed on no presents that year. Though I had made Edgar a quilt, I was going to give it to him the day after.

Before going to the door, I looked at myself in Mama's mirror. I found I looked presentable; I looked older than the sixteen years old that I was. I laughed, and said out loud, "A lot of living has been done in the past eight months." With that, I opened the door for my guests.

"Merry Christmas," I said in greeting them at the door.

"Merry Christmas," they replied as they stepped inside.

"Smells good," Molly added with a grin and then added, "Can I help you with anything?"

"What's for dinner?" Edgar asked, hearing Molly's comment. He looked over at the stove and he saw what there was. He then licked his lips indicating he was ready to eat.

"The turkey, of course, yams, potatoes, some greens and corn bread," I answered with a smile. I was proud of myself for having learned how to cook. I knew I owed Mary in the village a lot as well as Molly. I wondered what Mama would have to say about it all.

"Not too bad of a day," Jacob said commenting on the light snow that was on the ground.

"No, I like the snow," I answered as I took her coat. Our snow was never too much. When it did snow, it usually melted in a day or two. Then turning to Edgar, I asked him, "I thought we agreed on no presents?"

With a sheepish grin, he answered, "This isn't a present, really."

"What do you mean, it's wrapped like a present," I reminded him as I held it up to him.

"Yes, because it's special," he told me as he handed it to me.

"He made it himself," Jacob told me, and he gave me a funny look.

I took the gift from him, turning it repeatedly wondering what was in it. It was light in weight and rectangle in shape. Then feeling the center, it felt hollow giving me an idea what it was. I wondered why he was giving me a frame. I had hung up some of Mama's paintings but they were already in frames.

"Open it," he told me.

"We want to see what it is," Jacob said with a grin. He then grabbed Molly and wrapped his arm around her. She smiled up at him and they waited for me to open the package.

I opened it with a little hesitation, to find it was a frame for a painting or picture. It made me wonder more what the significance was with there being nothing in it. Looking at his face, I worried there was more to it than what it looked like. I commented to him, "It's empty."

With a boyish look, he tells me, "I would have put a picture of you and me as man and wife if I had one."

Not being able to catch my breath, I knew this was the best Christmas ever.

Matt's search for a life after the war

I left the old homestead with mixed feelings. Losing my father, three brothers, and an Aunt gave me an empty feeling. Then to top that off, my last two surviving brothers left thinking of me as a deserter or something worse. Looking back at the old place, I knew I should go back and make something of it. Otherwise, Father's work and ours had all been for nothing. With that line of thought, I kept coming up with an answer of why. Knowing what I did of the place, I again answered why. I decided, as father should have, to start living again. Now looking back, I know I was both young and dumb. At times, that's what it takes to do something meaningful as starting over.

With a few hours sleep, I was off to make something of myself. Not having any experience, other than farm work, wagon driver and killing people, I didn't know what I would do. I figured the best plan of action was to go out and find what there was for me. The closest place I could think of was Nashville. Having never been there, I worried at first how to find the city. Then asking a few of the people along the road, I found they were heading that way. This information made it easy for me, so I followed the string of people.

Thankfully, I found some fresh berries that helped satisfy my hunger. It didn't take long and the energy the berries gave me was gone. Then not long afterwards, a woman threw me a chunk of bread.

"Good luck, soldier," she shouted out at me.

"Thanks Ma'am," I answered her barely catching the bread.

"Where are you going kid?" A voice asked from under a tree.

"Nashville," I answered him. I saw he was an amputee and wished I could give him a ride. I knew if I tried I would probably finish my horse off.

"Me too," he shouted back at me, and then added, "You'll get there before I do." As I continued, he gave me a wave.

I waved back feeling sorry for him, as I did for most of the guys I passed. I wasn't sure about the Yankees, but I figured there were many more like that guy.

"If you see Maggie, tell her I'm coming," I heard him shout out to me.

With a smile, I gave him a wave. I got to wondering what my chances were of running into her. Then if I did meet her, what would she be like? At the same time, did she know he was an amputee? Maybe it didn't make any differences to her. I prayed it worked out for him, for he had enough to worry about as it is.

Along the way, it was obvious no one person or place was missed by the war. It seemed the bigger the home the more damage done. Not that it helped win the war one officer told me, it demoralized the population. Without the support of the people, their army was sure to lose. I personally, think the burning of homes was more out of jealousy than anything was. As in our little shack of a house hadn't been touched at all. Maybe the furniture was stolen or broken up, but the house was still standing. Others like ours were in the same condition as when the occupants left them.

Something told me the original idea was to ruin the supply line, but then it got out of hand. Many stories were being passed around that women had been raped as their homes were being burned down. Raping women had nothing to do with stopping the supply lines. The more I thought about everything that had happened, the sicker I got. I was glad I hadn't done anything like they did. I wouldn't be able to sleep, I wonder if they can. Oh, the actions one does in the name of war.

Coming to the top of a ridge, I saw between some trees what might be Nashville. With the city being in sight, I wondered about Robby and Mark. I wondered if they had made it to their destination. In fact, I was more worried if they were all right. Maybe I could go west and find them. I doubted that they would stay mad at me. At the same time, they needed to hear about Peter dying and all. The one idea I knew that was going to keep me going was the knowledge that they were out there.

"You've almost got it made," I told one soldier I rode past.

"For what good I ask," he answered, and then went on to add, "my wife Julie has probably been sleeping with everyone she could."

"It might not be that bad," I told him, understanding what he was saying. Then being ahead of him, I shouted out to him, "*I'm sure it was hard for her also.*"

In talking to many women in Richmond, I heard some horror stories that were hard to believe. Women with children found themselves with no way to tend fields. Even if they could, they were not strong enough to do the work by themselves. The answer was to move to the cities and find a job. Unfortunately, very few in the cities had any money. Even then, there wasn't anything for them to spend it on. The food that came from the farmers was not making it to the cities. The two armies were taking whatever was left with nothing else being grown.

Then about the money, there wasn't much around. I wasn't the only one that was without any money. Most of the people in the south were without money. Merchants printed most of the money themselves. The merchant that printed it only honored this currency. In the end, people had nothing but a bartering system. One favor was exchanged for a favor and another for another. A woman doing wash for someone might get a loaf of bread. Ironing might get a leg and a wing of a chicken. Even these opportunities were rare. Most women found it easier to surrender their bodies to the soldiers for food or favors. Many of these women had approached me, but I never slept with any. In fact, many of my fellow soldiers gave me a bad time about not having slept with a woman. I was keeping myself for one woman and one woman only; I just didn't know whom she was yet.

With this thought going through my head, I found myself in the city. Though the city had seen severe fighting, it didn't look as bad as Richmond. There were several ruined buildings, but the rubble was cleared. At the same time, there were people running around, taking care of business. I didn't see any bodies or wounded lying around. In fact, many women were wearing frilly dresses, hats and carrying parasols. Men were wearing long flock coats and top hats. It seemed Nashville was on the road of recovery.

"*Hey you,*" a voice shouted out from my side.

Bringing my horse to a stop, I turned towards the voice and asked, "Speaking to me?" The voice reminded me of a couple of soldiers I had met. I didn't like them and something told me I wasn't going to like this one. Yet, he might have something to offer that would be worth stopping for, so I stopped.

"Yes I'm speaking to you," he answered. He gave off an impression that he thought he was important.

"Your mother didn't teach you any manners, I see," I told him, finding him to be a little irritating. I didn't know if he was important or not and I didn't care right then.

"I'll teach you some manners for wearing my boots," he said coming at me.

"Wearing your boots?" I asked, surprised by his comment.

"Those are my initials on the top of those boots," he said as he grabbed for my foot.

I spurred my horse into action, and as I made it down the street, I shouted out, "*They're mine now.*" I laughed to myself thinking of the time Private Dick had given the boots to me. I had assumed the owner was dead, but it seems he was very much alive. The boots even felt better now, knowing they didn't come off a dead man.

Thinking about that day Private Dick gave me the boots seemed so long ago. Right then, I found myself feeling old. Though I was only eighteen, I had seen and done so much. Some things I was proud of, and of course as a soldier I had to do some I wasn't. I wondered when I changed from a kid to a man.

Slowing my horse down to a trot, I looked for job openings. I saw many signs advertising meals for twenty cents and shaves for fifteen. I also saw signs saying baths for ten cents. In reading that one, I felt like I had bugs crawling all over me. I knew right then I was over-do for a bath. At the same time, I felt the hair on the back of my neck, and it didn't feel too bad. At the same time, my beard didn't feel too shabby. A soldier in our company a few weeks earlier had given me a haircut. About my beard, I was young enough; it didn't grow that fast.

Yet at reading all the signs, my mind was on money. The signs were inviting, but I needed to get a job first. The first item on my list was still to find work. With that thought in mind, I didn't care what the job was.

As I rode on, men were giving me waves, and women were winking at me. I found myself sitting straighter in the saddle, as if I were royalty. I don't mind telling you, it felt good to be noticed. No one in my whole life gave me any attention so this felt good. Now why I was getting attention, I didn't know, nor did I care.

Having reached what appeared to be the busiest part of town, I pulled my horse to a hitching post. Getting off, I found myself slipping and catching myself on the side of a wagon.

"What do you think you're doing?" A man asked coming around the wagon.

"Leg went to sleep, I slipped and fell against the wagon," I told him.

"Be careful, there are some valuable items in there," he told me sounding a little rough around the edges.

"Sorry," I replied as I looked around, to see where I might try to find work.

"Looking for something, or are you lost?" The same man asked.

"Need a meal and a job," I answered and then I went on to add, "Just wondering which place to check out first."

"Can you drive a wagon?" He asked, as he looked me over as if I was a piece of meat.

"Drove one through the war," I answered trying to sound as good as he wanted.

"Name off the different parts of the wagon," he told me.

I swallowed real hard, worried I didn't know the names of each piece. Private Dick and I just got the job done and nothing more. Occasionally, he would refer to a part with a name, but not often. I began by pointing out the first piece that caught my eye, "That's the tongue, 'T's' there and there…" I went through every piece I knew and explained my situation.

He laughed, and told me, "It doesn't matter if a driver knows the pieces as much as can he handle a team. Even at that, I can teach you. The name is Sam, just plain old Sam, yours."

"Matt Duncan," I answered taking his hand and shaking it. I found myself glad my leg had gone asleep now. My slipping got me a job without having to look for it.

"We'll be hauling supplies to different army outposts," he told me. As he reached into his pocket, he told me, "We leave first light. Here's an advance on you wages. Want the job."

"Yes sir," I answered him, taking the money from him. I didn't even count it, nor did I ask him how much he paid. Then thinking about it, I asked, "How much are my wages?"

"Let's see…" he began. Then taking a breath and went on to finish, "Mind you, you only get paid when you are on the wagon. We are normally out for a month and back two or three days. Then at our destination, we are there for another two or three days. Your pay is sixty-five cents a day and I provide the coffee and meals as we travel."

"Sounds good to me," I told him as I walked away taking my horse with me.

"You won't be needing that nag," he said as I left.

"I'll be keeping him as backup, if you don't mind," I answered as I kept on walking. With each step I was scared he would take the job back if I kept my horse. Then as I got out of sight, I began to breathe again. "I must have the job," I said.

Getting down closer to where all the eating places were, I reached into my pockets to count the money I had. Taking the money out, I found he had given me twenty-five cents. I knew I could get a decent meal and still have change left over.

After a good meal, I walked around the streets of Nashville. Though most of the stores were closed as you might expect, the saloons weren't. Women were hanging on each porch column teasing all the men. Inside the saloons, music was loud enough to be heard in the street. Some had fancy dancers and others had singers, most just had a piano player. I walked into a few of them just to look around. I had tried drinking after a couple of battles and decided it wasn't for me. Still, I had never been in a saloon before and I found them exciting. Finally, I picked up my horse and went back to the wagon.

Taking the saddle off my horse, I looked inside to see if there was room enough for me. I saw Sam sleeping in the only spot available. I gave up trying to find a place, sat against a post, and slept sitting up.

"Good morning," Sam said waking me as he climbed out of the wagon. Then looking at me closer, he asked, "Slept there?"

"From what my back is telling me, it feels like I did," I answered with my legs not working right. Then seeing the look on his face, I told him, "No I didn't go out drinking. I learned that drinking does not work with this body."

"No problem. If you drink it's your problem not mine," he said with a grin motioning for me to join him. After a few feet, he asked, "Think a cup of coffee would help?"

"I have never been able to turn down a cup of coffee," I answered him with a grin. I was also thinking a few eggs, grits, ham, and biscuits would go nicely with the coffee.

"Good enough, and maybe some food to get us going," he said, slapping me on the back.

My first trip out was to San Antonio, Texas. I was glad to see San Antonio when we finally got there. My father had fought in the Spanish American war. Many times, he would tell us about the battle of the

Alamo in 1836. With my friends and neighbors and with their love for Davy Crockett, seeing the remains of the Alamo was exciting. To me, it was a long time since the battle. In reality, it was only twenty-five years back. That battle was followed by the Spanish American war. This war lasted for another twelve years. In talking about the secession, he related the south to the American that fought at the Alamo. The Americans were rebels, trying to take over a part of what the Mexican government owned. In the same way, the south was trying to take away what belonged to the United States. It wasn't that he didn't agree with the other southerners, he just understood they were not totally in the right.

On the trip to San Antonio, we weren't out a full month, but long enough considering the heat we went through. Other than the heat, we didn't have any problems. When we got back, the whole city of Nashville was a roar.

Coming down the street to the stable, I shouted out, "What's going on?"

"*President's assassin killed*," a paperboy cried out.

"Where've you been? Lincoln was assassinated."

"What?" I asked again not sure if I heard him correctly.

He held up a paper that said:

Lincoln Assassinated at Ford Theater:

Assassin killed

I jumped off the wagon and tore the paper from his hands. I began reading it and couldn't believe what it said. "Hey Sam, did you see this."

"What you talking about?" Sam asked me.

"Don't forget where you got that paper at," the man on the street reminded me.

"Sorry," I told him as I handed the paper back to him. Then turning back to Sam, I told him, "Some Actor named John Wilkes Booth assassinated Lincoln."

"He got his just dues, that's all I can say," Sam said heading back for his wagon.

"So the war was for nothing then?" I asked.

"The slave issue was going to happen one way or the other. In fact, stop and think about it. How many landowners do you know had slaves? I would be willing to bet you know very few. Most had learned having slaves was an expensive proposition. If the idea had been presented right, the landowner with slaves would have given them up without an issue. We weren't fighting a slave issue; we were fighting the issue of being told what we could and could not do by northern bankers and politicians. Until we can learn to work for one another and not ourselves, we will always have trouble," he said as he rode off towards the stable.

"The paper also said this Booth fella was killed in a barn in New Jersey," I told him.

"I guess that's what he deserved, but…" he answered, but not finishing his thought.

I wasn't sure exactly what he meant, but some of it I did. His issue about most of the landowners not having slaves was true. My father didn't have any, and no one I knew did. I was told there was a slave here and there, but I never saw one. Fighting for something we didn't have was a joke to me. As I originally felt, just don't tell me what I can and can't do. Explain it to me, show me the benefits and I'll change. If you do that, I'll even help you to make others understand. Our way of life took years to come about. To ask us to change overnight without reason was dumb.

I disagreed with Sam in that Lincoln didn't deserve to die. He had his opinions as I had mine and Sam had his; should the three of us be killed because we differ, no.

I doubt if the true answer will ever be decided. The one thing I did know was Lincoln's death and the war was talked about for the next few weeks.

I doubt if you need a detailed story of how I drove the wagon. A pair of horses pulling a buggy or wagon is all the same. Still, there were trips that ended up being a little more exciting than others are.

Indians never attacked us but we did meet and saw a few. One time, we were going through a corner of Texas on our way to Kansas. On a ridge there was a war party lined up watching us ride by. Sam and I drove separate wagons most of the time. This was one of those times and he gave me to signal to continue on. I knew why he gave me that signal, because there wasn't any place for us to go. We were out in the middle of nowhere and it was obvious we were out numbered. We continued, not stepping up our pace but continued. The Indians left the ridge and we never saw them again.

Another time, we came up the top of a rise and I saw a feather sticking up. I tried to stop my horses, but there wasn't enough time. I grabbed my rifle as we reached the peak. Once stopped, I found myself staring at an old Indian holding the reins of a horse. The horse was pulling a litter with what was probably all of his belongings. Then on the horse was an old woman slumped over who was probably his wife.

He dropped the reins and held up both of his hands. Then in his tongue, he rattled off a batch of words. By this time, Sam had come up to see what was happening. He couldn't understand the old Indian any better than I could. We didn't know what to do. The old Indian didn't seem threatening but he did seem intent on what he needed. The longer we stared at him, the more frustrated he became. Then he cupped his hand and put it to his mouth as if he was drinking something. Thinking that might be the case, I got out my canteen and gave it to him.

If you ever wanted to see a grin, you should have seen his. His little old feet got to moving and he took the canteen from me. Not wasting his time to say anything, he turned and ran back to his wife. She took the canteen and took a long drink. She returned a grin equal to her husbands. The old man never took a sip of water from the canteen, but brought it back to me. With having a couple in the wagon, I pushed it back to him shaking my head.

As with him trying to tell us what he needed, I had the same going the other way. I almost got so frustrated I wanted to shove the canteen down his throat. Then after I showed him I had two more he finally took it.

He handed the canteen to his wife, still wearing that big grin. Turning back to me, he said a few words that I could not understand. Then reaching up to his neck, he pulled the beaded necklace/pouch and took it off. Holding it out in front of him, he signaled for me to take it. Not knowing what to do, I turned to Sam. He nodded to say go ahead and accept. I felt funny about accepting something so pretty for a little water, but I did. Taking it from him, I bowed to the old man and put it around my neck. Both of us grinned at each other, happy with the exchange. The old man grabbed the reins of his horse and they were on their way.

Now like I said, driving a wagon is no big deal. No matter who you are some things happen. We had our broken wheels get stuck in mud and we even got lost a few times. When you are traveling country as we were, it is to be expected. Still, there are those memories that really stand out. Some you find scratching a particular spot or rubbing another in memory of the event. My first trip to Fort Dodge was one such memory.

The first time I went to Fort Dodge, I will never forget. If memory serves me right, it was 1871. The weather went from hot to warm and back to hot. Then it would be dry and then rain solid for three to four days. The trip took a week longer than it should have. Both of our tempers were on the edge. Oh, I remember the trip well.

"You're going to make more on this trip than I am," Sam yelled at me one day.

"I've been breaking the trail for the past three weeks, so I should make more than you," I yelled back at him. I then snapped the reins to get the horses moving a little faster than his did, as if I was leaving him.

I could hear him cussing and then he shouted out, "They won't pay you. You'll have to sit and wait for me to come in. You'll pay for it in the end."

"All right, have it your way," I shouted back to him. With that, I slowed down, and laughed for the next hour or two.

Finally, we made it to Fort Dodge, and both of us could not have been any happier. With it being as early in the day as it was, we unloaded the wagons. Most the soldiers were out scaring up some Indians so we ended up doing all the work. We only stayed long enough afterwards for Sam to get paid. We still made it into the town of Dodge long before dusk.

"I'm going to have the biggest drink the bartender will serve me," Sam told me as he strutted to his wagon.

"I'm right behind you," I answered as I got into my wagon. I wasn't planning to have a drink, but I was going to have a bath and a change of clothes.

As we drove through town, we saw a busy little community. On one side, there were thousands of cattle in pens ready for shipping to the eastern market. Also going the same way, there were tens of thousands of hides stacked up, ready to ship east.

Later I learned the hides were from buffaloes. Having never seen a buffalo, I was dying to see one. Before we left, I would take a ride out and see one of these animals for myself. I have to tell you, they are the most fascinating animals you could ever see. Buffalo hunting is a story in itself. The decaying hides in the yards with the cattle in another made for one stinking place.

In contrast, several of the men were dressed as we were, workingmen. Most of the men wore a pistol on their hip and every saddled horse had a rifle on it. Then on the other side of the coin, there were as many in long black flock coats, vest, ties, and top hats or derbies. The women were wearing long colorful dresses, high-top shoes, and supporting a hat. Again, on the other side of the coin, there were several women hanging over railings on the second floor advertising their goods. Most of them seem half dressed, making me blush. With the boardwalks full, kids were running all over the place.

The city itself appeared to be growing yet from what I could see of the buildings. The actual buildings were made of wood. Then in equal number to the wooden buildings there were tents. Some of the tents were used as sleeping quarters for travelers, as others were used to sell liquor or dry goods. With the stench in the air, all of this made for an interesting and exciting picture. At the same time, as I had learned, Dodge City was typical of the boomtowns in the west, but on a grander scale than most.

Sam had pulled his wagon in front of a saloon called the Long Branch, which I found to be an interesting name for a place. From looking at the signs outside, there was little that a man couldn't get that he could here.

"If you need me, I'll be inside," Sam told me as he tied up his horses.

"See you later," I answered, as I looked around and saw a dry goods store.

Once I tied my horses, I went to the store and bought a clean change of clothes. Then with Sam being at the Long Branch, I went there to get a bath. As I got to the door of the saloon, the place seemed to be alive in a manner I had never known. Not seeing anyone else to ask, I went over to the bar to see about my bath.

"Yes sir?" The barkeep asked as he wiped up a mess on the bar in front of me.

"A bath," I told him.

"Fifteen cents," he told me. Then as I handed him the money, he pointed to a door for me to go to.

I found the door led outside the saloon. From ropes, curtains were hung to give the bather some privacy. A woman pointed to a curtain and I went in. As I entered the tub, I remembered fighting my father not to take a bath. Then entering the water, I felt it very satisfying.

Once dressed in a fresh change, I gave her my dirty clothes. She promised to have them for me the following day. With my bath over, I was ready for something to eat.

While eating, I saw Sam at a card table. From where I was, I couldn't see if he was doing good or bad. I decided to check it out when I was finished. I had learned a few trips before that Sam didn't drink much. His bad habit was cards and he was very serious about them.

Knowing he didn't like to talk when he played, I stood back and watched. Most of the players at the table wore the black or brown flock coats, one man stood out from the others. Everyone referred to him as Doc, and he seemed to be a cold individual. It didn't make any difference to me, but I found him interesting. I had only watched three of four hands played and everything changed.

"I'll take one?" Sam asked Doc.

I watched Doc deal the card closely and he dealt it from the bottom of the deck. Though I had only played one game in my life, I knew that wasn't right. I bent over and whispered in Sam's ear, "He dealt that card from the bottom of the deck."

Sam laid his hand down and proceeded to tell Doc, throwing a thumb my way, "The kid here saw you deal from the bottom of the deck."

I vaguely remember a commotion but it was like a bad dream. The only thing I did remember was waking up in a jail cell. Waking up I found I had the biggest headache I could remember.

I saw Sam sitting next to me, and he told me, "The Marshal clubbed you."

"Was it something I said?" I asked wishing I had the strength to scream.

"Not your fault, though it did cost us the money I had on the table," he told me.

As I looked around the cell, I saw it was about as full as it could be. There were eight of us in a ten by ten cell. "All the comforts of home," I told him as I continued to rub my head.

"Cattle have more room in those pens than we do," he answered.

"Would the two of you shut up, I'm trying to sleep," a guy told us from the top bunk.

"We don't need any of your lip either," another told the man in the bunk giving him a slap.

"A friendly group," I whispered to Sam. Then I gave out a little moan.

"Better to have a sore head, than Doc having given you a third eye. The Marshal did both of you a favor as well as himself I guess," a guy next to me told me.

"He did himself a favor?" I asked him, not understanding what he meant.

"He gets three dollars for each prisoner he brings in," he explained.

"That doesn't sound right. He could lock up anyone for any reason then," I commented still rubbing my head.

"That's the deal the city made with him. When the cards are not running his way, he makes up for his losses by arresting people," he added to his explanation.

We were released later that morning and we didn't have to pay any fines. I had never been so happy to get out of a place as I was then. In years to come, much was printed about a particular Marshal and his friend a dentist. I have always wondered if it was them we ran into at Dodge City.

Still my visit then and afterwards brought back memories of the piles of buffalo hides. Though I was making a livable wage as a wagon driver, buffalo hunting seemed interesting to me. If I were to make a change, I thought I would try my hand at it.

Early fall of 1871, we had made a run to Texas and back, and my life was going to take a change. I wasn't thinking seriously about making a change. Other than a few meals and some clothes, most of my wages I had saved. I could have lived a few years without working. With me being in this financial position, that helped bring about an offer.

"That's another profitable trip," Sam said as he got down from his wagon, for we had just got home from a trip to Texas.

"Yep, no major problem, just the way I like them," I said as I began to disconnect the horses from my wagon.

"Same here," he answered giving me a smile. Then reaching down to give me a hand, he told me, "I was, supposed to have had a talk to you on this trip."

"Oh," I answered wondering what he was talking about.

"Let's just say, Beatrice is tired of me being gone as long as I am," he began to explain.

Beatrice was a woman he had met a year or so ago. Then six months ago, Sam married her. It wasn't until their marriage that I learned Sam's last name was Butts. He warned me if I gave him a bad time about it, he would shoot me. Being my best friend, I kept my thoughts and jokes to myself. As it had been for six years, we were gone most of the time. I could see where she might get lonely and want her husband home with her. Though she had enough money, money wasn't everything.

"And with that, she doesn't love me anymore?" I asked him, giving him a bad time.

"I wish that were the problem," he answered grinning, and then he went on to add, "No, but you might be an answer to her problem."

"How's that?" I asked him.

"Let's say, I buy another wagon or two and expand the business. What do you think about that?" He asked.

"There's plenty of business out there," I offered, wondering what else he had on his mind.

"If I did that, someone would have to run the business here, as the wagons are on the road," he stopped to get a breath and put his thoughts together.

"Understandable. But I wouldn't know what to do," I told him, knowing he didn't mean me to run the business.

"Man, you're dumb. I would stay here and you as my partner would run the wagons," he suggested to me, looking relieved that he had gotten the offer out.

"Partner? Your partner?" I couldn't believe what I was hearing. Then thinking it was going to cost me, I asked, "How much do you need?"

"With the money I lost because of you last fall at Dodge City… plenty," he answered with a smile and shook his head at the same time. He went on to add, "Keep your money; you have earned the position as my partner after all these years."

"There's no way I could say no, yet a simple yes doesn't seem to be enough—" he interrupted me, which was good. I was beginning to choke up and probably wouldn't have gotten any more out.

"Then it's settled. Now I can go in and tell Beatrice she has her husband full-time. I hope I can handle staying here all the time," he said giving me a pat on the back. Then as I began walking towards the stables, he said, "Well partner, with the wagons your responsibility, you can undo my team. Then the three of us can have dinner."

"I knew there was a catch to this partnership," I answered laughing with him.

That night we had dinner and all three of us were happy. The next day, Sam went out and bought the wagons, horses and everything else we needed. At the same time, I began looking for three more drivers. Dave, one driver that worked with us occasionally, joined our company. The other two drivers took awhile to find. It wasn't that there weren't men available, for there were, but none I would trust.

Still after a week, we had drivers and wagons. At the same time, Sam had gotten enough loads lined up for the next three months. It looked as if we were on our way to fame and wealth. I wondered what I was going to do with my share of the profits.

Getting on my horse, I took a ride through town. Nothing had changed as much as my life had in the past hour or so. I almost thought about having a drink to celebrate, but I didn't knowing I would get sick and I didn't think getting sick was any way to celebrate. Then seeing a sign in a window I began to get ideas. There was a house for sale, not far from our stable. It would be the answer of getting out from under Sam and Beatrice's way. As it was, my bedroom was next to theirs, and I felt funny about it. Now that I would be in the money, it gave me an excuse to move out. I thought I would buy the place when I came back. Then letting it out to a couple, keeping one room for me. I didn't know it at the time, but the other shoe would hit the floor or did it hit me?

I got back from my first trip as partner of the new company. Pulling up to Sam's place, I saw the house was draped with black ribbons.

I hadn't seen the use of black ribbons often, but when it was used it meant a death. I pulled the horses to a halt and ran to the house. Beatrice was sitting at the dining table dressed in black. I got the picture long before she opened her mouth. Standing there at the age of twenty-four, I had lost brothers, a father, and now my best friend, when was it going to end.

"Oh Matt," she said sobbing, and wiping her eyes at the same time. She grabbed me around the neck and told me, "He knew you were going to be so proud of him…and then…"

"Why don't you sit on the sofa and tell me about it," I suggested, pointing her to the parlor.

Once seated, she began telling me the story, "He had just gotten a contract to haul machinery for this company on the other side of town. We celebrated that evening, and made plans on how to tell you about it…" She stopped to blow her nose.

"There's no rush. Take your time," I told her, wishing she would speed it up a little.

"We went to bed feeling good about everything and how it all was working out," she told me, and then she went on to add, "I never wanted to be rich. Just to have someone that loved me. Then I met Sam and I knew I was going to be the happiest woman alive…and then this happened."

"What happened, Beatrice?" I asked her.

"I used to go with this guy named Phil. He left Nashville a year or two ago, and I almost forgot about him," she told me. Then wiping her nose again, she added, "Sam and I were sleeping and the bedroom door opened. Being startled, Sam and I sat up wondering what it was. Before we knew what happened, a pistol goes off. A man's voice that I recognized said, "That'll teach you to sleep with my woman." I was stunned and called out Sam's name and he didn't answer. Then Jody, our cook, came running in with a rifle. Seeing movement in the corner of the room, she fired. As I reached over to check Sam out, I heard a body hit the floor."

"What about Sam?" I asked her, knowing I would hear rest of it later. I wanted to know about Sam.

"He was dead. I don't know what I'll do without him," she said leaning over to cry on my shoulder.

"Can I get you something?" A female voice asked.

Looking up at the woman, I figured it was the cook Jody. I told her, "No thanks. However, you might help Beatrice to her bed so she can lie down. I have to take care of my team and the wagon."

"Don't worry about her. I'll take her upstairs to rest," Jody answered.

When I got outside, I saw that Dave had taken care of my team. I was thankful that he had, for I had forgotten about them. I saw him propped up against the stable wall, and I told him, "Thanks for taking care of the team."

"No problem," he answered as he put his cigarette out. Then looking back at me, he went on to add, "Frank told me about Sam. It's a shame."

Frank was Sam's stableman, and a good guy. He had gone to work for Sam long before the war started. Then when Sam began working with the confederate army, Frank helped him. If there was anyone that knew Sam, it was Frank.

"I agree with you on that. I lost the best friend a man could ever have," I answered not knowing what else to say.

"Sorry to have you come home to such sad news," Frank said coming out of the stable.

"I am also. The two of you have been together a long time," I said feeling sorrier for him than I did for Beatrice.

"That we were. Now the Misses has gone and sold the business. I don't know what I'll do," he told me.

"She what?" I asked him, not sure I had heard him right.

"From the way it sounds, it was part of the contract with the company Sam made a deal with. If anything was to happen to him, they would have the option to buy the business," He told me. He then gave me a shrug indicating he didn't understand it either.

It turned out Frank knew what he was talking about. The next day

Beatrice walked me through all of it. A provision was in the contract, giving me a part of the sale. I told Beatrice she could have my share, which she refused. Unknown to me, she had her own money. She was willing to give me everything, but I wouldn't take it. At the same time, the new owners offered me a job. Beatrice decided on going back east to live with her mother. I found myself with no one around again.

I worked with the new company for the first year. I can't say they were hard to work for, because I was traveling and never saw them. Still, it wasn't the same as working with Sam. In coming back from my last trip, I began to make plans. I knew I didn't have to work for a while, but still wanted to find Mark and Robby. At the same time, not knowing how they were doing, I didn't want to use all of my money. The money I had might make it easier for them. Thinking of them, I knew I needed to find a job.

Dropping my wagon off and giving the owner my resignation, I went into town. I knew enough guys in the business area of Nashville; I figured I would be able to find something.

"Hey Paul, what's going on?" I asked the guy that had taken care of our wagons for years.

"Not much. How you're new bosses, not the same as old Sam?" He asked as he checked out his inventory sheets.

"I don't have a boss anymore, or at least for the past hour," I told him as I looked around his shop and the street. There were a lot people milling around, with six Conestoga Wagons lined up in the middle of the street. As I passed them, I tipped my hat to the women.

"Sorry to hear that. What do you plan, on doing now?" he asked as he sat his pencil down, showing some interest in what I had to say.

"I'm open to any suggestion, though I would like something that took me west," I answered being honest with him.

"This might be your lucky day," he told me with a smile. He then motioned me to follow him. As we got closer to the Conestoga Wagons, he told me, "I think the head man's name is Buchanan. There are six of them wanting to meet up with a wagon train taking the Oregon Trail. Maybe the two of you can be of help to each other."

"I'm not sure, but it's worth talking to this guy," I answered. In driving our wagons, there had been several times we were part of a wagon train. My limited experience didn't make me a Wagon Master, but I thought I could do it. As if it were planned, a man walked around a wagon coming toward us.

"Mr. Buchanan, I might have your problem solved for you," Paul told him, suggesting I was the man to talk to.

"I'm Edgar Buchanan, Edgar will do," he said in greeting me.

"Matt Duncan, good to meet you, Edgar. Most call me Matt, I doubt if I have used my last name but once this year," I replied and we both laughed

"I'll let the two of you talk details over. Good luck, Matt, and you also, Mr. Buchanan," Paul said as he went back to his shop.

"As I was telling your friend there," Edgar began to say, but a woman interrupted us. Taking the woman's hand, he introduced me to her, "My wife, Ida. Ida darling, this gentleman is Matt."

"Nice to meet you, Matt," Ida said with the prettiest grin I had ever seen.

"Same here, it's nice to meet you also," I replied. I didn't know if it was a dream or if it was fact, but I thought I had seen her before. I didn't bring it up then, for it wasn't my place.

"As I was just about to tell Matt, we were supposed to meet the train in Independence Missouri two days from now. Everything just didn't work outright for us. If there were any way we can meet up with them, we would like to try. There are few wagon trains leaving now. As you know, most people are going from town to town by wagon or by rail. We can't afford to take the train, so we need the company of as many wagons we can get together," he told me.

I understood what he was saying. Going the distance was hard to do, on both the people and animals. Still it was being done but not by many any more. I told him, "If we leave tomorrow and push hard, we could catch up with them at Fort Kearny. With them having more wagons, they won't be able to travel as fast as six wagons. Still I can't guarantee we will make it. You might find yourself stranded until the next train."

"We'll take the chance," Edgar answered. His wife looked at him as if she knew he could do it.

"You understand the trip is going to take six to seven months, and you need to take everything you might need during that time?" I asked him.

"We understand that," he answered, and then he went on to ask me, "How much are you going to need for your services."

"Forty dollars," I answered and watched their two faces.

The two looked at each other and they didn't seem too happy about it. Edgar still looked at me and said to his wife, "That's only a little over six dollars per wagon."

"And I take it we provide meals?" she asked.

"Yes," I answered.

"It's a deal," Edgar said with a smile.

"Then let's go through the wagons and see what you are taking," I told him, not wanting to waste any valuable time.

I knew that in the old days, seed and the like were needed going across country. Now with the shipping lanes going to the West Coast now, everything could be bought there when they arrived. My main concern was the amount of food they had. At the same time, the condition of the wagons and the animals pulling them.

"Where are your animals?" I asked Edgar.

"In back of the stables," he answered pointing to Joe's stables.

"Edgar, Ida just told us you found a Wagon master," a black man said sounding excited as he approached us.

"Matt, this is my good friend Jacob, and Jacob, this is Matt," Edgar said introducing us.

"Good to meet you, Matt," Jacob said extending his hand to me.

"Pleasure meeting you," I answered taking his hand and shaking it.

"Matt wants to see our animals," Edgar explained to his friend.

"Sounds good," Jacob answered as he followed us to the stables.

Want to Go West Lady?

Once we go to the pens, I found fourteen oxen, and one horse the little group owned. I turn to the two men and told them, "Fine looking animals. I was afraid you might have horses or mules. They would never make it."

"I was told oxen would be the best for this trip. For safety though, we bought two extra. If it turns out we don't need them, we can always turn them loose or sell them. We also have a few horses," Edgar told me.

We went back to the wagons and checked what they had in them. I was surprised there wasn't as much as I was afraid there might be. The more they had, the slower the trip would be. The Buchanan's were the only ones with some excess. There were a few paintings, but no furniture. Then, as the other wagons, there were some basic tools. Still I checked out their supplies, and they had plenty.

While checking out the wagons, I got to meet everyone. The total number of people making the trip was going to be twenty-five counting myself.

"I guess everything is good for tomorrow morning," I told them all getting a round of applause from them.

My intent wasn't to take them all the way west, but to Fort Kearney and no further. Ida can tell you about the trip because she made it. I should tell you about two events about my part of the trip.

The first day had gone without a hitch. We didn't have any breakdowns and we made good time, considering we were using oxen. That night, I ordered a circle-up order and everyone understood what I meant. Some years later, I read that circling up the wagons was done to fight the Indians. First off, there were few Indian attacks back then. The second is the circling of the wagons was to keep control of the animals. I find the eastern writers understanding funny.

Then the final point is we got to Fort Kearny. We made it shy of a month and beating the main body of the wagon train by three days. In leaving the six wagons, I did with a clear conscience.

I hung around Fort Kearny for the three days they were there, waiting for the main train. All twenty-five of us had become friends and I didn't feel like heading out on the trail again so soon. At the same time, I didn't know what I was going to do next. I thought about going rest of the way with them. This would get me closer to Mark and Robby. Then the memory of Mark's letter kept coming back saying we don't want you. With that, I didn't know what I would do out west; I had never been there.

As they left for Oregon, I headed for Dodge City. At twenty dollars a hide, I figured I would try it. Along the way, I found some ranching jobs that I took for a month or two. In the end, it took me longer to get to Dodge City than I had expected. I did gain some experience in ranching. I decided if worst came to worst, I would try it. Still I got there before Buffalo hunting ended for good.

To be honest, I didn't even make it into Dodge City. I ran into a hunter on his way to a herd. He stopped me before I went past him.

"Need a job?" He asked.

"Thought I would try my hand at buffalo hunting," I answered.

"Tie you horse off and we will be on our way," he told me as his way of hiring me.

As I tied my horse off, and climbed into his wagon, I weighed my options. By, myself, I would have to buy a wagon and a rifle big enough to take one of these animals down. At the same time, I would be doing it all myself. The two of us could get twice as many and splitting the sale, I would make the same.

"Fifty-fifty split?" I asked as I sat beside him on the seat.

"It's my wagon and you don't have a rifle," he pointed out.

"And these will get you how many?" I asked, hoping he would see it my way.

"After the first day, I would get tired of it all and quit," he answered. Then he went on with his thinking, "The two of us might make it a week. Giving me a couple more days of profit. All right, fifty-fifty."

"Let's go then," I told him feeling good about everything. As I took my seat, I introduced myself to him, "I'm Matt Duncan."

"Peter Mathew. Good to have someone to hunt with," he told me.

"Likewise," I answered as we bumped along out to the herd. I then got to wondering if he had ever hunted buffalo. With this question on my mind, I asked him, "Ever hunted before?"

"Once," he answered not adding anymore.

"My first time," I told him as a warning more than anything.

"First chance you get, you might want to get another cap," he suggested.

"What's wrong with my cap?" I asked not having thought about it for a while. It was Private Dick's Kepi cap, and I was proud of it. My pride wasn't as much because of it being a part of the Confederacy but because it was Private Dick's and he was my friend. Now for those of you that don't know what they look like I'll tell you. They are a little cap made of cotton, with a small bill and a flattop. The flattop is angled towards the front of it. Around the bottom edge there is a leather band. The Confederate cap was gray and the Yankees were blue.

As I got into the wagon, I asked, "Well?" I had seen him check out my cap as I got on aboard.

"It'll do," was his only answer.

"People take a bad attitude to Rebels. That hat says you're a Rebel and out here one shot more or less wouldn't be noticed. I would hate to lose a partner too quickly," he answered.

"At least not until we have filled the wagon?" I asked with a grin.

"Something like that," he answered laughing as he snapped the reins.

The first time we were in town I bought a new hat to make him happy. Though it looked like everyone else's and felt good, it wasn't the same as the Kepi cap. Then out on the range, I learned the broad brim sure helped keep the sun out of my eyes, not to mention rain. Occasionally, I still put the old Kepi cap on and thought of Private Dick.

Trust me when I tell you buffalo hunting is dirty work. Skinning the beast takes better than a day in most cases. As long as you are skinning, you are in blood up to your neck. Then it's getting the hide onto the wagon. A hide can weigh two hundred pounds. When you have twenty or thirty on the wagon, it takes every ounce of energy to get it on top of the pile.

The actual shooting was the easy part. Peter had bought a Sharps single-shot rifle, with a breechblock. You set up a stand (a rod with a "U" shape piece on top of the rod) to take the weight of the barrel. This rifle had no problem bringing the Bison or Buffalo down. With his rifle, we had no problem bringing them down, just skinning them. I also knew I wouldn't like trying to bring one down like the Indians do with a bow and arrow on horseback.

When we brought our first load in, we were in for a surprise. Along the tracks, buffalo hides were stacked higher than a man.

"They say, there's more than 30,000 hides piled there," Peter told me. Then looking at the pile again, he added, "They expect another ten to twenty thousand to be in by the end of the week."

"My mind can't imagine numbers like that," I answered, and then I added, "It's a shame; all of that meat is going to waste." Then watching what we brought in, it didn't even make a dent in the pile.

I made it in the buffalo hunting business for two seasons. By the end of the second season, it was almost impossible to find a herd. It wasn't that I didn't like the work or I didn't make enough money, there just weren't any buffaloes around. Where as a wagon driver I would be getting sixty-five cents a day, I was getting better than six dollars a day. I had gotten into the business a year or two too late.

For the next year, I worked as a Deputy Sheriff for a short time. It was an interesting but boring year. I had wandered around for a few days and ended up in the northeastern corner of Kansas. While walking around, I saw two men having words. As I got closer, I saw the guy away from me supporting a badge. The guy nearest me seemed like he was drunk.

"I should take you out like the gunfighters do in them dime novels," the drunk told the sheriff.

The sheriff shook his head and told the drunk, "You know you don't want to do that. It's going to be bad enough when the booze wears off."

The drunk froze for a second and he got into a crouching position he asked the sheriff, "Are you saying I'm drunk."

The sheriff had seen me, but the drunk didn't realize I was even there. Seeing the stance he had taken, I worried he might pull his pistol on the sheriff. Not knowing either one, I took out my pistol and kept it in ready.

"Think about it, would you be doing this if you were sober?" The sheriff asked him.

As the guy went for his gun, I hit him over the head with my pistol. The sheriff had his pistol out about the same time the drunk fell to his knees. From his knees, he made a graceful tilt to one side and he was down for the count.

"Good thinking, stranger," the sheriff said as he put his pistol back into its holster.

"Any time I can be of help," I answered laughing as I looked down at the poor man. Then looking up at the sheriff, I told him, "I've see enough deaths."

"Fought in the war, I take it?" He asked.

"Like many did, unfortunately," I answered, happy he didn't ask which side I fought on. I had learned since working with Peter the war was still going on. If you said anything to suggest you were with the confederate side to a Yankee, it was an automatic fight. I had learned to get around the question without lying.

After helping the sheriff, he told me, "That was some good thinking. You wouldn't be interested in a job would you?"

"Might consider it," I answered as we carried the guy off.

"The guy is a good guy as a rule. But his wife took off with some drifter, and he's out to take it out on the world," he told me. Then he added, "The towns not too large so the pay's not much. Most of the time, all you do is collecting taxes from the farmers and businesses."

He was right it didn't pay much. Most of my real pay came from the ten percent I collected in taxes. Still, it covered my cost of a room and food. I stayed there for a year and got bored. It turned out the town was too quiet. Farmers don't have the time to cause too much trouble.

The job did remind me of when I went to jail in Dodge City though. I told the sheriff the story that first day and we both had a laugh. He told me there was no bonus for locking someone up. At the same time, the city fathers frowned on killing people. It turned out the first reaction I did coming to town was the correct way of handling a situation. The funny part of it all was the entire town knew about it before I had even been there for five minutes.

From there I worked on ranches and migrated towards Idaho for some reason.

Mrs. Ida Buchanan

The day after Christmas, Edgar and I were on our way to see the Reverend. Jacob and Molly wanted to throw a party, but we declined the offer. I told Molly we might get together for dinner but no party. I grew up with parties and I didn't think I needed another. Just the fact I was Mrs. Ida Buchanan was more than enough for me. In fact, in private, I would say my new name repeatedly. Our marriage brought together plans Mama and Father had. At the same time, it was a new start for me by dropping Marsh from my name. Still, if Mama had been there, there would have been a party. I might have even enjoyed it for her sake. I prayed that Mama and Father were able to see us get married from wherever they were.

You can't believe how thrilled I felt being married to Edgar. Though there were a few things to get used to, it was as if it was suppose to be that way, him and I together. Then nine months later little Harold came into our lives. Of course, we named him after my father.

Our little one's timing though wasn't the greatest. During the planting season, I was beginning to show (I was getting bigger around than I was tall), by harvest time I couldn't help. I have never felt the pain before as I did delivering the little guy. I was so thankful Molly was around, because Edgar would have been a total waste. Unlike some, I was up and around the next day. I have heard so many stories about other women, I'm glad I had it so easy. It wasn't that he couldn't stand blood, but he was a person that's all thumbs.

With me laid up with my big belly and Edgar and Jacob working all day, we didn't get everything harvested. Still, we recovered our cost and made a few dollars. We should have been able to make enough to support both families. The problem was the same as after the war. Most people didn't have any money. The ones that did weren't spending it. Then, too, there were those northern Carpetbaggers.

If I wasn't busy enough taking care of the little ones I was teaching, Edgar added to it. One afternoon's event became a regular happening, starting with him running to the house.

"We have company, Hon," he shouted out as he came running into the house.

"Who?" I asked looking out the window. From what I could see, there was a covered wagon coming up our lane. The wagon had two adults and three kids. Tied to the wagon were cages of chickens, pots, and pans. Then from behind it was a cow. It was easy to see they were on the move.

Edgar had gone back outside to greet out guests, so I went out to join him. I wondered why they were there; I didn't know them. Then at the same time, it might be relatives of Edgar, I didn't know. I knew I was about to find out though.

"Hon," Edgar said motioning me to come closer. Then as I got to them, he tells me, "This is Mr. and Mrs. Wilcox. This is my wife, Ida. These nice people are on their way north."

"Nice meeting you," I offered as a greeting. Then thinking of my mother, I asked them, "Care for some water? I could put a pot of coffee on if you would like?"

"Nice place you have here," Mrs. Wilcox told me as she touched everything. Sitting down, she told me, "We tried to get our lives back together like you have, but we didn't make it."

"It isn't easy," I agreed with her.

"It wasn't for Frank not trying, he did. It was like everyone and everything was fighting us," she said and then she went on to add, "wasn't it enough giving up our loved ones? Now we are giving up everything we worked for."

"We ask ourselves the same question everyday. Is it worth it? Edgar has been talking about going west for some time now. I expect someday soon we will be, heading that way ourselves," I told her understanding exactly what she was saying.

"Are we going somewhere, Mama?" Little Harold asked me, having overheard our conversation.

"Not right now, honey," I answered, as I motioned for him to go outside.

"You have such quiet children," she commented on the children as she watched them.

"Oh, they are until they get to know you. A little shy at times," I answered giving her a motherly smile of thanks.

In the end, we put them up for the night. Then over the next three weeks, we had four more families that spent a night or more. One family had a sick little girl and we kept them for a week. The Wilcox family opening the gates, the stream of migrating people just continued on and on. Every one of the ones that stopped had a similar story as Mrs. Wilcox told me. I knew we weren't the only ones having problems. Then as each one left, Edgar would say, "Why don't we join them." For one reason or the other, we didn't.

Over the next four years, we had four more children. Our children's names were Harold, Mark, Luke, John, and Annabelle. Most people wonder about the names for our children. It's simple, I tell them, and our first son was named after my father. The next three boys were named after books of the bible. I wanted to name one after Edgar's father, but he didn't want to. Then, of course, our daughter we named after Mama.

With every addition to the family, it seemed we were adding onto the house. Edgar even got me a real cook stove for our third Christmas. That meant I had to have a kitchen. He went right to work adding it on. It wasn't something we had to have, but it was nice having. I think he built it to work off his frustrations. Still with his building, I now had separate rooms for different functions and windows. The old sharecroppers would never recognize the place.

We had plenty of frustrations. As if only getting a third of the market value for our crops wasn't bad enough, there were our neighbors. Two years after our marriage someone built a place on Mama and Father's place. They supposedly had connections up north and got full value for their crops. For me, just having them live where I used to was bad enough. Still we tried to make a go of the place.

After selling each crop, Edgar would come home and announce, "For one little cent, one little cent, I would move west. There everyone is equal and you have a chance to be free, unlike it is here."

In reality, I think he would have liked to move to an island with no one around, than to live where we were. Our lives had been in so much turmoil he was tired of it. I understood the feeling, but knew it was only a dream. I think he also felt that way, but still he needed a total change. Living where his parents had died was more than he could handle. Myself, I just wanted to go on with our lives and put the past where it belonged, in the past. My family was my main concern and I wanted them to be happy. I couldn't see how my children were going to be happy people with everything that was going on. I had come to feel more than willing to leave what we had and to start again.

"Then why don't we pack up and move?" I asked him one year.

"John and Annabelle are not big enough to travel. In another year, if we don't have anymore, I might be talked into it," He answered me.

The following fall and winter, our neighbor kept bothering us about selling our place. He said it would be perfect for his brother.

I reminded Edgar, "You realize Annabelle will be two in a few months." The ages of the children would then be, Harold 7, Mark 6, Luke 5, John 3, and Annabelle 2. Not that these are ideal ages for traveling we were going to be doing, but better than nothing.

"Yes," he answered not understanding what I was getting at.

"She should be able to make it out west," I told him.

"That's true, if we had the money," he said looking as if his dream was lost. Then sitting down, he went on to add, "It's going to take money to make the trip."

"How much do you think we will need?" I asked him. He didn't know I had some money stuck away. I hoped I had enough to outfit us, but I didn't have any idea what it was going to cost.

"I don't know with prices of supplies changing like it is," he answered still looking discouraged.

I didn't say anything, because I wanted to surprise him. I turned and went into our bedroom and got Mama's steel box. I brought the box out to the parlor and handed it to him and watched his expression.

"What's this?" He asked taking it from me.

"Open it, dummy, and you tell me," I told him, remembering him doing about the same thing some years ago at Christmas.

He carefully opened the box looking at me as he did it. With it open, he looked inside. He seemed to freeze in shock from what he was looking at it. Then sitting down, he began taking money out of the box. He stopped after pulling a few bills out and stared at me.

"Something wrong?" I asked.

"Several things," he answered.

"Can I go outside?" Mark asked his father,

"Yes, and take rest of the kids outside with you. Your mother and I have to talk," he answered looking at me with a questioning look.

However, we had a good marriage and never really had a fight. We did practice keeping our conversations to ourselves. We felt some things the children should know and other things they shouldn't know. This was the reason he had sent the children outside.

Once we were alone, he told me, "I have couple of minor questions, as you might guess."

"Yes Hon," I answered, leaning over to give him a kiss but he pushed me to one side.

Setting the steel box down, he asked, "Where did this come from? No one around here has this much money that you could have stolen from them?"

"I wouldn't steal from anyone. It came from Mama," I answered, and then hearing my answer, he began to relax. Seeing him relax, I began to tell him, "I didn't know it was in one of those boxes in the root cellar. I never looked in it until last year for some reason."

"That explains why the dates on the bills are 1860 and older," he looking at the bills.

"And they're all Union bills," I reminded him and then I went on to explain, "With it being during the war, Mama must not have thought they were not worth anything. Still not liking to throw money away, she kept it safe in the cellar."

"Why didn't you tell me about finding it?" he asked.

"I knew we would need it more going west than here," I answered.

"But we—" he stopped mid-sentence because of me interrupting him.

"For all of your talk of going west, I knew we would someday," I told him.

"We owe your mother more and more every time I turn around," he said sitting back in his seat.

"She wasn't the dumb plantation owner's wife everyone takes them to be," I told him with a short laugh.

"I agree with you there. I guess we are going west then," he said getting up and giving me a kiss.

"Is everything all right, father?" Harold asked.

"Yes, everything is definitely as good as you can expect," he answered and then he went on to ask me, "How much is there."

"A little over three thousand, I think," I answered him.

He seemed to relax more than I could remember after seeing all the money in the box. He sat down and said, "I'll talk to Carter about buying the place. I'll check as to the best ways of traveling and all of that. I also want to talk to Jacob and you can talk to Molly for they might want to join us."

"When would we leave?" I asked him.

"Probably the first week of April," he said getting up and acting as if he had ants in his pants. The next five weeks were busy getting a couple of big wagons. One wagon was for us and the other one for Jacob and his family.

At the same time, he sold everything that wasn't nailed down except the children, our horse, and me. I asked him why we were keeping the horse and he said for emergencies. At the same time, we would need a horse out west anyway, so why not keep it.

The night they brought the wagons to our place Molly came with Jacob and their son Little Joe.

"*Little Joe,*" Harold cried out seeing Jacob's son.

"Hi," Little Joe answered as his father let him down from the wagon. The two of them were good friends, even if Harold was two years younger.

"You boys go and play," Molly told her son.

"You too, Harold," I said agreeing with her.

"They get along better than if they were brothers," Molly said watching the two.

"They had better, we have a long trip ahead of us," Jacob said.

"I doubt they will ever be anything other than friends," Edgar assured them with a laugh.

"What do you think? Are we going to do better out there than here?" Molly asked me.

"We can't do any worse," I assured her.

"I don't think it would be possible," Jacob added and then he went on to comment, "These wagons are the top of the line."

"For as much as they cost, they had better be," Edgar added.

"Let's go inside," I suggested, tired of standing there. The rest of the evening we discussed our soon coming trip. Not having talked to Molly that much in the past few weeks, I asked her, "What do you think of being on the trail for six months?"

"Having my man around every hour of the day worries me," she answered giving me a wink.

"It is a long time," Edgar pointed out.

"We can stay here if I bother you that much," Jacob answered as if he had taken her seriously.

"She was kidding," I told him laughing, with Molly laughing harder than I did. Then turning to Molly for Jacob's sake, I told her, "He might have a problem having you around him."

"That's right," Jacob answered making us all laugh.

We continued to discuss the trip for a while longer. Then the six children began to tire out. Realizing how late it was, Jacob and Molly took Little Joe home.

Later that evening, Edgar told me, "I hope you don't mind, but I bought the wagon and supplies for Jacob."

"Not if we have the money," I answered and then giving him a kiss said, "He has done a lot to help us not even taking a meal." At the same time, I remembered how we had grown up with each other. I knew father would be the first to suggest that we do it.

"That's what I thought you would say then with buying two, I got a break on the cost," he added as if that justified buying two. In reality, he wouldn't be so willing to leave if his best friend didn't go also.

"I'm not sure how that works, but if it works for you, it works for me," I told him with a smile of understanding.

With him getting the wagon, oxen, and supplies needed, all there was left to do was pack up what we wanted to take with us. Most of our furniture we were leaving behind, making it easy to load the wagon. Edgar had learned that most making the trip had to throw out furniture and the like. We decided why bother trying to take it if we had to throw it away.

The wagon Edgar bought was one of the biggest wagons I had ever seen. He told me they were called "Conestoga Wagons." The wagon bed was twelve feet long, with a canvas cover, with seven curved bows holding it up. He also told me the reason for the sides to, angled out as they were was to keep rainwater from going inside. All I knew was that it was large enough for everything we needed and for the children.

In finding out when the next wagon train was leaving, Edgar also found four more families that were going our way.

We said good-bye to the place a week later than we planned. We didn't care, we were on our way. The only problem was trying to catch up with the main group. The first night though, we stayed at Jacob and Molly's. When everyone was asleep, I walked back to the old place. With a can of lantern oil, I burned the house down. By the time anyone knew it was burning, I was in bed with Edgar. To this day, I still don't feel bad about burning it. For the way we had been cheated so many times, it was my turn.

When Edgar heard the place was on fire, he went to help put it out. When he got there it was too late. He came back to the house looking defeated. I understood why, after putting all the work into it that he did.

"No one else is going to benefit from our labor now," I told him, and then I went on to add, "Now they have full value of what they paid for. Hopefully we didn't leave a candle burning."

He didn't say anything then or afterwards. I had the feeling he knew I had burned the place down. I think he felt better thinking I wasn't the type to do something like that. With not saying anything, he didn't have to learn the truth. He did smile occasionally, giving me the idea he appreciated it.

"We'll never make it to Independence in time," Edgar told me. Then motioning for everyone to follow us, he told me, "We'll cut across to Nashville, Tennessee. From there we should cut off a few more miles and catch up with them further on."

I didn't have any idea what he meant, but I asked him, "You have been talking about the Oregon Trail. Where does it take us?"

"The route begins at Independence, Missouri, to Fort Kearney, Nebraska, to Fort Laramie, Wyoming, bypassing Fort Bridger, onto Fort Hall, Idaho, to Fort Boise, Idaho, to Whitman Mission and ending at Oregon City. Something over two thousand miles they say," he answered. Then looking back to see if everyone was behind us, he went on to add, "They say if all goes well, it will take six months to make the trip."

"Isn't somewhere up there a General Custer and Sheridan?" I asked him.

"The General Custer that accepted Lee's terms of surrender at Gettysburg?" he asked as if it was a big deal.

"Yes, him," I answered thinking it was the same General.

"From the way it sounds, the two of them are keeping the Indian uprising down," he assured me.

"Are you telling me we don't have to worry about the Indians then?" I asked.

"Not from what I have been told and what I have read," he answered.

"I don't want my children captured and raised by Indians is all," I told him, grinning only on the outside. I was used to where we were. Now he wanted me to go into country full of Indians on the warpath.

I learned that driving a wagon with oxen was different from driving with horses. The first item I noticed was they were wearing a single piece wooden yoke rather than a leather halter. At the same time, rather than controlling them with reins, you guided them with a stick or whip. This meant the driving was really done from the ground. The idea of walking two thousand miles seemed outrageous. Then again, this was something that Edgar had to do, so we were going to do it.

"Where are we going mama?" Luke asked.

"We're moving to another place," Harold answered him.

"Yes we're moving," I confirmed giving him a smile saying it was all fine. Though he was going on six, he was my worrier.

"I want you all to sit down and not fight," Edgar told them.

"Do you think you can find our way to Fort Kearny?" I asked him, remembering he had never been out of our area except during the war.

"I think I can find Nashville, but we need help from there on. There has to be someone there that can get us to Fort Kearny," he said coaching the oxen along.

I wasn't sure we would make it with the oxen for as slow as they were. However slow their speed might have been, it was easier riding than with horses. After a week and a half, we made it to Nashville.

"Where are you going to find a Wagon master?" I asked Edgar.

"Can we get out mama?" Harold asked me. Then before I could answer, he went on to add, "I'm tired of riding."

"Pretty soon," I answered waiting for Edgar to answer my question.

"I'm going to follow a freight wagon or something until we see a likely place I can ask for help," he finally answered as he watched what was going on around us.

"There's a wagon," I told him pointing out one to our right. Then looking around, there were hundreds of wagons and carriages filling the streets. Then there were men on horses, and people filling the boardwalks. I had never seen so many people in one place. Richmond was large, but when I was there last, most places were burned or torn down. Then, too, most of the men, wagons and horses were in the battlefields yet.

"Good," he said as he pulled in behind the other wagon.

With the oxen being so slow, we couldn't keep up with the other wagon. Still we could see it ahead of us and others joined us going down the street we were on. With this being the case, Edgar continued following the wagons. It wasn't long before we saw a sign saying:

NASHVILLE STABLES

Edgar brought us and the oxen to a stop and left me in the wagon. He went into the stables not saying anything to me. Coming out, he waved for everyone to join him by our wagon.

"As you know, we need to find someone that can guide us to Fort Kearny," he began, but Mr. Williams interrupted him.

"Why don't you take us there, you got us this far?" Mr. Williams asked him.

"Only by luck more than knowledge or skill," Edgar told him. Then holding his hands up to quiet them, he went on to tell them. "It might take a day or two, so I have asked the man at the stable if we can keep the oxen there. He said it would be all right and he won't charge us."

"Bless him," one of the women uttered.

"I agree. Anything we can save is good," I said for the group.

"Anyway, let's get them out of their yokes and boarded. Once that's done, I'll see about finding a wagon master," Edgar told them.

We let the children out of the wagons to play. At the same time, the men took care of the oxen. Us women put some food together for everyone. I have to admit, we were a spectacle that everyone in Nashville enjoyed watching.

I was glad to see that Nashville wasn't like Richmond. Though it had been some years since I had been there, the memories seemed fresh. Nashville had a whole different feel about it. Though I hadn't seen all of it, I felt comfortable with what I had seen. At the same time, the people seemed friendly.

"Can I be of some help?" A man asked coming up to us.

"We're heading west," I told him.

"I see. Why did you stop here, may I ask?" Then he went on to add, "My name is Paul Dennison, I own the business over there." As he talked, he pointed out his shop.

"Glad to meet you. I'm Ida Buchanan. My husband is over at the stables and he can give you more information."

"That's all right. There's no problem with you stopping here, I was just curious is all," he said as he tipped his hat leaving us.

"Who was that?" Edgar asked as he came up from behind me.

"A shop owner by the name of Paul Dennison. He said if you need any help just come on over," I answered.

"Where?" Edgar asked.

I pointed to the shop the man had pointed out and I called the children, "Okay everyone, let's eat."

Edgar came back and grabbed a piece of dried meat and a piece of bread. He didn't say anything but ate his food. As I was wiping the faces of the children a man on a horse wearing a Confederate Kepi cap road by. As he went by, he tipped his cap to us and continued on his way.

It wasn't long afterwards Edgar got up and said, "I think I had better talk to a few more people. Mr. Dennison wasn't able to help us."

"Okay, here's hoping you find someone," I answered cleaning up the children's mess.

Then needing to talk to Edgar, I followed in his footsteps around the wagon. As I got all the way around, I saw he was talking to a man. I knew it was the same man from his cap. I advanced up to them to find out what was going on. Edgar saw me and motioned for me to come over to them.

"My wife, Ida. Ida darling, this young man is Matt," Edgar said in introducing me.

"Nice to meet you, Matt," I answered in greeting him. He appeared to be a nice man and all, but I had no idea what Edgar was talking to him about. I guessed he was about five ten in height and a hundred and eighty pounds. He had reddish blonde hair, long in the back and a mustache. Curious to what Edgar was talking to him about, I decided to stay and listen.

"Same here, it's nice to meet you also," Matt replied.

He went to the stable, checked out our oxen, and then began going through the wagon. Matt was friendly and informative, but most of all thorough. In ways, he was just like Edgar. I also could understand why he was the way he was. Having the responsibility of so many people, I wouldn't want to leave anything to chance. With the open country, we were going to be going through you have to be prepared.

The next morning at dawn, we were leaving Nashville. Matt throughout the trip to Kearny kept an eye on each wagon. A couple of times we thought he was God or something. The fifth or sixth day out he made an announcement.

"*A storm is coming and we have to keep moving,*" he shouted out as he passed us.

By the sun, we could see the sunset was about to take place. Throughout the day, he pushed us hard. At dusk, he wanted us to circle up and rest. He was doing his best to get us to Fort Kearny in time to meet the main group. This one night, though, he wanted us to keep going.

"*My legs are about to drop off,*" Mr. Anderson shouted out to him from behind us.

"*Then let your wife handle the oxen,*" Matt answered.

Mr. Anderson was too proud to let his wife handle the oxen and we continued. Though we didn't fully understand his need to continue, we did it. We finally stopped a few hours later, circled up the wagons and ate. He sat down some time after us and told us why he had pushed as he did.

"Look back where we came from?" He asked all of us to do.

Every head turned, and we saw lightning striking not too many miles back. Everyone was in awe of the sight, as if we had never seen lightning before. The open range gave you a different understanding and view of it. Finally having seen enough, we turned our attention back to him.

"If I'm right, the storm will miss us by a few miles. If we had stopped back there, tomorrow we would be fighting mud all day and getting nowhere," he told us. Then he got up and crawled into his bedroll.

"I think the man has an idea what he's doing," Edgar told all of us.

"But I'll be dead before we get there," Mr. Anderson said getting a laugh from everyone.

The men went about checking out the wagons before going to bed. We women got our children down for the night. Then we sat down with a cup of coffee and talked for a while.

"Missing home yet?" Molly asked me as she sat down beside me.

"Not really. I think I learned some things are meant to be and some are not. At the same time, I know I will never have what I miss the most. Mama and father are gone, and I have something just as important if not more. My life has changed over the past seven plus years. My life now is Edgar and my children."

"I know what you mean," Molly said, looking around the group, she went on to add, "Unlike most of you, I lost my family before the war. I don't have any idea if they are dead or alive and that's behind me. Jacob and Little Joe are enough for me. All I want now is a chance to live."

"I think that about says it for all of us, just a chance to live," Mrs. Schmidt said agreeing with her.

Looking around I was surprised to see the change in some of the women. When some of them learned that Jacob and Molly were joining us, they were shocked. I even heard the term "That Black Family" used. Then after explaining who they were, they were accepted. Now I wonder if those people accepted them as being our slaves, rather than a family wanting a new life.

"An early morning coming," Edgar said walking up to me.

"Far too soon for me," I answered trying to smile.

"Good night everyone," Mrs. Anderson said as she got up to join her husband.

That first night after bypassing the storm, interesting conversations and emotions came out. Then every other night when problems happened or were avoided, conversations went the same way.

That wasn't the only storm we avoided. Though some he let us go through them. He also changed our directions of travel a couple of times for no reason. At least at the time, we didn't see any reason for the change. When we got to Fort Kearny, we were there three days before the main group. With what he had done, we knew he must be God. This isn't just my opinion but of the others also. Our true wagon master didn't have half the skills Matt did.

In Fort Kearny, we didn't take any chances. We spent the three days going through our supplies and restocking. It was the last day there I noticed a problem.

"Mama, I feel cold," Luke told me that afternoon.

Though the temperature had dropped from the day before, it wasn't cold. "Put another shirt on," I told him.

I went about making sure everything was packed away for the following day. We would be one of eighteen wagons rather than six. I didn't see any problem with that, but Matt had warned it would go slower. Then having put everything away, I checked on Luke.

"How are you feeling?" I asked him.

"I feel fine," he told me as I reached down and felt his forehead.

"What's wrong?" Edgar asked, coming up to me.

"I think he's a little warmer than he should be. He was complaining about being cold an hour ago," I answered wondering if there was a problem.

Edgar reached down a felt Luke's forehead with the back of his hand. Pulling his hand away, he told me, "He might be a little warm." Then turning back to Luke, he asked him, "Feeling okay?"

"Yes Father," he answered.

"He'll be all right. The traveling is catching up to him," Edgar said roughing up Luke's hair.

"Stop father," Luke told his father.

"I know it's got me feeling tired," I told him, thinking another five months and I'll get there in a pine box.

The next morning of the fourth day, we began looking hard for the main group. We knew if they had kept to their schedule, they should be coming in. Late that evening, they showed up. We waited for them to pull up by our wagons,

"I take it you are Phil Madison," Edgar said in greeting a man on horseback.

"Yes," Mr. Madison answered hesitantly.

"My name is Edgar Buchanan, from Virginia; we had a late start, and took a shortcut to catch up with you."

"Oh yes, I was wondering what happened to you folks. Just get in?" Mr. Madison asked.

"Four days ago," Edgar answered with a smile.

"You have to tell me about this," he said as he got off his horse.

We met everyone and discussed our adventures getting to Fort Kearney. It turned out they were caught in a couple of storms. They found themselves have to spend a good part of a few days pulling one another out of mud. When they heard about our trip, some said they wished Matt had been their wagon master. I had to laugh to myself, for my husband had found Matt and supported him all the way.

I have to say, during the month we were on the trail to Fort Kearny, the two men got along like brothers. I in fact got tired of hearing Matt this and Matt that. I thought my husband was pretty darn special and

I didn't want to hear about some other man. Then like everything, change happens.

When we left we had been at Fort Kearny for six days. Not that we were tired of the place, but we wanted to get to Oregon City. We found ourselves on our way and it took over an hour to get us out of Fort Kearny. Being the new members, we were put in the lead. This was to change everyday, putting us in the rear to eat the dust the next day.

"I'm glad Luke's feeling good today," I told Edgar as we started the next leg of our journey.

"Same here," Edgar answered as he got the oxen moving.

Mr. Madison was impressed that we had two extra oxen. He related that several times an ox had died or broke a leg leaving people stranded. He said having an extra ox was a wise decision. Here again my husband was the thinker behind the idea. Then when he found out we were carrying two extra wheels, you would have thought he had been given a sack of rock candy. Five days later, we almost needed one of the wheels.

"That was close," I told Edgar when he had just missed going over the edge of a cliff.

He looked up at me and smiled adding, "Have to get lucky once in awhile."

I knew better but I didn't say anything. Edgar was too careful to have made that mistake. Unfortunately, not everyone was paying as much attention as Edgar.

"*Hold up,*" Mr. Madison cried out. Then coming back past us he said, "A wagon back there has one wheel over the edge."

"I'll get my pry bar," Edgar told him, and then shouting down to Jacob, he shouted, "*Get the block out, Jacob.*"

Mr. Madison looked at Edgar as if he was out of his mind. Then getting himself together he asked, "What are you doing?"

Edgar hesitated and then he answered, "I'm going to get the wagon back on the road." Then not saying anything else, he unstrapped the ten-foot pry bar from the side of the wagon. Then hauling it down towards the disabled wagon, Jacob met him with the block.

Edgar and Jacob went to work, setting the block into place and laying the pry bar on top.

Edgar told the driver, "When I tell you, lead them to your left."

"Okay," the driver of the wagon answered waiting for the signal.

"Okay," Edgar cried out as he and Jacob held the right side of the wagon up, letting them pull it across the pry bar. Once the wagon was on solid ground, he told the driver, "You're set."

All the time, Mr. Madison just watched as the two of them solved the problem. Once the wagon was on solid ground he said, "Good job. You are prepared for almost everything."

"Not all, but most," Edgar answered with a smile.

From that point on, Edgar and Mr. Madison seemed to have a problem dealing with each other. I realized that Edgar should have let Mr. Madison take command, but he had done everything himself for too many years. At the same time, he didn't like talking about doing something, when he could get it done himself in the same time. One problem that didn't help either was the admiration he had from the others.

"Did I overstep my position?" He asked as I remember.

"Maybe a little," I answered and then I went on to add, "the main thing, is you got the wagon back on solid ground."

"But I didn't want to step on his pride," he confessed. Having got the pry bar tied down again, he went on to add, "I have a feeling the two of us are not going to be getting along."

"I know you didn't mean to hurt his feelings. And I agree, he probably has taken a dislike to you," I told him. Knowing what the past month had been like, I knew two people not getting along would make this a long trip. We would get there eventually, no matter what happened. Over the next few weeks, I turned my attention to other problems, such as boredom.

"Finding the countryside beautiful?" Molly asked one night at supper.

"I didn't think I was going to get homesick. Now I find how wrong I was in my thinking," I answered. Then hearing what I thought was

Annabelle crying, I told them all, "I think my children are trying to kill one another." I put my plate down and went into our wagon to see what was going on.

"What's going on?" I asked seeing Annabelle was the one crying.

"Luke keeps taking her water," Harold answered taking another bite of his supper.

"I don't feel good, Mama, I'm thirsty," Luke, told me.

Not answering at first, I looked around and saw nothing. The landscape was completely bare, other than some wild grass, and rocks. Looking out, I began to fear the west coast might be the same. If it was, I would almost be willing to go back home. I found myself for the first time missing the trees and streams of home.

"I'll get you some water," I told Luke as I felt his forehead. He felt as if he was burning up and it began to worry me. He appeared to have gotten over what he had a few days ago, and I wondered about this fever, was it the same?

I went and got Luke another cup of water. I told him, "Once you drink this, I want you to lie down and rest."

I prayed that rest was all it was going to take to get him over whatever he had. Not that I trusted doctors or not, there weren't any around to take him to one. Then looking at Annabelle, she held her cup up.

I got her another cup of water and told them all as I handed it to her, "We have to leave early tomorrow morning; I want you all to go to sleep."

"Okay mama," Harold answered.

"I'm not tired," Luke told me.

"Go to sleep anyway," I answered feeling sorry for them. They were used to running around and playing. This trip was taking a toll on them as well as us adults.

"What's going on? You didn't come back," Edgar asked.

"Luke has another fever," I answered looking in at our children. Then reaching in to tuck a blanket over Annabelle, I told them, "Good night, I'll see you in the morning."

"Think he's all right?" Edgar asked.

Motioning for him to go back to the fire, I told him, "I don't know, I wish we had a doctor on the train."

"I'll ask around, but I don't remember hearing that one of them is," he told me as we got close to the fire.

"I don't think there is one here either," I confirmed. Stopping for a minute, the blaze of fire seemed so romantic I reached out and took his hand. Sensing my feelings, he stopped and gave my hand a squeeze.

We were up for awhile talking to several other people about the trip. We were all surprised how Mr. Madison kept to himself. One of the men said he had a talk with him, and he seemed like he was nice guy. Rest of us weren't too sure of it. Then, somehow, we began turning in for the night ending our conversation, not deciding anything.

Most of us adults slept around the fire, giving our children more room and the added protection of the wagon. Edgar and I crawled into our bedroll and proceeded to fall asleep or at least tried to. I just laid on my side worrying about Luke.

As I said a prayer for my son, Edgar's hand dropped over my body and his knees touched the back of my legs. Feeling them, I whispered to him, "You feel nice."

"You feel nice too," he answered giving me a squeeze.

Wiggling closer to him, I told him, "I'm glad there are so many people around."

"Why?" He asked in a low voice.

"We can't have me pregnant towards the end of the trip and having a baby just getting there," I answered taking his hand in mine and kissing his fingers.

"Humph," was his answer and he was snoring shortly after. In the morning, he was to find my blankets and me gone.

Coming around to the back of the wagon he saw me holding Luke, he said, "I was wondering what happened to you. Is he okay?" With me not saying anything, he saw I was crying. He jumped into the wagon asking, "What happened?"

Between sobs, I got out, "I heard him coughing and crying, so I came over to check on him. He was shaking so hard, the wagon was moving. I went to get my blankets to wrap him up. He was so still, it scared me…" I couldn't go any further, because of my crying. I saw and could feel Edgar take him from me.

"I'll take him," he said crying himself.

"I wanted to get you," I managed to get out. Then added, "But I felt he might be more comfortable if I wrapped him up in the blankets. I picked him up into my arms." Again, I had to stop, to get myself under control. Taking a breath, I went on to tell him, "He died in my arms."

"Something wrong," a voice asked. I, to this day, had no idea who it was.

"Our son just died," Edgar answered.

"Mama, I don't feel so good," Annabelle said crying.

I barely heard this person ask, "Can I help?"

"I'll take care of him," Edgar got out with some difficulty.

"*No God*, not another one," I cried out as I turned to check on her. Feeling her forehead, I found her burning up. I remembered the two of them sharing a cup of water. I felt my heart being torn out, and I cried out, "*Not Annabelle too.*"

"What's going on here?" Mr. Madison asked.

"Their son just died," a voice answered him.

"Oh…I was just…" he replied stopping mid-sentence and not finishing it.

I know I was there, but everything is blurry, but we buried our son. Everyone, I think, touched my arm and saying, "We're so sorry…it must be hard."

Once Edgar placed the last shovel full of dirt on the grave, he said taking me in his arms, "We have to leave now."

"I don't want to leave him," I answered crying.

"He's God's to take care of," Edgar answered as he guided me along. Then as we got to the wagon, he told me, "Mr. Madison said he won't kick us out of the train, but we have to stay behind everyone else."

"I'll take care of her," Molly offered coming up to us.

"Thank you," Edgar answered letting me go. Then as he walked off, he reminded me, "Annabelle may need you."

My heart sunk again, having forgotten her. I pulled out of Molly's arms and ran to my daughter. I found her sleeping as her brothers followed me to the wagon.

"I'm sorry, boys, it must be hard for you also," I told them, giving them all a hug.

"Why did Luke have to die?" Mark asked.

"He was sick, and God wanted him," I answered not knowing what else to tell him.

"I'll take the boys for you," Jacob offered.

"No, I wouldn't want Little Joe get whatever they have," I answered, seeing the tears in both his and Molly's eyes.

"Can't I play with him?" Harold asked. Then looking up at Jacob, he told us, "I'm not sick."

"Your mama is right, you might feel okay now, but you might be a little sick. Let's wait for awhile," Molly told him. Then as I was climbing into the wagon, she told me, "If you need anything, let me know."

"I had better get the oxen into their yokes and us ready to leave. I loved the little guy," Jacob said as he left with Molly not far behind.

That night, I slept in Edgar's arms no matter what the others thought. We both cried as we laid there thinking of our loss. Then, I found myself wanting to be intimate with him. I needed something to take my mind off our loss. The thought made me feel ashamed with it being the day my son had died.

Later, as we made our way to Fort Laramie, Edgar told me Mr. Madison said drinking lots of water, might have helped Luke as well as Annabelle. What we needed was "Quinine."

As we progressed, I almost poured water down her throat on a regular basis. By the next day, we were within sight of the Fort. Annabelle was feeling tired but otherwise was feeling good. Still I asked to have her seen by the Army doctor. In checking her out, he didn't find anything wrong with her. He was good enough to tell Mr. Madison that we were all doing fine. This allowed us to continue with our trek west.

Being worried, I asked him, "Do you have any Quinine we can have?"

"With the war, supplies haven't gotten to us yet. Sorry," he told me giving me a shrug of not knowing what else to say.

I cried as we left as if nothing had happened. If it made a difference, we left Fort Laramie in the lead. It did give us the appearance of being all right to be with the group. Other than weather, we made it to Fort Hall without any problems. Though Luke would never be forgotten we did get back to a normal life.

A week from the Fort, Mr. Madison called us all to a halt. He announced that Jacobs's wagon had a broken wheel.

"Just because we bought spare wheels didn't mean you had to break one," Edgar told Jacob.

"Thought you needed a break," Jacob answered as he untied a wheel from the side of his wagon.

"Don't get rid of the old wheel," Mr. Madison told the two men. He went on to explain, "We can get it fixed maybe at Fort Boise."

"He's not even offering to help us," Jacob said as Mr. Madison went by.

"Probably because we have proved we're better than he is," Edgar answered with a laugh.

"Can I help?" Little Joe offered.

"Me to," Harold also offered.

"You're not big enough, but thanks," Edgar told them with a smile.

I didn't know it at the time; Edgar was having a problem helping Jacob. I thought it was just that he was tired. Even with his problem, they got the wheel on. With this being done we all took a break and got some food out so we could eat and then got going.

"Are we ready?" Edgar asked as we were starting to leave.

"Yes," I answered, being hesitant about telling him about Annabelle. I had allowed the children to get out and play. Annabelle decided not to join rest of the children, so I checked her out. I found she was running a slight fever.

I watched her over the next few days and she was better one day and very warm with fever another. Edgar and I both shared concern for her, but we had no choice but to continue. I made her drink as much as her body could hold, hoping it would pass.

Midday we, all heard a shot ring out. Mr. Madison rode by at full gallop to check it out. Coming back by, he stopped us all.

He told us, "Don't worry, it's not Indians. Mr. Wilson just shot a big elk."

I remembered seeing the elk and thought he was a beautiful animal. At the same time, I thought some fresh meat sounded good.

Mr. Madison went on to add, "We've been doing good for the past few weeks, so we might as well stop for the night. Maybe some fresh meat is called for."

"It sure will beat the salt pork and dried beef we've been eating for months," Edgar said as he joined the rest in circling up the wagons.

"I'm not one to argue," I answered him giving him a smile.

"I'll fix some beans," one woman shouted out, with the same thought as we had.

I'll help," another one replied.

"I'll make some corn bread," I heard Molly add.

"I'll eat anything you fix," a man answered.

"I'm going to need some help butchering the beast."

"I'll help you," Jacob answered.

"You're on," the man replied.

"What's going on, Mama?" Mark asked.

"We're going to be eating fresh meat for dinner," I answered him.

"I'm hungry," John, told me.

"We'll be eating soon son," Edgar told him giving me a smile.

"Maybe it's time to celebrate. We're over halfway there," I said feeling good about everything.

"Yes that we are. Tomorrow we should be almost to the end of the shortcut to Fort Boise," he said, and then he went on with a smile, "And then it's Whitman Mission and then Oregon City."

"Where to after Oregon City?" I asked. He had talked about staying in Oregon but also talked about going even further south.

"Don't know yet. I want to get this trip out of the way first," he answered as he walked toward the other men, giving me a wave. I saw him help Jacob and Mr. Wilson pulled the Elk closer to the wagons.

I went back as the boys got out of the wagon to check on Annabelle. She was warm, but not as bad as she had been.

Supper was great, with most of the women contributing to it. The boys had their supper and I had taken some to Annabelle.

"Eat this honey," I told her as I gave her a plate.

Watching her for a little bit, I went back to the fire. I was in hopes of getting another piece of meat but only found bones to chew on. Edgar laughed at my disappointment.

"You have been saying you needed to lose some weight," he told me giving me a kiss.

"That was before we started on this trip," I reminded him. I knew my weight wasn't a problem, for all of my clothes were fitting a little loose.

"Annabelle lost her dinner making a mess in the wagon," Harold said pulling on my shirt.

"What?" I asked.

"It's all over the place," he told me.

"What was that?" Edgar asked listening to some music some of the men were playing.

"Annabelle got sick in the wagon," I answered and seeing he was coming with me, I told him, "I can take care of it."

"Okay," he answered, as I walked away.

Looking into the wagon, I found Harold wasn't joking about the mess she made. She was covered with her supper as well as her corner of the wagon.

"You sure did make a mess," I told her as I picked her up.

"I don't feel good, mama," she told me.

"I'll clean you up and you'll feel better," I promised her. I washed her off and changed her. With that done, I attacked the mess in the wagon. I wondered how long it was going to take to clear the stench out. I laughed telling myself, "We'll find out."

"What's so funny," Mark, asked me.

"Nothing honey," I lied to him. I was surprised to see him.

"Is Annabelle going to be all right," he asked, then looking down at his feet, he said, "she's not going to die like Luke did…is she?"

"No honey," I answered praying I was right.

"Damage cleaned up?" Edgar asked as he walked up to the wagon.

"As usual, your timing is perfect," I answered.

"Remember I offered to help," he reminded me.

"Yes, with those eyes saying you would rather do something else," I told him, taking his face into my hands, and giving it a kiss.

"At least my eyes didn't lie to you," he answered as we both laughed. Then giving Annabelle a kiss, he said, "I think I'm going to lie down myself, I've been feeling tired the past few days."

"I'll be with you shortly," I told him as I went to see what I could do to help the women.

"Anything wrong?" Molly asked as I got to the women.

"Just a little sick to her stomach is all. What can I do?" I asked her.

"Think everything is about done, other than you getting your things," she answered me.

"I think I can do that. Your corn bread was fantastic," I told her.

"Thank you," she said looking proud of herself, and then went on to add, "a few of the women made the same comment."

"That's because it was good," I told her.

She laughed and told me, "Good night, see you in the morning."

"Good night Molly, see you in the morning," I replied, as I took our things to the wagon and put them away,

When I got back to Edgar, he was sound asleep. I eased myself into the blankets, and proceeded to fall asleep myself. Not being able to sleep, I found myself waking up a number of times. One time, Edgar groaned and turned over, and I reached out and touched him. I was surprised to find he was warm to the touch.

The next morning, thinking how warm he felt, I asked him, "Are you feeling okay?"

"I'm fine," he answered, as he made ready for the days journey.

Mr. Madison warned us the day's journey wouldn't give us too many miles. He wasn't wrong in warning us. Though we had been traveling through hills the last week or so, they were nothing like we were facing then.

"We're getting up pretty high," Harold said looking out of the front of the wagon.

"We sure are," I said agreeing with him. Over the side, I could see valleys below. I could make out an animal stirring up dust, but I couldn't make out what kind he was. Then looking ahead, I could tell we had to go up a lot further. I had to say one thing about the area, it was a lot better than it was around Fort Kearney, and the next few hundred after that point. Though these trees were not like the ones at home, they were more majestic. I thought I could easily learn to live here.

Now you have to understand, our trail was not a trail well marked. For as rough as it was, Mr. Madison might be off by a mile from where the last train went through. He only had a general idea where to go to find different passable passes. The reason I bring this up is to illustrate the terrain. The trail was full of fallen trees and boulders. This meant we had to make many stops to clear a path for the wagons. I knew making any time it would have taken an act of God. It was strange, though, seeing the mess, when you are also looking at ruts made by hundreds of other wagon. These ruts were two to five feet deep.

In the back, I had a little girl I couldn't do much for. I went back often to give her some water to drink. Even though she was asleep sometimes, I would wake her and feed her more water. From the warmth I felt, I knew she wasn't going to make it. I found myself crying with each step of the oxen.

"She's not doing so well?" Edgar asked, as we stopped to clear another boulder.

"No," I answered. I knew as he did, there wasn't anything either of us could do.

At the same time, if we made it to Fort Boise, it would probably be too late for our little girl. What made it hard was that she was my only girl. I had dreams of raising her as Mama did me. I hoped I could be more to her than Mama had been. I knew no matter how I tried to fool myself, my dream was never going to be.

As we reached the summit the next day, we were so happy. Mr. Madison had told us this was the last rough spot until we got to Fort Boise. Everyone would stop at the summit and look back from where we had come. Going down the other side I was worried the wagon would overrun the oxen. If this were to happen, I wouldn't have to worry about Annabelle or her fever.

"Keep your hands on the brake. If it appears you're going too fast, pull hard," Edgar told me, as he stumbled.

"Maybe we should trade places," I suggested and I went on to add, "I have a pretty good idea how to handle them."

"Okay, maybe I should take the break. But when you get tired, you let me know, and I'll take over for you," he answered.

Stopping long enough to change places, I saw other couples doing the same thing. For his own purpose, Edgar kept forgetting Mr. Madison had us women learn to control the animals. The hardest part was the constant walking. Then on the other hand, riding the bumpy wagon seat was hard on me also.

After what seemed like days, weeks and years, we finally made it down the other side. Thankfully, it wasn't as long of a way as the climb had been. We understood it meant more downhill traveling; we were glad it was over for a while.

"Back up there, your highness," Edgar said as he got back down to take control of the oxen.

"Yes sir, I think I did a good job," I answered as I took my seat on the wagon again.

"Not bad for a beginner," he answered as he got the oxen moving.

He didn't take more than two steps and his body kept falling forward. I pulled the brake and the oxen fought me for a short time.

"Is something wrong with Father?" Harold asked.

"Something wrong?" Mr. Madison asked. Then seeing Edgar lying on the ground, he jumped off his horse and checked him out.

By his side, I touched Edgar's face and he was burning up. I collapsed the rest of the way to the ground crying. I knew I was going to lose him. The hands helped me up as others picked Edgar up and put him into the wagon.

"I'll be all right shortly," he got out between coughs. Then as the men lowered him into the wagon, he let out a terrific moan.

Jacob and Molly just stood there, not knowing what to say. I told them, "He'll be fine, just tired."

The three of us knew I was either lying or I was dreaming. The two of them nodded their heads turning to go back to their wagon.

Molly stops and turned to tell me, "We love the two of you."

I didn't say anything, but nodded to her as I got the wagon on the move.

Then seeing our wagon going, Mr. Madison shouted out, *"Let's get them animals moving."* Then as he came up to me, he told me, "It's another hundred miles to Fort Boise."

"I know," I answered. Oh how I knew this was going to be the longest part of the trip.

"Is father going to be all right?" Harold asked from the wagon.

"I don't know, Honey," I answered him, not knowing and thinking he wasn't.

Thankfully, we didn't have too far to go before we found a clearing. Looking at the position of the sun, I knew we could have traveled further. I figured Mr. Madison was stopping early to give me time to be with Edgar.

Mr. Madison rode up to the wagon and stopped. He asked, "How's he doing?"

"I was just going to check on him," I answered. I got up so I could see Edgar and he looked bad.

As I was climbing up, he told me, "Edgar told me five days ago he thought he had the fever. He said for me not to tell you because your daughter was bad enough. He wanted to make sure you got out west, and that was his main concern."

"At least I got you and the children this far. I love you," Edgar said, not taking another breath.

I fell back off the wagon, onto my back crying. I could hear Jacob's voice ask me, "You okay?"

"I think he just died," Mr. Madison told him as he reach down to help Jacob in getting me up. Having gotten me up, he went on to add, "I think we have another case in the rear."

"Mama," I heard Mark's voice call out. "Annabelle got sick again."

I put Edgar out of my mind, and went over to check on her. I was afraid I was going to lose her also. I knew I needed to let her know I loved her. With all the traveling we had done, I hadn't spent that much time with her.

"Come with me, boys," Molly told my three boys.

I could hear the three of them crying for the loss of their father. I was torn between the loss of Edgar, my little girl that was dying, and the boys. I knew I had to be with her when she died, but the boys needed me also.

After cleaning up her mess, I held her until she went to sleep. Carefully I got out of the wagon and found the boys. As I comforted them, the men were digging a grave for Edgar.

"What are we going to do now, mama?" Harold asked.

"I don't know, but we will make it, just wait and see," I answered giving them a squeeze.

"Is father dead? Did he go to Heaven, mama?" John asked.

After the men buried Edgar, the boys and I sat by his grave. Molly was good enough to keep an eye on Annabelle. From somewhere, I heard Edgar's voice saying, "You have to be strong for the boys." I stopped crying and listened to the wind. Looking down at my three sons, I knew he was right.

"Let's get something to eat," I told them as we got up.

As I passed the wagon, Molly told me, "She's sleeping yet."

"Thanks Molly, I think I'll get the boys some supper and then I'll check on her," I told her as she climbed out of the wagon.

"No problem, I had better check on Little Joe, come to think of it," she answered as she headed to her wagon.

As I sat with the boys watching them eat, I saw Jacob get up and leave. In doing so, I realized he had been sitting a ways from the rest of us.

I didn't watch where he had gone, I just knew he had left. The rest of the group would pass me, and give me a loving tap on the upper arm. Then I heard some pounding and I turned to see who and what was going on. I saw by Edgar's grave Jacob pounding on a piece of wood.

I went to see what he was doing as he was getting up. There above Edgar's head was a board. On the board in white paint, it read:

Here lies

My best friend

Edgar Buchanan

1873

"The paints wet," Jacob said as he left me at the grave.

I stood there and cried. It was the second time Jacob had taken care of a lost man in my family. I finally went back to the wagon, woke Annabelle, and gave her a drink. She was so limp; I knew the end was near.

The next morning, Mark told me, "Mama, Annabelle won't wake up."

I jumped back into the wagon and found she had died in the middle of the night. I picked her up crying, "I hope you know I loved you, Edgar, and always will. Now it's up to you and Mama to take care of Annabelle."

The men carried her over to her father's grave. Then we buried her alongside of him. As I got our wagon ready to leave, I looked back at the grave and I saw a change. Getting close to it, I saw the writing on the board was added to. It now read:

Here lies
My best friend, Edgar Buchanan
1873
And his daughter, Annabelle

Now anyone passing by would know who was there. I prayed some passersby would pull the weeds from their graves. I found Jacob before we took off and gave him a kiss. I didn't have to say anything, for he knew how I felt.

Driving the team, I had plenty of time to think. I began remembering the time Edgar and I would play on the plantation. The one birthday celebration I had threatened father that I would talk to Edgar about having children. Then going through the war, and I never learned his part in it. I just knew he had a bitter taste of it, and was putting into his past. Then with the help of Jacob and Molly, we began with nothing and built up something. Then because of attitudes and greed, we lost it. The only things we had from it all were five wonderful children. Now two of them were lost seeking his dream. Hardly a moment of our lives was spent enjoying each other or life in general. Now the one I loved more than life was lying beside our daughter. "Is it ever going to end?" I asked myself.

Thinking of the horse tied to the wagon, I thought about jumping onto it and riding away, not telling anyone where I was going. I came back to reality when my children's faces came to my mind.

After a few days, we were in sight of Fort Boise. Mr. Madison rode by and I told him, "We won't be going any further."

"Oh," he answered.

"I've had enough. I'm going to stop long enough to enjoy the children I have left," I told him.

After a few days outside the Fort, we waved at the wagon train as they left. Jacob and Molly felt the same as I and stayed behind with me.

We stayed a few more days in our makeshift camp to be sure the boys didn't have the fever. Then for safety's sake, we burned my wagon. We didn't want to take the chance it was carrying the fever. The last thing I wanted was to pass it onto others.

The seven of us made it to Boise City to start a new life.

Matt's search for happiness

I found I didn't care for ranching and something was missing in my life. At first, I thought it was my brothers and my father. Then thinking about it, I knew I did miss them, but it was more. I personally, needed something everyone else seemed to have, but I didn't. I didn't have stability and a family. Stability, I knew I could have had many times over. Being a wagon driver, hunter, deputy sheriff or rancher, but nothing worked for me. This problem just didn't make any sense to me for I had seen many men happier doing nothing more than I was, so I knew it was me that had a problem.

"Maybe I should go back to the old farm?" I asked myself with a laugh. I knew that wasn't the answer, being part of this reconstruction of the south that was supposed to be going on. From what I had heard, not much was really happening in the south. The only noticeable thing was the political verbiage being used in the papers. Not being there anymore, I was still sure, the south was being remade in the northern image.

Unlike many men I had met, money wasn't the issue with them either. Not that I was rich, because I wasn't. I had saved most of my wages over the past eight years. This gave me enough money that I could have started a small ranch or a farm. Though the idea sounded good, it still seemed empty. Then I heard of logging going on in the Northwest. I had seen logging in the northeastern part of Kansas, and it was different from what I had known. Still the northwest sounded interesting. That feeling might have been because of Edgar and Ida were heading that way, I'm not sure. For whatever reason, I began working my way in that direction.

About the family side that I needed I was at a loss. The only family I knew was from home. There wasn't enough there to give me any idea what to look for. It in reality wasn't until I met the Buchanan's that I had any idea what a couple could be like. This one couple seemed to share everything. At the same time, they were willing to make sacrifices for each other. Between them there was something, I had no idea what it might be. Using them as an example, I was willing to look for something for me.

With making that decision, I headed to the northwest. It was in the fall of 1876 I packed my bedroll, jumped on my horse and headed out.

After riding for three hours, it began to rain. Patting my old mare, I told her, "I think it's time to get out of the rain." I decided, no matter what town was ahead, I was taking a few days off and dry out.

Getting down from my horse, I got out my slicker. The slicker would at least keep me a little drier, but it wouldn't help my eyes. The rain was being driven with such force, I could hardly see. Getting back on my horse, I looked around through the rain trying to make out where I was. The rain made it hard to make out what the countryside even looked like. Not being able to make anything out, I continued on. I hoped I was heading into Nebraska but I wasn't sure if I was or not. Looking around again, I really didn't know where I was going, or what I would do when I got there. All I knew was I was on my way, with the intent of getting something out of life.

Coming over a rise, I made out a few buildings among a clump of trees. It didn't look like a town really for there wasn't enough buildings around. Stopping for a better look, I was glad the rain had eased up. As I spurred my horse, I saw a flash of light, and a clap of thunder. Before I could take a breath, I saw a building burst into flame. I spurred my horse again to see if I could be of help.

"*Don't worry about the shed, save the church,*" I heard a man shout out, as I rode up.

"*Let me help,*" I called out to the men.

"There's a bucket by the well," a man told me.

Stopping for a second, I looked up at the church. I saw why they were worried, with it being a wood construction. I saw a couple of things that would work in our favor. The building was only one story and the roof was flat. Looking it over, I got an idea.

"Mind if I go up the bell tower…Then with my rope, I can raise buckets of water up, and put out any embers flying up there?" I suggested.

"Good idea," the man answered.

I ran to my horse and grabbed the rope off my saddle. Running towards the church, I called out, *"Give me a minute."*

"Where's he going?" another man asked passing me.

"Roof of the church," the first man answered. At the same time, he was passing a bucket of water to a man.

"Better get some water on that dry hay. If it catches, the roof will definitely go," I shouted out, as I entered the church.

"I'll get a ladder and go up with him," the second man returned to the first.

I stopped and waited for the second man to get back to me. While I was waiting, a couple of wagons drove up and stopped. The men and women in the wagons got out, and began filling up their buckets with water.

"We can get up now," the second man said with a ladder in his arms. Without waiting for me to say anything, he set the ladder against the church. Without checking the ladder, he began climbing it to the roof.

"Hurry up with that water," someone called out.

"Watch your step, it's a little wet up here," the second man warned me.

"Right…Here's some rope to bring the buckets up with," I answered making my way up the ladder, tossing up the rope. As I stepped onto the roof, I saw the shed was engulfed in flames. Whoever was worried about the straw had a point. If the hay caught fire, the roof was going to go. The shingles would fly around and probably land on the roof and the church would go.

"Bring us a couple of buckets…tie one on each end of the rope," I called down as I lowered both ends of the rope down.

"Yes sir," a woman returned.

"I'll keep track of any embers flying up here," the second man said and then he added, 'I'm Pastor Paul Swanson."

With a smile, and a wave of my hand to get him moving, I answered him, "Matt Duncan."

"*Here you go mister,*" the woman called up to me.

Barely hearing her, I began pulling the buckets up, and answered, "*Thanks.*"

As the shed burned, ground level, there was a lot of shouting and crackling of wood burning. On the roof, the Pastor and I were being covered with soot and embers. Though we were keeping up with the embers, it took a number of buckets of water. Unfortunately, as we fought the fire, the rain eased up. The heat made the roof dry out real quick.

With my back turned, I heard a loud, "*Whoosh.*" I didn't have to turn around, for I knew what it was. The hay had caught fire, and the roof of the shed had exploded. With that thought, the air was full of burning shingles and straw.

"*Keep that water coming.*" I called down as I turned around.

"We might be in trouble," the Pastor said coming up to me for more water.

The Pastor was not to far wrong. Another two men came up to the roof and gave us a hand. I don't have any idea how long we were up there, but we kept stomping out ember and wetting the roof. Finally the shed had burnt to the ground and the people were able to put the remaining flames out. One corner of the roof was burnt, but it wasn't going to take much to fix it. Standing back after it was all over, I felt good and didn't care how wet I was.

"We did it," the Pastor said slapping me on the back. He then stepped over and talked to another man, before he came back over to me.

"We sure did," another said giving off a nervous laugh.

"I'm glad it's over," I added with a smile. Looking up into the sky, I saw nightfall was on us.

"How about some coffee?" the Pastor asked as we climbed down the ladder.

"I would be happy to set somewhere dry, until I can dry out," I answered him.

"I might even be able to find some stew and a piece of cake," he said getting off the ladder.

Looking around, I saw more than a dozen faces. Every face was black with soot, and looked very tired. Though tired and dirty, everyone was slapping each other on the back with smiles on their faces. I looked down at myself, and saw I was just as dirty as rest of them. What surprised me was that I was fairly dry considering how much rain had come down.

"Thanks everyone…I think it can be said we did a good job," the Pastor told everyone.

"Thank you mister," a couple of people offered as they walked passed me.

"One heck of a mess," one said to someone he was walking with.

"Let's see what Mother is doing," the Pastor said walking up to me.

"Let me get my horse," I told him looking around for my mare. I was surprised to see she hadn't wandered off that far. I didn't have to go but a couple of hundred feet, and she was eating some grass. Taking her reins, I walked back to the Pastor.

"My place is just at the end of the block," he said leading the way.

"One heck of a fire," I said trying to keep a conversation going.

"Thankfully we had God's help," he returned continuing down the road.

Inside his house, we were met by an attractive woman in her twenties. At her sides, were two small children hanging onto her skirt. The little girl looked at me, as if I was going to bite her. When I smiled at her, she pulled her mothers skirt around to cover her face.

"My wife Helen, my daughter Sara and my son David. This is Matt Duncan, if I remember correctly. He came by to give us a hand with the fire," the Pastor said introducing all of us to each other.

"Nice to meet you Mr. Duncan and thank you for your help. Any damage to the church?" Helen asked offering her hand.

"My pleasure," I returned taking her hand.

"One corner of the roof, over the storeroom. Harry checked it out, and there is some water damage but not much. It shouldn't take much to fix the roof though," he answered her.

"That's good to hear…Want to wash up Mr. Duncan. I was just about to set some food on the table, when the lightning struck," she offered.

"If you have enough…and washing up sounds like a good idea," I returned looking down at myself.

"And you can help us celebrate Sara's birthday," the Pastor told me hanging up his hat.

"Well happy birthday, Sara," I told the little girl as she hid behind her mother.

With a little laughter all around, I agreed to eat with them. Helen began setting out the dishes as I washed myself up. Supper was good and I enjoyed the Pastor's family and their company. Talking to them brought back many memories of home.

The Pastor and his wife were kind enough to allow me to spend the night on their floor. With a dry change of clothes, and a bowl of mush, I set out the following morning feeling good about life again. I always felt a chance of helping people and putting smiles on faces had to be the best reward a man could receive. In leaving the little community, I remembered I had forgotten to ask where I was.

As I went down the road, I said to myself, "Oh well, just as long as it doesn't rain." As the thought left my mind, it began to rain again.

A new life for Ida

Thinking it over, my life was still a mess and I prayed it was over. In just a few days I had lost two of my children and a husband. I wasn't carefree to search for a life. To make everything worse, I was in an unfamiliar area. My children were going to be depending on me, and I had no idea what to do. Yes, my life quite often was hanging from my skirt, wanting something to eat.

Looking at Boise City one morning, I stood up and shouted out, "*Ida Duncan is Coming…Watch out.*"

"What was all of that about?" Jacob asked me.

"I realized waiting here to make sure the fever is not with us still, I have to do something. Just sitting here, feeling sorry for myself is destroying everything the four of us have stood for. Yes, Edgar, Luke and Annabelle are gone, but my three boys and I are still here. With you and Molly nearby, I know we will make it," I answered.

"Good," Jacob told me giving me a slap on the back. Then looking solemn, he went on to add, "In reference to Edgar, I'm sorry I walked away when you needed me."

"I understand," I told him. I thought I understood what he might have been going through himself.

"His death, I think, is worse than losing a brother or even a father. Everything, other than marrying Molly and having our son, I did with him. Your parents gave me worth, not myself. Edgar taught me I was worth something. He appreciated me for me. With losing him, I felt like the best part of me was gone."

After the two of us sat there in our own thoughts, I knew how he felt. I told him, "Like you, I am the same way; my whole life was Mama and father. Then finding myself alone, I knew I was nothing. Then Edgar showed me my true worth. I never knew who or what I was until he came back. He had that ability with people he loved."

"Am I missing out on something?" Molly asked as she set down.

"Just talking about how we miss Edgar," Jacob answered.

"He is a legacy who will be missed," Molly said looking out into nothing.

With a laugh, I said trying to be honest, "He had his bad points. He was stubborn, opinionated, bullheaded and a few other things."

"Still, he was more," Molly added, looking over at Jacob. Wiping a tear from her eyes, she told me, "My father was that type of person. I saw so many of his traits in Jacob and I was drawn to him. Then after marrying him, I found he was so different. Jacob was so laid back I would get mad. Everything that went wrong was his fault and he hid, not fighting. Then Edgar came back, and they started to work with each other. At this point, everything began to change. Jacob was then coming home bragging he had done this or he had done that. He began coming up with opinions on different subjects. Not that he was repeating Edgar; in fact, at times, he disagreed, and it was good to hear. I finally had the husband I thought I was marrying. I owe your husband for that."

"Was I that bad?" Jacob asked giving her a pinch on the arm.

"Yes, but enough has been said," she replied.

"Thank you for Edgar's sake. That was good of you to tell me and I will never forget it," I told her as I gave her a hug.

"I'm hungry, mama," Little Joe announced as he came up to us.

"Me too, mama," Harold added.

"I guess we have our orders," I said as I began to get up. Once up I told the boys, "If that's the way it is, let's get going and we will see what we can find."

I prayed I would be able to instill some of Edgar into our sons, maybe not as harsh, but still some of his determination, self-confidence, and self-worth. I prayed I had it in me.

"After some breakfast, let's go into town," I told everyone.

"I have a few ideas but what's yours?" Jacob asked.

"Thought we would barge into town, and tell them we are taking over," I answered with a laugh.

"And as you are laughing, so might they," Molly said laughing at the idea.

"At least they will be getting a laugh for free," I replied as I began fixing some mush. I hadn't laid out a plan, but to go in and see what there was to offer. Turning to everyone, I made a suggestion, "Everyone in town, undoubtedly, knows we are here. Let's do something which will kill two birds with one stone."

"What do you have in mind?" Jacob asked.

"I'm not sure I want to keep the wagon, because it might be infected with the fever. I think it would be wise to burn it. At the same time, it will give everyone notice something is up," I told him.

"Like Gabriel blowing his horn?" he asked.

"Yes," I answered with a smile and then I went on to say, "We might as well announce our coming."

"I'm game if you are," Jacob said with Molly nodding her head with a grin. He then added, "What do we have to lose."

We transferred everything from my wagon into theirs. With some lantern oil, it didn't take long for the wagon to ignite. We watched it burn, not wanting to start a fire. Once we were sure it was safe, we headed for town. With four of the seven of us being white and three black, we must have been a sight.

What must have been everyone in town, they were all out on the street watching us. I tried to keep from laughing but it wasn't easy. I told Jacob, "If you see a sheriff or doctor's office, stop."

"Why?" Molly asked as Jacob opened his mouth to ask the same question.

"They more than any other might have an idea what there is to offer for us," I answered.

"Good thinking," Jacob answered, with a smile looking up at us.

"I see the sheriff's office two doors down," Molly told us.

"I see it," Jacob assured us, as he headed the oxen in the general direction.

The Sheriff met us on the boardwalk with a questioning look. He asked, "Hi, I'm Sheriff Johnson, may I help you folks?"

"I hope you can," I answered as I got down from the wagon.

We went into the sheriff's office and I told him our story. He just sat at his rolltop desk and shook his head. He looked up at me and down at the children. He got up, walked to the window, and looked out without saying anything.

Coming back, he roughed up John's hair with his hand, and said, "At one time, the people here were families of soldiers at the Fort. Then the shopkeepers moved in. Then the loggers moved in making the town too rough for most. I was hired and the town is now halfway safe. Hardly do we get someone stranded here. No one in their right mind would come to Boise City, let alone allow themselves to get stranded…here at least."

"We're here and we didn't have much of a choice about it," I told him.

"Ma'am, that's plain to see," he said with a smile. Then thinking for a second, he told us. "If your friend here was a blacksmith, I might know where he can get a job. As to housing and something for you to do, I doubt being a dancehall girl is an option for you."

"No, I'm not the type," I answered thinking what my mother had done for me. I knew there had to be another option.

"Do you know of any houses for sale?" I asked him.

"You might try June Whitehall on the hill above us," he answered and then turning to Jacob, he told him, "The blacksmith place is at the far end of this street. You'll see a stable sign. The old Blacksmith also had a stable."

"Thank you," Jacob told him, hoping it might turn into something. Molly was also grinning with hopes.

"Thank you, sheriff," I told him offering my hand, and I went on to add, "We'll be seeing you."

"Something says I will," he replied taking my hand and giving me a smile.

"Thanks again," Jacob said offering his hand.

With what seemed like a little hesitation, the sheriff took his hand and said, "I wish you luck. We need a good blacksmith."

"Thank you Jocko," I said as we headed for our wagon. I stopped because I saw my children running around the wagon, playing with other children. I told them, "Be careful of the oxen."

"Where to first?" Jacob asked.

"Let's see about the blacksmith job," I answered as I turned and told the children, "Time for us to leave."

"We're having fun, mama," Mark said looking as if I had shot him.

"There will be plenty of time later," I told him, pointing to the wagon.

Then looking inside the wagon, I saw John was still sitting where I had left him. Once Harold, Mark, and Little Joe got in, Jacob got us going down the street. Still people were out on the street watching us go by. I waved at them as we passed. I was hoping my friendliness would break down any resistance we might come against in the future.

After traveling five blocks, we found the stables. Jacob stopped the oxen and looked around. Molly and I didn't wait to be asked to join him, and we followed him into the stable. We saw the blacksmith shop to one side, and he went into it and looked around.

"May I help you? Joe's not here anymore, He died two months ago." A little old white haired lady asked coming out of the back shed.

"The sheriff said you might be looking for a blacksmith," Jacob told her showing his best smile.

"If I was planning on staying around this dump maybe. I want to get rid of the place and go to my son's," she answered.

"Oh," Jacob said looking as if he had died himself.

"Hi, I'm Ida Buchanan, and we just got into town. This is Jacob and his wife Molly," I said introducing ourselves to her.

"I'm Rose Haggerty, good to meet all of you," she replied, showing some interest in us.

I went on to ask her, "How much do you want for the place?"

"Not what it's worth. However, the house isn't much, but the business is good, if someone was to take care of it. Still, I want to get out of here," she answered but not giving me a price. Then seeing the expression of interest, she went on to tell me, "Two hundred, that'll get me to Denver with a few dollars left over."

Jacob turned to leave and I stopped him. I asked him, "What's wrong."

"I don't have that kind of money," he said looking defeated.

"And what will you do?" I asked as I watched Molly watching what her husband said.

"It appears there's a logging camp. I should be able to get some work there," he answered looking back at the furnace close enough for him to touch it.

"They're hiring all right," Rose told us.

"But would you be happy," I asked him.

"I can answer that, no," Molly answered for him, having an idea what I was about to offer.

"I couldn't ask you for that much money," he told me, looking determined.

"Edgar got you this far. He would want me to go rest of the way. Mrs. Haggerty, you have a deal," I said giving Jacob a hug.

"Between your parents, you and Edgar, I don't know what to say," Jacob said, with a tear in his eyes.

"Try thanks, dummy," Molly said kissing him on the cheek.

"Keep in mind, you might have to support the four of us for a while," I reminded him.

Looking at Molly, he told me, "To keep myself from being killed in the middle of the night, I agree. But, you will get your money back, for this, the wagon and everything."

"We can talk about that some other time. Let's get the paperwork done," I suggested.

"I can be out of here in the morning," Rose told us, motioning us to follow her.

As we entered the little house in back, I told Jacob, "It might be wise to check the house out first."

"Can't be much worse that what we had," he answered with a smile.

"My man's got a point there," Molly said stepping into the house ahead of me.

The house was somewhere between their house and ours in Virginia. Both Jacob and Molly were happy with it. As Rose got out her paperwork, the two of them looked the place over. I told her our story of getting here and she understood my loss.

"You understood, the furniture goes with the house," Rose told them.

"Oh," Molly got out, with a tear running down her cheek.

"I'll make a bed for Little Joe and we're set. Now to find you a place," he said giving his wife a hug.

"How many children did you say you had?" Rose asked me.

"Three boys," I answered.

"Well, something to think about, June wants to sell her place," she offered as an idea.

"On the hill?" I asked.

"Yes, I don't know if you know it or not, but it's a boardinghouse. You won't make much money, but with the garden in the back you'll make ends meet," she told me.

We walked to the bank with her, and got the papers taken care of. After having been taken by the Carpetbaggers, I had learned. I wanted everything done nice and legal. Unfortunately, June was a little pricier. She wanted four hundred for her place, because of the boarders that were there already. Though it was a comfortable home with six bedrooms, I thought it was a little much. Still with forty cents a day for a room and supper, I should make a little. Visiting the banker again, the two families were now business people of Boise City.

Matt continues looking

I found myself wondering how Edgar and Ida were doing as I rode along. It wasn't just that they were a happy couple, but they had a dream and they were out to reach it. I had one, but I didn't know how to reach it. The only thing I knew was to wander around until I could find myself. Not being in any hurry getting anywhere, I would stop here and there. Any place I stopped at, I would find work to pay my keep. Some of the jobs were cleaning saloons or in the stables. Once, I drove a stage when a driver was sick.

One afternoon, after riding in the rain all day, I decided to stop. I wasn't sure if I was going to hang around, but thought I would deposit the money I had on me for safekeeping. In seeing a bank, I stopped my horse at the hitching post in front of it. As I stopped, I saw a general store, thinking before I left I had better pick up some supplies. In my yellow duster I wore to keep dry from the rain, I got off my horse.

Halfway to the ground, I noticed four other men coming out of the bank dressed as I was. I thought it was interesting we were dressed the same. Then I noticed they had pistols and a rifle out. I had a funny feeling they were bank robbers. It wasn't long before I knew for sure.

Gunfire erupted, as my foot touched the mud. It was obvious they were shooting at the bank robbers. The men didn't know me from them and assumed I was one of them. A couple of shots whizzed past my head, and I knew I had to get out of the line of fire. As I reached for my saddle horn, a bullet grazed my little finger. It hurt like heck, but it didn't slow me down. As I got my other leg over my horse, I sped out of town, crouched over my horse. Thankfully, the men shooting at us were bad shots.

I noticed looking back, the bank robbers turned down a street I had just passed. For some reason, I decided to follow them.

Mind you, I was in a little town in the southwestern part of Nebraska. The countryside is full of rolling hills with only a few trees. With it raining, it's difficult for a horse to get its footing. In making it around the block to follow them, I lost some time. Still, I caught a glimpse of them going over a rise a couple of miles out of town. Looking behind me, it was clear the sheriff or marshal hadn't gotten a posse together yet. I couldn't see any sign of riders coming from the direction of town. Having this knowledge, I spurred my horse into a gallop. As I rode, I saw blood flying from my finger. I managed to get a bandanna, wrapped it up, and I continued after them.

I got to thinking as I rode that this was more action than I saw as a deputy sheriff. Looking down at the ground, I saw I wasn't going to have any problem following them. They way they rode showed their tracks perfectly clear. A half hour later, I slowed down a pace to give my horse a breather. I came upon three men on horseback and one in a wagon.

I stopped and I asked them, "Four guys dressed like me come by?"

"Yes, like greased lightning," one man answered.

"Help me catch the bank robbers and I'll give you a hundred dollars to split.

"Lead the way," the four of them said without hesitation.

Keep in mind I was going after these guys for a couple of reasons. One was to clear my name in case someone recognized me. I was the only one without a bandanna around my face, making it easy for someone to recognize me. The other was because it needed to be done. At the same time, I was bored and it seemed like fun.

As we rode, I saw the tracks were not as deep as they were. I reasoned they felt safe and they slowed their horse down to a trot. Within twenty minutes, we saw a house to the right of us sitting on a rise.

I told the men, "I would like not to shoot these guys, but take them in alive." Getting them out of the house, if they were in it, might not be easy. I decided I wanted one of them to take the rear, another on each side and then two of us in the front. Each of the men nodded their understanding and we split up.

As we made it to the house, I saw their tracks did lead to it. I waved my hand flat up and down, to signal to take it slowly. The man in the wagon followed me, since he couldn't make to the rear or sides too easily. Looking back at him, I saw he was carrying a can of Lantern oil. Seeing it, it gave me an idea how to get the men out of the house.

In front of the house, I signaled for the man to give me the can of oil. I got off my horse and took the oil from him. Taking my time, keeping clear of windows, I crept toward the house. When I got to the corner of the house, I dumped the oil all over the walls that I could get at without being seen. Taking my pistol out, I fired a shot in the air.

"You're surrounded...Come out with your hands up, or I'll burn you out," I yelled out to them.

"*I'll show you; burn us out,*" one of the men yelled back. The man inside fired a shot toward the trees in front of the house.

The man that had been driving the wagon fired a shot back at the house. I yelled out, "*No more shooting...I'm going to burn them out.*"

Though it took three matches, I got the oil lit. I ran back to the tree where the other man was standing behind to wait. When I got there, there was a bright orange glow. I didn't think it would take long for them to make up their minds, but I was willing to wait.

I yelled out, "*It's your choice and as you can see I don't play games.*"

As the flames began to get to the windows, I knew they would have different thoughts about staying inside.

"*We're coming out,*" a voiced cried out.

"*Throw your guns out first...rifle and pistols,*" I yelled back, realizing my finger was beginning to hurt. With the excitement of the ride, I hadn't noticed it. Now that I wasn't doing anything I could sure feel it and it was hurting.

Six firearms were thrown out the door. Then the door opened wider, and the four men began walking out.

"Call out to your friends to come on around," I told the man beside me.

"*Jack, Harry, Sam, come on out front…we need your help*," he shouted out to them.

I held my pistol on them, and told the man beside me, "Take the rope off my saddle and begin tying them up, if you would."

About the same time, the other three came around the house and joined us. Getting off their horse, they brought with them their ropes. They joined their friend in tying up the four men.

"That's the easiest twenty-five dollars I have ever made," one man said as he tied his man up.

"I would do this everyday if I could get this much money," the driver of the wagon told me. Later I was to learn his name was Pete.

"Let's get them into town, and I'll give you your money," I told them and then I went on to tell them, "Tie their horses to the wagon, if you would. I don't like leaving animals out to die. I'm going to check for the bank money."

"Gotcha," a second man answered as he grabbed the reins of a horse.

I found the money on a table near a lit candle. I picked all up and put it into the saddlebag hanging on a chair. Then blowing out the candle, I made it for outside before the house was engulfed in flames.

"It was a nice home at one time," one of the men said as I came out of the house choking from the smoke.

"Heavy on the 'was,'" I answered and went on to add, "At least we have them alive."

"Probably worth more that way," Pete pointed out.

Heading back to town, no one said anything in words. With nothing being said, all four of them were riding high with pride. I got to thinking how dumb I was to trust strangers. These four could have been friends of the robbers and killed me. Thankfully, an angel was riding on my shoulders.

Halfway back, I saw a group of riders ahead of us. I rode out to the front so I could meet them. As they approached, I raised my hand to stop them.

"Think you're looking for our four friends," I told the man in the lead wearing a badge.

"What," he answered rising in his saddle to look in the back of the wagon. Then sitting back in his saddle, he shook his head and told me, "I'll be. You're right."

I told him what happened showing him my finger. He laughed as well as I did as we kept going towards town.

I asked him, "I hope there's a reward?" Then before he could answer, I told him, "I promised these men some money."

"The bank usually offers two-hundred and fifty dollars," he answered.

"*We got a raise*," I shouted out to the four men.

When we got to town, one of the men that helped me asked, "What did you mean a raise back there?"

"Rather than twenty-five each, you'll be getting fifty each, along with my thanks," I answered.

"Mister, if you ever and I do mean ever need help again, just call on my brothers and I. And you won't need to pay us anything," he told me as we made it to the sheriffs office.

"Hey sheriff, that was quick," an older man wearing a derby said coming up to us.

"These five men caught them before we got to them. And you owe them two-hundred and fifty dollars," the sheriff answered as he got off his horse.

"No problem," the man answered taking off to the bank.

"What's your name, stranger?" he asked me.

"Matt," I answered taking his hand and shaking it.

"That was quick work if I ever saw it," he said motioning his men to take the prisoners into the jail. Then turning back to me, he introduced himself by telling me, "Call me Brad."

"I glad I was able to be of help, Brad," I answered him.

"Here you are, mister," the banker said coming up to me, with the money in his hands. Catching his breath, he went on to add, "You have my thanks."

I took the money and told him, "Thanks, otherwise, I was going to have to take my own money to pay these good men."

"Thanks to you guys also," he told them as I handed each one fifty dollars.

Taking their ropes back, they mounted and shouted out, "*Thanks again.*"

I didn't see them for another month. We had a good laugh about that afternoon's piece of work. They were more than willing, to help me again.

"Need a job?" The sheriff asked.

"Here I go again," I answered as I nodded my head yes.

Another year went by working as deputy sheriff. I had told him of my other experience of becoming a deputy.

Ida and a new beginning

At the time, I remembered Matt but that's all he was, a memory. After we left him in Kearny, I had no idea what he was doing or where he even was. After all of our talks around the campsites, I knew he was looking for a life. Now it seemed I had something in common with him, nothing but past lives. Once again, I had to begin a new life, and it looked like it was going to be in Boise City. Boise City was a nice quiet little town nestled among towering pines, which made for a beautiful landscape.

The community wasn't that large being only three to four hundred people. The main source of income came from the logging industry and the Fort. There was some farming and ranching, but not that much. Though during the day it was pretty quiet, the evenings could get noisy. With the soldiers stationed not far away, they would come into town to do their drinking.

With area as it was, it was similar to where I grew up in. The area was all green offering fun for the children. Harold was now old enough he could go fishing in the stream at the edge of town. At the same time, he had already learned to swim. My only hesitation was the winters I had heard about. Though we got snow in Virginia, it didn't hang around for months on end. Living on the side of a hill, I was afraid what it might be like going down to Main Street.

One event happened in town that never did in Richmond. A doe went walking right down the center of Main Street. Everyone was so shocked, they didn't even think about shooting her. Many, I'm told, kicked themselves afterwards. This event is an example of what you can see in the surrounding countryside.

We settled into the community with running the boardinghouse. The boys and I had even joined the church. I didn't have time for friends, because of the workload, but that was fine. I still had Jacob and Molly for friends. The boys though had made friends and were happy having playmates other than themselves.

Jacob had it easy in one way. With the community used to having a blacksmith, they were at a loss not having one for two months. Jacob had all that work waiting for him. He found himself working fourteen to twenty hours a day six days a week for two months. He did such good work; he earned the respect of everyone in town. He was referred to as Mister Jacob or sir.

Molly did her best to give him a hand whenever possible. She had enrolled Little Joe in school, so during the day she helped Jacob. At the end of the two months, Jacob replaced her with hired help. Both were as happy as when my son John gets rock candy.

At the same time, in taking over the boardinghouse, I had a lot to learn. I had to learn to manage my time, so my boarders could have supper on time. Then as June had warned me, the drunks renting from me could be a problem. I learned early how to take care of that. I had Jacob modify the doors, so I could lock the drunks out at eleven PM. Any one caught not being in the house by then was locked out. I lost a few boarders, but I didn't care. The following day, I would gain a replacement for the boarder that left. Finally, the house got a reputation of being a clean house. The cleanliness also included no liquor in the rooms.

Cleaning the place was not easy with three boys running around. Still, when the men got home, their beds were made and dinner on the table. The one thing that hurt was taking care of the garden. As each day went by, I got better at managing the workload.

Sunday being the day, I didn't cook supper for my boarders, I would visit with Jacob and Molly after church. The children would play and we had a good time. It was also relaxing seeing Jacob so proud of himself. We kept to this routine and it was my release from a hard week.

One Sunday about six months after we got to Boise City I had a strange experience. The boys and I were walking down the hill to Jacob's place after church. We ran into the sheriff and he had an interesting look on his face. He stopped me and asked, "I know you probably told me, but what was your husband's name?"

"Edgar Buchanan," I answered wondering why he asked.

With a grin on his face, he went on to ask, "A plantation owner's son that lived right outside Richmond?"

"You fought with my husband?" I asked. This was the first time I had heard anything about Edgar even being in the war, let alone what he might have done.

"Yes Ma'am I did. Yes, I did," he answered.

"Edgar never said anything about fighting or even having been in the war. Mind you we grew up with each other, but not a word," I told him.

"I think I know why," he answered looking troubled. Then looking around and at his feet, he went on to tell me, "He was ashamed of what he did."

"I find it hard my Edgar would do anything he would be ashamed of," I told him.

I guess from my expression he was worried and told me, "He didn't but he felt he should be. In fact, he told me not to tell our commanding officer what he had done. If I had, he would have been given a medal or promoted."

"What did he do?" I asked.

"It's this way, our commanding officer ordered us to do some scouting. He wanted to know where the enemy was and all. Come to think of it, he mentioned he didn't live to far from where we were. Anyway, we rode around for hours and we didn't see anything, not even a squirrel. Then just before we got back, your husband spotted a campfire through the trees. Well we couldn't just ride over and check it out, so we crawled on our belly. There, ten fifteen miles due north of Richmond, we had found a company of Yankees."

"What did you two do?" I asked him.

"Well, we were lying there on our bellies wondering what to do. There they were, camped out for the night. The only thing between them and us was a bridge. Edgar told me not to move, and he would be right back. He was gone about a half an hour. I almost thought he had deserted. Then about dusk, I saw him sneaking down the draw to the bridge. At first, I couldn't make out what he had in his hands. Then as he worked his way up a trestle of bridge, I could see it was a keg—"

"I know the bridge, the two of us used to play down there," I said interrupting him.

"As I was saying, I knew what it was when he got it up there. Then he came down and made his way back to where I was. I asked him what he was going to do. He told me he was going to keep those Yankees from coming over to our side."

"Did he blow the bridge up?" I asked.

"Yes Ma'am that he did. As we were discussing it, a couple of squads began marching over it. He took his rifle without thinking, and fired at the keg. Bridge, Yankees and all went up," he said with a smile remembering. Then losing the smile, he told me, "Seeing all the men that died made him sick. He made me promise I would never tell anyone he had killed so many men. It wasn't that he didn't shoot Yankees afterward, for he did. And, as he explained later, he didn't feel bad about shooting them. They were trying to shoot him, so it was even. The men on the bridge he said were different. They didn't have any warning that he was there, or that he was going to blow the bridge up. In the end, we went back and told the commanding officer we saw men across the gorge, but we didn't see how they could cross because someone had blown the bridge up," Sheriff Johnson told me.

"Thank you for solving many questions for me," I told him.

"He was one man I thought a great deal of. He even saved me and now you tell me the fever got him. A real shame. Have a nice day, Ma'am," he said as he continued down the street.

"Did he know father?" Harold asked.

"It seems so, it seems so," I answered, still in shock hearing something about Edgar and the war.

I was sure I had heard the explosion that night, and I wanted to laugh. Edgar had stolen it from us. I wondered why he didn't stop in and say hi. It wasn't that late when we went out for the seed. From the way it sounded, we had just missed him. Still I found myself saying, "Mama, I know where the gunpowder went to."

Getting to Jacob and Molly, they greeted me with, "Good afternoon, Ida. How are you boys?"

"Good afternoon," I return.

"We're fine. Where's Little Joe?" Harold asked.

"Around back," Jacob answered and turning back to me, he asked, "What's with the smile on your face?"

"There's something wrong with a smile?" I asked giving him a bad time, as I went inside with them.

"No, but that smile I haven't seen since Edgar proposed," he told me with a smile on his face.

"Funny you should refer to Edgar," I told him as I sat down. I then went on to tell them, "I just had a strange experience. Our sheriff just stopped me…"

I went on to tell them what he had said. The three of us smiled hearing something about Edgar.

"You know, there were a few times someone would come by the plant talking about their experiences in the war. Edgar would walk off, not even listening. There was one time I thought he might have been a deserter or a Yankee. I mean, what other reason would there be not saying anything. Now it makes sense, not that I understand it," Jacob.

"He was different in many ways," Molly added.

"Yes he was," I agreed.

"Can I get you something to drink?" Molly asked.

"Thanks, some coffee sounds good," I told her. Then turning to Jacob, I told him, "For some time now, I have had the feeling you have been up to something. Then at the hardware store, I went in to buy a couple of hinges. Guess what I found? Hinges made by Jac's." When I mentioned hinges, Jacob broke into a smile. I knew my suspicions were about right. He was turning out his own products.

"I have been meaning to tell you, but I have been so busy I haven't even seen you. Then, too, I wanted to make sure I had a product and a market…" he began to tell me but was interrupted by Molly.

"I was going to say something but he wanted the pleasure of being the one," Molly said, trying to keep herself out of trouble for not saying anything.

"I understand, Molly; I know about men and their secrets. Such as Edgar and his war experience. Now tell me about Jac's products?"

With a grin on his face, he told me, "That first week or so, if you remember I was real busy…"

"I think it was more like the first few months," I said interrupting him. Molly nodded her head in agreement.

"Whatever," he said and then he went on to tell me, "this guy came in to see if I could fix a hinge. Not seeing any problem doing it, I just made him another, rather than fixing the old one. He was so happy I decided to begin making utility hinges, nothing fancy for kitchens but everything for fences and barns. I was thinking about selling them, then I got to thinking about my workload. I took some samples of different sizes to the hardware store. Joe was thrilled, and agreed to sell them. Now I have orders from a couple of other hardware stores in the state."

"I'm happy for you," I told him feeling proud everything was working out for them.

"It gets better," Molly went on to add. "He designed a grappling hook for the logging industry."

"That and a few other items," he told me showing his toothy grin. Then getting up to get some coffee for himself, he added, "With the stables Molly takes care of, and having enough work to keep another four men busy, we just might make a living."

"All because of Jocko and Mr. Smiley," I added.

"I think most of it is due to Jacob himself, expressing something he found interesting as a child. Those two with Edgar's help brought his talents out," Molly said in his defense.

"Remember Molly, we grew up together. His talent was keeping me from riding my colt," I told her with a laugh at the memory of the colt.

"That wasn't me. That was Samuel," he said defending himself.

Molly and I got supper going and we called the children in. Jacob said over dinner he could pay me back anytime I needed some money. I told him to keep it for expansion of his business and if I needed some money, I would let him know. Rest of the afternoon and evening was a relaxing time. With it beginning to get cold, the children and I didn't stay too late.

The next day was a good example of my acceptance in town. I was on my way to the General store and I passed a couple of women. One of them, I later learned, was Mrs. Abbott.

Mrs. Abbot said in passing me to her friend, "That's the hussy."

"I know. She's the one living with all those men," the second one answered.

In hearing what I did, I began to understand some strange events. Whenever I walked down a street, people would cross the street or make a wide path around me.

The third time I heard Mrs. Abbot making a comment like she had the first time, I stopped her. I told her, "If you're so worried about your husband and me, maybe, you should take better care of him." I didn't wait for a reply but I did hear her as I walked away.

"Well I'll be," she said, driving her heels into the boardwalk and continuing on her way.

Later in the week, I had a nice conversation with the wife of the owner of the General Store.

"I hear you put Mrs. Abbot in her place the other day," she told me with a sparkle of enjoyment in her eyes.

"I had a few words," I admitted.

"Your problem, not that I like talking about people, but you deserve to know. June was a little loose, if you know what I mean."

"With me buying her place, I must have bought everything, gossip and all," I said summing it up for her.

"That's what some have thought. Then hearing you had put a curfew on the place, people began to think otherwise. Still those few like Mrs. Abbott kept the thinking alive."

"I find it hard to believe someone would think a mother of three boys would do anything like that. Other than laundry, what other business can a woman do in a small town like this?" I asked her.

"And those that don't work have nothing better to do than start rumors," she said. Then as she began to total up my purchases, she told me, "I wish all I had to do was start rumors. Maybe my back wouldn't hurt like it does."

"I know what you mean," I replied with a laugh.

"That'll be two dollars and seventy-three cents," she told me.

"Thanks," I told her feeling better about my little talk with Mrs. Abbott.

"You know it seems those friends of yours, Jacob and Molly, are doing good," she said. Then wrapping up my purchases, she went on to say, "Our son started working for him last week. He's so happy getting out of here and learning something new, and Jacob is getting more and more business everyday."

"I know, and my late husband would be very proud of him," I replied.

As I left, I wondered what she would have said if she knew he was once my slave, or at least my family's slave. Then there are some things best left alone and I wouldn't want to jeopardize Jacob and Molly in anyway.

Still in the days to come, people were a little friendlier. Not that I was being invited to Teas or anything, but better. I was nice to get a friendly "Howdy" from people.

Then as the first snow began to fall, I was on the front porch watching the snowflakes fall. Each one drifted down so gracefully. I wondered how many of these storms it was going to take before I got tired of them. As I turned to go back inside, I noticed a man walking towards the house.

I stopped dead in my tracks thinking I had seen him before. The closer he got, the more I was sure I knew who he was. The only difference about him from this distance was he wasn't wearing his Kepi Cap.

"Matt, how are you?" I asked before he got more than thirty or forty feet from me.

"Ida?" He asked, stopping and then picking his pace up to greet me. As he got to the steps, he told me, "I have thought of you and Edgar many times. How are the two of you?'

I invited him in, and I poured him a cup of coffee in the kitchen. I told him about losing Edgar and Annabelle and Luke. I then promised to take him down to visit Jacob.

"The reason for coming up here was to see if you have a room," he told me with a smile and went on to add, "If I had known you were here, I would have been coming to visit."

"Now you can do both," I told him. Thinking how great it was seeing someone from our past, I asked him, "What are your plans?"

"I am gradually heading west in hopes of finding my brothers. Not knowing where they are, I'm trying to find a purpose in life," he told me. Then added, "The only two jobs I have had for any length of time is wagon driving and as a deputy sheriff in a couple of towns. In fact, the last job I had was in Cobb, Nebraska, as a deputy sheriff. I thought I might try logging and stay around long enough to feel like I belong somewhere."

"Tired of running?" I asked the pointed question.

"I don't know; I haven't been running away from anything, other than myself. I do know my backsides are getting tired of traveling," he answered.

"Then take the room at top of the stairs, on the left and stay awhile," I told him. Then thinking about it, I told him, "I may be wrong, but the hiring at the camp may be ending, with winter coming and all. You might check with the Sheriff and he might know of a job. In fact Jacob might need someone."

"Once I told the sheriff of my experience, he put me on as a deputy," Matt told me when he got back. He laughed and told me, "Maybe my destiny is to be a lawman. You know, I find your place here to be familiar in ways. The boardinghouse in Cobb set on a hill just like yours does."

"Might be you were born to be a sheriff. Supper is at six thirty," I reminded him. I then told him, "In most, cases curfew is eleven PM. Since you are a member of the sheriff's office, that won't work. I'll get a key made for you tomorrow. It is interesting the similarity in the two places."

"Thanks," he answered with a smile.

"Oh, have you taken care of your horse?" I asked knowing I didn't have a place for his horse.

"Yes, the sheriff told me where Jacob's place was, and that he also had a stable," he answered, and then went on to add, "I meant to tell you Jacob said to tell you hello."

"Mama, is supper ready," John asked coming into the kitchen.

"I haven't even started cooking it yet," I answered chasing him away.

"Jacob sure seems busy," he said, and then he went on to tell me the sheriff had referred to him as being Mr. Morgan. I always wondered what his last name was. Then I remembered with him being a slave, he probably didn't have a last name."

"He didn't. However, when he bought the place, he needed one. I decided to give him my Mama's surname," I told him.

"He's the first black I have seen getting so much respect," he said shaking his head with approval. Then accepting my offer of a chair, he sat down. Then taking a cup of coffee, he told me, "When I went in, there were four customers waiting. One man was giving him a good sized order. I was—" He stopped when another man interrupted us.

"Mrs. Buchanan, so you have any towels?" the man asked.

"Sorry George, I brought them in from the line and forgot to put them away," I answered reaching over to grab one. Then as he took it, I told him, "George, this is a new boarder, his name is Matt Duncan. He's also a new deputy in town."

"Good to meet you, Mr. Duncan," George said offering his hand to Matt.

"Good to meet you also, George," Matt replied shaking his hand.

"We're both new to town then. I'm the new barber in town," George told Matt.

"I guess I'll be seeing you occasionally then," Matt told him with a smile.

"Sorry to have interrupted your conversation Mrs. Buchanan. Stop by anytime Matt. I'm next door to Jacob's place," George said.

"It's Ida, George. It's no problem, I should have put the towels away," I told him.

"As I was about to say, Jacob sure seems busy for being just a blacksmith," He said.

"He's more than a blacksmith. Though, originally shoeing and stabling horses was the only thing done there, Jacob has a line of products he makes and sells," I told him. Then I added, "I would bet in another year his business will double."

"That's great. Well if you don't mind, I think I'll freshen up for supper and put my stuff away," he said in excusing himself.

Matt worked out good with the sheriff. After the second year, the sheriff moved on and Matt took his place. I, on the other hand, kept plunking away with the boardinghouse. Jacob and Molly built a new house four blocks away, nicer and larger. Their business outgrew the old place, so Jacob built a big place on the edge of town.

The most interesting news was with Molly. On a few Sundays, Molly's cooking was done in a pit outdoors. The aroma got to all the neighbors, driving them nuts. They kept asking her to cook for them. Then one summer Jacob set up a tent up for her and she sold beef, chicken and pork cooked over the pit with corn and cornbread. Once winter came, people got irritated with the cold, and that convinced her to open a café. Then she became pregnant, and had a little girl. They surprised me by naming her Ida. That had to be the biggest honor I had ever been given. I learned to love her as I did Annabelle. My love for her worried them at first, but they learned she would never take the place of my own daughter. In having the baby, she had to let someone else run the café.

The café by itself made a decent amount of money. With having a twelve-year-old and a new baby girl, she sold the place. They made a good profit off the sale of the place. The two of them were doing great. It seemed everything couldn't do anything but go right for them. I was happy about that.

In fact one day Molly brought their new daughter over and told me, "You remember that day we talked about Edgar?"

"Yes," I answered, remembering well.

"I wish I could thank him; he made my man the hardest working and loving man a woman could ever have. As you might guess, money is not an issue with us. To me, I wouldn't mind going back to what we had in Virginia. The self-confidence and determination in him is something else."

"I'm happy for the two of you. Like I have said before, don't let him kill himself," I warned her.

"Trust me, I won't. You might not know it, but he's taking two days a week off so he can be with his children."

"I know, because Harold joins him and Little Joe," I reminded her.

"That's what I am thinking. I guess I found myself so happy this afternoon I forgot how close we are," she told me.

"I'm just glad you're so happy," I told her and then I let her go home. I had a few chores to do other than talk.

With my sons, they had a great time over those three summers. With Matt and Jacob both taking them fishing and hunting, I wasn't needed. In ways, they gained a father when Matt came to town, which was fine with me. A mother can only do so much with sons and I know it.

The biggest surprise came after the first snowfall. I was looking out the front window looking at Jacob's old place. He had just sold it to a man that wanted to run the stables. I found it strange not looking at it as being Jacob and Molly's place. Then I saw Matt running up the hill carrying a piece of paper in his hands.

Coming into the house he saw me, and asked, "Want to go west, Lady?"

"*What*," I asked, not sure if I heard him right. I then went on to ask further, "What do you mean go west? When? I have the boardinghouse and three boys."

"First I marry you. The boys have wanted me to for the past year. We sell the place, get a wagon, and move to northern California," he rattled off not waiting for me to say anything.

"Marry you?" I asked him. Then before he answered, I got to thinking he would make for a wonderful husband. Though he had similar traits to Edgar, he was gentler, unless he was madder than Edgar. We had several picnics and suppers, of course, and we did work well together as a family. Thinking about it, I was convinced I should marry him. Then I realized he was talking to me.

"...?" He said, but I didn't catch a word.

"Sorry, you startled me and I was thinking," I explained to him.

"Okay, I understand. I was saying, two weeks ago I got this post. It concerned a stagecoach robber. I looked at it wondering why I would get a copy of it. I saw the contacts name was Robert Duncan. Seeing the name, I almost messed my pants. I knew it had to be Robby, so I sent him a letter. I got the answer today," he said with tears in his eyes. Wiping tears from his eyes, he told me, "He wants to see me. I can't go, not without you and the boys."

"And why not?" I asked.

"I've been in love with you since I met you and Edgar," he confessed.

"In three years, you haven't said a word?" I reminded him.

"Well there are two reasons..." he stopped looking embarrassed.

"Knowing you, this should be good," I answered dying to hear his answer.

"The first is out of respect for Edgar. The second is the hardest," he told me stalling.

"You think Edgar wanted the boys not to have a father, or me to die a widower?" I asked him.

"I guess I know the answer is no. The second reason is the hardest and probably the main reason. I have never been with a woman."

I got to laughing so hard I began to cry. In seeing the hurt look on his face, I ran over, jumped into his lap, and told him, "*I'm yours.*"

"Really?" He asked shocked.

"Yes, yes, yes," I answered giving him a kiss. Then thinking what Edgar's reaction might be, I shared a simple thought with him, "Keep in mind, I might be a widow, but I'm only twenty-seven years old. Like, I'm not old and dead." I was sure he hadn't heard a word I said. I then realized I had said it more for me than him. Yes, I should remarry and share my life as well as my sons with someone.

"Whoopee," he replied looking as if he was going to faint.

I got off him and asked, "Are you all right, am I to heavy for you?"

"Just relieved," he answered getting up and taking me into his arms kissing me.

When he finally released me, it took awhile for me to catch my breath. Having all those years pinned up waiting for someone, it was hard to take all of it at once. I managed to ask him, "When are we leaving?"

"First, I want to marry you, then give you some time to get used to being Mrs. Duncan. We need to arrange the sale of this place. At the same time, it's whatever you would like to do with it. Then we wait for spring to come and then we head west," he answered, giving me a big smile.

"Sounds like a good plan," I answered him.

"May I tell the future Mrs. Duncan that I have kept a secret from her?"

"Oh what have you kept from me?" I asked.

"Mama, Jacob and Molly are coming," Mark announced.

"Just a minute," I answered him, looking out the window seeing them.

"I've made a fortune off my investments from my wages for all of these years, and so have you," he answered me with a smile.

Then, Jacob knocked on the door.

"*Just a minute,*" I shouted out.

"Ask them to give me a minute would you, Mark?" Matt asked him.

"Yes sir," Mark answered going to the door.

Matt pulled an envelope out of his pocket and handed it to me. As I took it, he told me, "I have had a talk with Jacob and Molly about asking you."

"You what?" I asked him as I opened the envelope. Inside, there was just a note that said:

Ida,

We wish the five of you the best. It's about time you found some happiness in life. We pray that you accept Matt's offer of his hand. We know he loves you very much. Good luck.

Since we started the business, there has been an account in your name at the bank. Since opening it, fifty percent of what we made has been deposited in that account in your name. Last count the total was in the $10,000.00 range.

Without yours and Edgar's support, we would not be where we are today. Take the money and live a good life. We will continue to make the deposits on the future income of our business.

Jacob

Note–If I haven't thanked you before, thanks for giving me your mother's name. It means a lot to me.

I fell back, not knowing what to say. I just stared at the letter and began to cry. The money its self was enough, but the reference to Mama was the nicest.

"Let them in, Mark," Matt told him.

"Well, did you accept?" Molly asked being the first to get it out.

Crying, the only effort I could do was shake my head yes. Then holding up the letter, I tried to say thanks, but I couldn't get it out. I fell back into the chair I had been sitting in.

As I fell back, Jacob helped me into it, saying, "As you can guess, we have lived and are living right fine without that money. We don't want to hear anything about you not accepting it, you understand."

Want to Go West Lady?

"This is too much for one day," I finally got out.

"Are you all right, Mama?" Harold asked coming into the parlor with John following right behind him.

"I'm fine," I answered him, giving him a smile.

"I was worried from the way you looked," he told me.

"You might not be, young man. I was told you have been having conversations with Matt about me marrying him?" I asked him.

I wanted to laugh, seeing him tense up. At the same time the grins on everyone else's faces.

"While we talked a couple of times, it was Mark's idea," he answered.

Matt shook his head agreeing with his statement. Seeing me, I turned to Mark making Harold wait for my response.

I asked Mark, "What do you have to say about it?"

"I thought it was a good idea," he answered with a quick and simply reply.

"What do the three of you think about me marring Matt?" I asked them praying they were for the idea.

Thankfully, all three thought it was a good idea. Matt looked weak and sat down. Jacob and Molly also looked relieved.

"Well, let me tell you three something," I began telling them but I thought I would drag it out some. After waiting a minute, I told them, "Matt is going to be your new father." The three boys jumped up and down with joy. First, they kissed me and ran to Matt. They didn't know to shake his hand or kiss him. In the end, they did both.

"All I have to say, it's been a wonderful day full of surprises from the people I love the most. Now what Edgar said was going to happen, Matt is going to finish, for I'm going west. The only problem is buying a wagon and making the journey."

"You think I would make my wife ride in one of those dusty wagons?" He asked with a smile. Then went on to add, "I wouldn't make her travel five to six weeks that way."

"How else would we get there?" I asked him.

"Where have you been? This is the day of railroads, woman Three days and we will be there."

"Guess I'm getting old. You're right, we could take the train. I hadn't thought about them," I answered with every muscle in my body saying thanks. Looking around at all the smiles on their faces I told them, "I still have men to feed tonight and I need to see the Reverend about a wedding come Saturday."

"Tonight, I'm buying dinner for everyone, boarders included," Jacob said looking at Molly getting her okay.

"Jacob," I said getting his attention." About your last name, your closeness to Mama made you a Morgan. You don't have to thank me, for what she did for you. That's between the two of you, with me doing what she couldn't."

"I don't care what you say. Thanks," he told me giving me a hug.

"And thanks to the two of you. Matt, the boys and I may need the money if we are going by train," I told them giving them what I hoped was an appreciative smile.

"We're going on a train?" John asked excitedly.

"Later, I'll explain it to you," I told him.

Somehow it seemed everyone in town learned of our wedding. When we arrived to meet the Reverend, we had to wade through people. Even Mrs. Abbott showed up giving us a wedding gift and her blessing. Somewhere I had changed from a "Hussy" to something respectable. I greeted her as if we had never had any problems. I was leaving, so I figured there wasn't any point in fighting with her.

Our reception by everyone was wonderful. I had to wait until after the wedding to find out what it was like. Afterwards, Jacob and Molly threw a party for us. Not having any idea they were going to do it changed some of my plans. Though I knew some of them could wait until the boys went to bed.

The party afterwards reminded me of the parties Mama would give when I was young. The major difference was I was the center of attention. The only problem was the rice thrown at us when we left the church. I knew Mrs. Abbott or someone had it in for me. Someone hit me in the eye with rice.

Come spring, we were ready to make our move. I had given my banker power to handle the house. If he could find someone just to run the boardinghouse that was fine with me. I was hoping he could, because my boarders had become friends of mine. I hated to toss them out into nowhere.

Matt had heard again from his brother Robby, or Robert as he went by then. He told him we would be arriving April 5, 1878. I'm not sure who was the most excited, Matt, the boys, or myself. The worst part was leaving Jacob and Molly. Still, they were pushing as much as my sons were. I found myself thinking a strange thought, wishing Edgar could see us off. I knew he was glad I was happy being Matt's wife.

The first of March finally arrived. We would arrive on the first leg of our trip on the third of April and change trains on the fourth. Then the afternoon of the fifth of April, Matt's brother would be meeting us at the train station in a small town in Northern California. Jacob, Molly and the kids showed up to send us off. Half of the town was behind them, which I wasn't expecting. There was even a band playing, making it a different way to leave town. I realized the send off was more for Matt than myself. He had been a good sheriff even though it was short-lived. Everyone loved him as much as I did.

As we sat in our seats, we were still waving at the crowd. Matt handed me a letter he had received from his brother Robby.

Dear Matt,

One item I have neglected to mention is Mark. A few years ago, Mark got to feeling bad about leaving the letter he left you. He felt guilty for what he had said. He felt guilty more for what he might have missed and for what I might have missed. In the end, he left me a similar note.

I don't have any idea where our brother is. I'm just looking forward to seeing you. At least two of us will be together.

Love, Robby

"Sorry," I told him looking at the letter.

"As he said, at least there will be the two of us, and you and the boys," he said correcting himself.

"Once we get there, do you have any plans? The last time we talked, you hadn't made up your mind." I asked him.

"Playing it by ear," he answered.

I waited to find out. I understood that not knowing his brother he might find it better to keep on going. If they got along, then we could look for a way to stay in the same area. Everything depended on them getting along.

We got off the train in Portland, Oregon. For some reason, we had to pick up our baggage and take it to another window. As we got to the baggage area, there was a baggage man with his back to us. Matt stopped midstep and watched the man.

"That's Mark," he said poking me in the ribs.

"His back is turned toward us," I pointed out to him.

"He looks the same as dad did and he's missing his left hand. There's a hook on it now, but it's him," he explained. Then taking a big breath, he called out, "Mark Duncan."

The man turned and began looking around. His eyes missed us, and he started looking around everywhere. Matt didn't wait and ran over to give him a hug.

Pushing Matt away, he looked at him with reality setting in and asked, "Matt?"

"None other than Mathew D. Duncan, the 'D' is for dumb," Matt answered him.

"When we were kids you were dumb, then I took the title away from you and I became dumb," he answered with a tear in his eye. Wiping the tear, he told Matt, "I'm so…I'm so sorry."

"No problem. These few years has given me time to grow up and get smarter than when I left you two," Matt told him. Then turning to the boys and I, he told his brother, "I would like to you to meet my wife and the boys."

"You have three boys?" Mark asked.

"A long story, but I knew their father. But this is my wife, Ida; this tall guy is Harold, then Mark, and John."

"A pleasure to meet you folks," he replied. Then looking around, he told us, "The boss is apt to get mad if he catches me not working. Where are you heading for?"

"We're off to see Robby," Matt told him.

"Another major mistake I made," he said shaking his head.

Matt gave him Robby's address and told him we would be seeing him soon. When we got on the train heading south toward California, Matt was almost as happy as the day he married me. Seeing Mark again erased away many memories for him.

Matt sum's up their life

Finally, my life was coming around to where I had always dreamt it should be. Laughing to myself, I figured the reconstruction of the south had finally hit me. From what I had heard, the south was still fighting things like poor land, lack of funds, discrimination and the Ku Klux Klan.

I, on the other hand, had a wonderful wife. She was the same woman I had used to measure every other woman by. She was a wife every man only dreamt about, and most never had. With her came some children I had learned to love as if they were my own. Since we married, I had met one of my brothers, and now I was going to see the second one Robby. My meeting him at the station is a story in itself. Even telling Ida of my feelings was difficult.

Walking up to my brother, there was no question of who he was. In seeing him, I felt as if we had never been parted. It was as if we were still back home with Dad, Peter, Samuel, Henry, Mark and the two of us. The only difference was Robby had a wife and two children. Of course, this foursome wasn't anything I could remember from our days at the homestead. They were a wonderful addition to the family. Father would have been proud to have Robbie's wife Helen and children as part of the family.

Ida, the boys and I bought a home in the same town that Robby lived. I even worked as a part-time deputy under Robby. He liked me working for him the best.

Ida and I also bought some property south of town. We built a little house for us, for the times we were there. I also planted a small orchard of pears, apples, oranges and a few date palms. To this day, we have lived in the same home for twenty plus years. We now have five grandchildren living not far from us.

Other than still breathing, there's not much to say. Having to grow up with the Civil War and the losses was hard on a person. Unlike me, Ida's life was hard for many years after the war, and it might still be hard? All I can say is it was a growing process for the two of us. At the same time, the past is the past.

The past twenty some years have been a touch of heaven. I see tomorrow being the same.

I'm glad we came west and I know many that did that feel the same way. For some, it was a mistake, others a blessing. It's a shame people such as Edgar didn't make it; we did.

Amen

From the author - This may be the end of my Grandfather's interview with the Duncan's, but it's not the end of their story. The following is what I learned much later from Ida's own diary, with a note from their son.

What wasn't said, from Ida's diary?
(And a note from their son)

Note from the author–This chapter are excerpts from Ida's diary her relatives, let me take notes from. As with most, Ida did not make entries every day. At the same time, some entries are of no interest, so I have not included them.

I had so much fun talking to that nice young man that interviewed Matt and I. Though some of the memories, I could have done without remembering. On the other hand, it might help him full fill his dream of becoming a reporter. As he learned, Matt and I have had our share of our own dreams. With that thought, I feel I'm living a dream now, and will continue living it. In meeting this young man, I wished Matt had been more open with him. There is so much more to Matt than what he let's others know. Maybe some day, I'll get in touch with that young man, and fill him in on what Matt didn't tell him.

"Why didn't you tell that nice young man, about our life here?" I asked Matt.

"He said he was interested in hearing about our move west. It's bad enough explaining to people circling wagons on a wagon train wasn't done to protect one from Indians. The reason was really to corral the horses and oxen," Matt answered me.

"But…?" I began to ask knowing there was no sense in going any further.

Looking at Matt in the other chair, I find him smiling at me. The only other person that ever loved me as Matt does was Edgar. Yet, in my heart, I have always felt Edgar's love was more of a brother than

Want to Go West Lady?

a husband's. Part of that might have been from his resentment of what he had lost in the war. However, most of it was with having grown up together. Until marrying Matt, I never thought to ask Edgar any questions relating to our feelings. All I can tell anyone is he was devoted to our children and me. At the same time, there was something inside I never really got to know. In many ways, Matt and Edgar are alike. Both are strong, self-sufficient, dedicated, and ran there lives by their own rules. Then thinking about my sons, I realize there is a difference. Though both Edgar and Matt are both hard workers, Matt takes time for the boys. It wasn't that Edgar didn't love the boys, he just didn't have the time for them very often. Matt, on the other hand, makes time for them. This little difference is probably why the boys took to him so easily.

Again, looking at Matt, I find myself smiling thinking of his proposal to me. His asking me, "Want to go west, lady," is not a usual type of a proposal but it was effective. Still I knew what he meant.

We left Boise City on March 31, 1878. As we left the station, I gave the past twelve plus years a lot of thought. In 1865, still at the age of fifteen, I was married to Edgar. The following five years I had a child every year Harold, Mark, Luke, John, and Annabelle. By 1873, Annabelle was two and we headed west. Our best friends Jacob and Molly and their son, Little Joe, went west with us. By the time we got to Boise City, I had lost Edgar my husband, Luke my son and Annabelle my daughter.

Sitting there watching trees go by the train window, many thoughts go through my head. I find myself thinking that I'm just a few months from my twenty-eighth birthday, with a new husband, and sons eleven, ten, and nine. The five of us are on a train heading for Portland, Oregon. From there we would be transferring to another train to some little town in Northern California, after an overnight stay on April 3. We are to arrive at our final destination on April 5.

After a few days on the train, I feel comfortable with the trip. Every one of us was looking forward to getting to Portland and ready to start over. Then looking up I see Harold coming down the aisle towards me.

Harold sat beside me, and told me, "This is a lot better than it was in the wagon riding."

"Mabel's trying to find you," Mark tells Harold as he comes up to us.

"Who's Mabel?" Matt asked Harold with a grin.

With a red face, Harold answers, "A girl I met in the other car."

"*Oh*," I comment. I found both the reference to our wagon trip to Boise City and Harold meeting a girl interesting. Thinking about it, I realize Harold is at the age of being interested in girls. For a second, I wonder what it's going to be like being a grandmother. That thought sends chills up my spine and I put it out of my mind.

"I bet there's some good fish in that stream," John mentions to Matt.

"I think I would rather be down there fishing than sitting here," Matt returned and then he added, "Maybe when we get to California, we can go fishing."

"Harold's got a girlfriend," Mark tells us, then running off to keep from being hit by his brother.

Getting up, Harold asks his two brothers, "Lets go for a walk?"

"All right," the other two answered getting up also.

"Harold wants to see his girlfriend," Mark whispers into my ears as he passes me.

"They don't seem bored," I said commenting to Matt.

"It doesn't look that way," Matt said with a chuckle. I notice he also has a grin, as he winks at me.

"I guess not," I replied as I watched the boys go down the aisle.

"This seat is more uncomfortable than my old mare was on a long ride," Matt said shifting his body in the seat.

"Are we getting old?" I asked, only get a forced smile from him.

I found myself feeling uncomfortable in my seat. I knew it was time to get up and move around a little. After two nights sleeping in these seats, I can tell you they are not that comfortable. I also find it hard not to curl up to Matt's back. I find myself thinking about the first thing we might do when we get to Portland. I decide I might try to talk Matt into sleeping away a day or two to make up for the loss.

Setting a on a train for days isn't the only bad thing. The food isn't all that good either. Still, as Harold pointed out, it's better than the dried beef on the trip by wagon.

"Writing a book?" Matt asked. He had the look of being bored out of his mind, doing nothing.

"I've been keeping a diary since I could write. What have you been thinking about?" I asked him as I showed him my diary.

"I'm looking forward to seeing Robby. It's been what…fourteen or fifteen years? I just wish Mark were around. It would be fun to see both of them," Matt told me. He raised his book up and shrugs as if he can't get interested in it.

"You found Robby. Keep trying, you'll find Mark. Who knows, Robby might know where he is," I offered him as hope.

I let him go on with his reading and watched the scenery go by. I found the view of the mountain to be beautiful. I even saw some wildlife. Watching them, I wished the train could stop so I could have watched them a little longer.

Feeling the way I did, I got up to take a walk. In getting up, I told Matt, "I need to walk off some cramps."

"Walk off a few for me also," he responded looking back out the window.

In walking through the cars, I found Harold sitting with his little friend. When he saw me, he got a funny look on his face. Without saying anything, he moved away from his new little friend and blushed. I was nice and didn't say anything, but walked right past them.

Waking up the last morning, we knew we were going to arrive in Portland soon. All of us almost wore the windowsills out trying to see Portland coming up. Finally getting cramps from leaning over each other the boys gave up. With Harold in the lead, I knew he was going to find his little friend. Finally the Conductor announced we would be in at Portland station in an hour. I went to get the boys. I found Harold sitting with his little friend. His brothers weren't to far off making it easy on me. Pointing toward our seats, they went back to where Matt was. Harold walked back with me. As I came back by the little girl,

I stopped to talk to her. Harold seemed to freeze where he was, and turned red when I stopped.

"Hi Mabel, I'm Harold's mother," I said introducing myself to the little girl. I have to admit my son has good taste; she was a cute little girl.

"Nice to meet you," Mabel answered while Harold was squirming.

"We had better get everything ready for when we arrive," I told Harold. "Then you can come back and visit some more," I told my son.

"Are you going to Portland or are you going somewhere further?" I asked Mabel.

"We're leaving for Sacramento tomorrow," she answered.

"Then I guess Harold will be seeing you tomorrow then," I told her with a smile.

As I walked back to our seats with my son behind me, I thought how young love was so sweet. I wanted to warn my son though there were dangers. Then realizing how young he was, I decided Matt could do it later.

"I hope what we are doing is right," Matt said as I sat down.

"We are" I told him, and then turning to the boys, I told them, "Put everything away now."

In getting off the train, Matt was irritated that we had to claim our baggage. I was glad, so I could take a bath and get a clean change of clothes on my body. It wasn't that I wasn't use to being dirty, but sweaty was something different.

Going to the baggage department, Matt saw an employee with his back to us.

Matt told me sounding a little excited, "That's Mark."

"How can you tell, his back is to us?" I asked him.

"He looks like father did from the back, and he's missing a hand." He explained. Not waiting for me to say anything, he ran ahead calling out, "Mark Duncan."

Mark turned looking confused, and realized it must have been Matt calling out to him. Then something happened, I knew I wouldn't ever tell Matt. Mark gave me a look that gave me a feeling as if bugs were crawling all over my body. To tell the truth, looking at the man, I wanted to get sick. The boys even looked up at me, giving me a funny look. Yes, he was dirty, but he was working, so it could be understood. It wasn't the dirt, that bothered me, but the way he carried himself, the way he stared at me and acted that bothered me.

The boys and I continued to go over to where Matt and his brother were and Matt introduced us. I was happy for Matt having found his other brother. At the same time, I felt bad about my feelings I had about him. I prayed my first impression of him was wrong. I told myself, "You could be wrong."

Later that evening, Matt told me, "I hate to say it, but something's wrong with Mark. It's as if he's not quite right, or he isn't all there, you know what I mean?"

I told him, "It's been years since you have seen him. First appearances are not always the one you want to judge."

"I hope you're right," he answered as he got ready for bed.

Though I would have liked to have stayed in Portland for another day or two, I knew we couldn't. Getting up early the next morning, I got the boys something to eat. We then headed for the train station, to head south to California. Though that was going to be our final destination, seeing Robby was more important to Matt.

I turn to my sons and told them, "Remember today. It is April 5, 1878, and we are now in California. We should be pulling into the station any minute now." Sitting back, I prayed Robby isn't like Mark. *If he is, should I be married to Matt*, I asked myself? With brothers that are alike, it made me wonder.

Getting off the train it wasn't difficult to spot Robby. He was wearing a badge and a woman was beside him, with a baby in her arms and a little boy beside them. I have to admit, the four of them were easy to like. It didn't take long, and he introduced his wife to us.

"Matt, Ida, this is my wife Helen," Robby said with a smile.

"I find it hard to think of you as being old enough to be married. A pleasure to meet you, Helen," Matt told Robby's wife.

"A pleasure," I extended to her.

"A pleasure to meet the five of you also. Robby has been worried for years something had happened to his brother in the war," Helen said.

Though we talked for a long time, we knew there was more to learn of each other. I personally found it interesting Robby was a lawman. Matt had also worn a badge a number of times. As it turned out, the two brothers had similar jobs. I was also glad that Robby wasn't like his brother Mark. I also got the feeling Matt might be right about something being wrong with Mark.

Later the evening of our arrival, we found out that Robby had passed his law exams. We also learned he had sent out applications to different cities, applying for positions as prosecuting attorneys. He also hired Matt as a part-time deputy.

Before doing anything important, we relaxed a few days. Then it was time, and the boys are enrolled in school. We also bought a home and furniture. It didn't take long to sign the papers on the house and we were moving in.

There was one problem with our new home. The well had caved in, and we needed a new one. It took Matt a little longer to dig the well than what he thought it would. The well ended being eight feet across and forty-eight feet deep. He lined it with stones to keep the sides from falling in. He finished them just in time for the rise of the water table.

The well wasn't the only thing wrong with the place. However, we didn't buy the place for the living quarters. We bought the property because of its location, an orchard, and the scenery. Matt fell in love with it, because it reminded him of his father's place. The living quarters or house was a dugout type of place. I'm not too fond of the dugout house, but it's better than a tent I guess.

"It's not going to be our permanent place. We'll get a place in town for awhile or at least until we build a house," Matt told the boys and me.

We had only been in the area but a few weeks, and we started to get mail. I got a letter from Molly and she said they missed us. She also said everything was going well.

"I got a letter from Molly," I told Matt when he got home.

"Anything interesting happening back there?" he asked.

"She didn't say anything, other than everything was all right and they miss us," I told him.

"I need to go up and see Mark. Do you want to come with me?" he asked me.

"It might be better if you go alone. The two of you have a lot of catching up to do," I answered him. From my first visit, I really didn't feel comfortable seeing the man. I did feel too many hard feelings had festered between them. Knowing how Matt felt, I knew it might be wise for him to go alone.

"I might be gone for a couple of weeks," he told me.

"The boys and I can make it alone. If we have any problems, we can go to Robby," I assured him. I didn't understand why he had to be gone so long, but I wasn't too worried. He knew what he had to do, and I was comfortable with it. If nothing else, it would give the two of them time, to get to know each other.

A little over two weeks had gone by, and Matt finally got home. He looks tired. In fact, he looked like he had fought a war while he was gone. He hardly said hello or gave me a kiss for the first three hours he was back.

He finally told me as we went to bed, "Mark got himself into trouble, and I got him out of it."

As was the case with Matt as with Edgar, nothing else was said. After a few times of things like this, I asked him why he never went into detail. He always answered, "No need to make you worry. I don't want you to grow wrinkles over something I can handle." With that knowledge, I went to bed that night not asking him anything.

I found myself laughing looking at my husband and how hard he has been working Matt had only worked a total of nine days in the last few months. He's happy about it because it gives him time to work on the orchard. I couldn't see much having being completed. Then if he's happy, I am.

One afternoon, when Matt came home, I told him, "I met with the women from the church and we are planning a church social. Wouldn't Mama be proud of me?"

"She would be proud of you anyway," he told me, giving me a kiss, and then he asked, "What are we raising money for this time?"

"That was nice of you to say. We think the church could use some paint," I answered letting him go.

"Let's go out and check out the orchard this weekend? Then you girls can talk me out of some money. I might even find time to do some painting for you," he suggested.

"I guess we can do that. The boys don't have anything going on that I know of," I answered as I picked up some dirty clothes.

"You realize I want to plant some more trees this fall don't you?" he reminded me.

"I would think so. The dozen or so trees, isn't going to give us enough money to make it worth our while." I told him, wondering when he was going to do it.

That following weekend we were out at the orchard. The boys were happy, because they could go hunting with Matt. Again, we stayed in Matt's dugout while we are out there. I hadn't gotten used to it but I put up with it. To me it was terrible, even if it did keep the weather off us; it's damp, dingy and just terrible. It reminds me of the place Mama and I had lived in while we were in Richmond. The only thing good is the well.

When Matt had first dug the well, the water was muddy. Not that I was surprised, having been part of digging a well a couple of times. I did wonder if it was going to ever clear up though, because they didn't always clear up. When we got back to the place, the mud had cleared from the water; it tasted good.

Getting back to town Sunday, we found a note on our door. The note was from Robby inviting us to supper. Not feeling like cooking we went to Robby's for supper. After we ate, Matt and his brother went outside and talked a long time. When they came in, nothing was said.

Still the four kids had fun playing and Robby's wife Helen and I got to know each other a little better.

In bed that night, Matt told me Robby had told him; Mark did have problems. In checking him out, Robby had heard from several cities that they had files on their brother. These files were on a number of offenses Mark had committed. Again, Matt didn't go into details, but I knew he wasn't happy.

The school year came to an end with the boys getting good grades. They also had taken on part time jobs to earn money for their future. At the end of the summer, everyone was happy that we had made the move. I wasn't too happy knowing winter was coming. I had gotten used to the rainy weather, but I wasn't looking forward to the snow. It wasn't that I hadn't lived in snow; I just didn't like it. Needless to say we weren't living on the orchard yet. All summer, Matt always had something else to do. Though we did go out to it occasionally, it didn't seem as if anything was done. Then when harvest time came, Matt arranged for someone else to pick the crop.

Knowing Matt's history as a lawman, it was funny when he came home one afternoon. As he walked through the he had the biggest smile on his face I had seen for weeks.

He told me, "I made an arrest this afternoon."

"You mean after six months of wearing a badge something happened? Who did you arrest, the town drunk?" I asked him.

"It seems there was a little marital dispute," he answered with a smile.

I told him, "You have arrested your first person. The boys' grades were among the highest in their classes. All three of them have settled in nicely. We own a little orchard…how much more could we ask for?"

As far as the job went, the next day Matt had more fun. He was asked to take care of a drunk being the only deputy available. Matt said the hardest part of taking him in was getting him into the wagon to haul him to jail. Over the next few weeks, Matt finally had been going out to the orchard to plant the trees he had bought. He came home from one trip out there, smiling from head to toe. He was also covered in dirt from head to toe.

He told me coming in, "The last tree is planted. I don't have to worry about not getting them in before the first frost and killing them off."

Again, Robby invited us over for dinner. Something told me this wasn't just a family get together. As we entered his place, everyone was smiling.

Robby announced, "I got an offer to start as a law clerk in Los Angeles. I have to say, the pay is quite a lot better than I'm making now as sheriff."

Matt warned him, "Don't forget difference in the cost of living."

Robby smiled, and told us, "I'm not worried. I should be getting an increase after a while."

Knowing how he felt, I told him, "We both are happy for the two of you and maybe we will come to visit occasionally.

"When do you start?" Matt asked his brother.

"The first of the month," Robby answered, then turning to his wife, he added, "It will be our first Christmas without snow. In fact, I might take the children swimming, if it isn't to cold."

The end of November, they appointed Matt temporary sheriff until another one could be hired. Luckily, he only had to hold the position for a couple of weeks, when the town had found a replacement for Robby. Matt confirmed we are going down to visit Robby soon.

After a few weeks, Helen wrote they were doing fine. Robby thinks the job is different from what he thought it would be. He still planned to keep it long enough so he could actually try some cases. He was going to keep with it, until he could open his own law office. She also sent their love and they are looking forward to seeing us Christmas.

After reading the letter for himself, Matt asked me, "When did you tell her we were coming down for Christmas?"

"I only said we would come down occasionally, I didn't say when, I thought you might have," I told him.

"I never said anything…at least I don't remember saying anything. Would you like to?" he asked.

"The boy's might enjoy it and they are our only family, other than Mark," I told him. Hearing me mention Mark, I got a funny look from my husband.

With another train trip we went down to Los Angeles for ten days. We had a nice visit with them, and Robby seemed happy with his job. Our boys were unhappy about us not going swimming though.

I wasn't until May, we went out to the orchard, and Matt said that half the fruit trees were dying. He debated with himself about planting any more. We have so little time to care for them, I don't think it's going to be worth it. At the same time, if we were to move, we would have to take the boys out of school. Having grown up in the country as Matt had, we felt it wasn't fair to the boys.

Matt came home one afternoon, and told me, "I got a message from the sheriff's office that Mark's is in trouble again. This time he's in Seattle."

"So you're telling me you are going to be gone awhile again?" I asked him. This time like a few others, he didn't ask if I wanted to go with him. He knew my answer would be no, if for no other reason than the boys.

"Yes. As before, I don't know when I'll be back," he told me, looking tired.

"I'm sorry, darling. When are you going to leave, tomorrow morning?" I asked him.

"Thanks. I'll check with the office first, but yes. I'll take the early train and be there tomorrow afternoon," he answered.

Matt finally got home. The boys weren't home so Matt had no problem talking to me when he came in.

"Where are the boys?" he asked as he came in.

"At the library working on some papers or something," I told him.

"Oh," he returned as he sat down.

He told me, "There's definitely something wrong with Mark."

"What?" I asked.

Hesitating a little, he answers, "Take too long to tell you. I just wish I knew how I could help him. Let's just say, I don't think I can do anything for him. I have about run out of ideas."

"He could sleep in the spare bedroom, if you think having him here would help," I offered as I kicked myself.

"I don't think that would work. I think he's another casualty of the war," he answered.

"How's that? His hand?" I asked.

"Yes. When he came home, I had a feeling he wasn't the same kid I grew up with," he answered.

Matt wouldn't talk anymore about his brother Mark. I got the feeling he wished he had never found his brother. I didn't know what he was keeping from me, but I appreciated his need to help his brother. I began to worry, because it seemed Matt was being dragged down more and more. I wished there was something I could do to help. Then to help, he would have to tell me what was going on.

The first of October, I got a letter from Molly. I was opening it up when Matt walked in.

"Who from?" he asked.

Reading it quickly I answered, "Good news, Molly says we might be seeing them soon."

"It'll be good to see Jacob again. I have some bad news," he replied.

The bad news was he had to chase down Mark again. I hoped he wasn't going to be gone as long as he was last time. Being a mother of three boys can make one old not having your husband around. They have more things going on than I can keep up with by myself. Thinking to myself, I said, "Thank God, Harold is graduating next year." He had been accepted to college. He wanted to follow his Uncle Robbie's example and become a lawyer.

Matt got home quicker than I expected. He told me, "It wasn't anything."

I wished he would tell me what the problems were that Mark kept getting into.

I told him, "I received a letter from Helen yesterday. She said Robby is now a prosecuting attorney. She also said they will see us for Christmas this year."

June of 1880 came around and things were a little easier for us. Harold had graduated and was going to work as an office boy at Matt's attorney's office until he started school. I figured it would be good experience for him. It would also give him a better idea what it was going to be like being a lawyer rather than just knowing his uncle was one.

Seeing the boys grow up, Matt had been asking about us having another child. I understood his need for a child of his own. At the same time, I knew what it would mean. I told him I didn't think I could handle a newborn at my age. I reminded him in a few years the boys will be starting a family, having their own children. He could play with all the grandchildren then. I knew he was disappointed, but he seemed to understand.

Mark hasn't decided what he wants to do. I reminded him he had another year in general school, so there was time yet. John, on the other hand, wanted to be a doctor.

Come October, we had a surprise at our front door. There was a knock on the door one afternoon. Our housekeeper answered it. To my surprise, Jacob and Molly with little Ida were standing there. Little Joe stayed at home to take care of a cabinet shop he and Jacob had started for him. Still, Ida was with them and she sure had grown.

We had a good dinner. Jacob rubbed it in that it was like the old times. The only difference was he was sitting at the main table. Still, I had a housekeeper and a cook, just like Mama. Matt was nice to remind us how many years had gone by since then.

During supper, Jacob announced they had sold the business. After adding another fifty products, the business had taken off. He offered me a check with more zeros than I care to try to count. We refused most of the money, electing to put it into a fund for the five children, theirs and ours.

It was lucky they came when they did. The following day, Matt was going off to help Mark out again. Robby had told him to forget they had a brother. Matt won't have anything to do with the idea. He said he wouldn't be gone more than three days. Jacob said he would be staying until he got back. Then they were going to see the country, and were thinking about going to Europe.

Again, I was lucky and Matt came home a few days after he left. He came into the kitchen and told me, "We don't have to worry about Mark for awhile. He's going to be in jail for a few years this time."

"I can't say I'm unhappy, but it's still a shame," I told him, as I got a drink of water.

I had to laugh, it took Matt until August of 1881 to get the message I didn't like the dugout. Finally understanding, he had a little house built near the orchard. He never told me about it until I saw the place. He even provided it with simple furniture and everything needed to live in it. I was surprised to learn a neighbor's wife set the place up for Matt. Her husband even had a laugh, saying, "She was able to spend money and not touch our own."

With two of the boys down in San Francisco visiting with their brother, Matt and I went to the orchard. I was hesitant thinking of the dugout, but I was willing to suffer through it for Matt. What I found made me so happy I almost cried.

The following morning, I was even more surprised. Standing at the kitchen window, I saw Mark walking down the road towards the house. With a bundle hanging from his hooked hand over his shoulder, as he got closer I could see him wearing a smile.

"*Matt, your brother Mark is coming this way,*" I shouted out to Matt.

"What?" he asked running into the kitchen. Looking out the window, he sees his brother and he says, "Good."

He then goes out onto the porch; he waited for his brother. He didn't bother to close the door, so I was able to see and hear everything. From what I could see, Matt was tense.

"Good morning, brother," Mark said in greeting him.

"Good morning, what are you doing here?" Matt asked him.

"Looking for a new start," he answered. Then setting his bundle down he added, "I'm on my way to Frisco, thought I would stop and visit for a few days."

"Sounds fair, I guess. Maybe you can help around here while you're here," Matt told him, suggesting for him to come inside.

"Then it's settled," Mark said with a grin looking toward the house.

"You mind if Mark stays a few days?" Matt asked me.

"Of course not," I answered biting my lip.

"You can have this room," Matt said showing him where to go.

Settled in, I found it hard to be in the same room with Mark. He kept staring at me, giving me a funny feeling. Still after two days, there hadn't been any problems. The only problem was Matt being on edge. I wondered what was bothering him. The two of them were getting along just fine.

The morning of the third day, I could hardly stand Matt. He was almost worse than Mark's stares. I suggested that he get out of the house and go for a walk. He told his brother he was going to do some shooting. While he was gone, maybe he could clean out the stalls.

"I can handle that," Mark told him, giving him a big grin. As he was going out the door, he told Matt, "Good hunting."

Shortly afterwards, Matt grabbed his rifle. Heading for the door, he told me, "I won't be gone long." Then giving me a kiss, he headed out through the orchard.

I finished the dishes and made up the beds. Having everything done, I decided to sit on the porch and catch up on some sewing. As I sat in the chair, I could see Mark standing, staring at me. I decided that he wasn't going to chase me away; this was my house not his. I sat there and let him stare at me.

Then out of the corner of my eye, I saw him coming towards me. I looked around in hopes of seeing Matt, but I didn't see him.

"Thought I would get a drink," Mark told me.

"It is warming up. I'll get you a drink," I offered as I set my sewing down. Turning to go into the house, he lunged for me.

I found myself pinned between him and the wall of the house. He laid the hook of his hand across my throat, with the point digging into me.

He asked me, in a guttural tone of voice, "What is it that you have that keeps my brother happy."

Then with the wrist of his hooked hand, he pushed up on my chin. I found myself grasping at him, not being able to get a good swing or hold of him. I did scratch his face but it didn't stop him. I felt his other hand reaching under my dress, going up between my legs. I was so scared I couldn't get a scream out. As I continued to fight him off, I heard Matt's voice.

"Mark, let her down," Matt told him. Not getting any response from Mark, he fired one shot at him.

Startled, Mark feeling the bullet hit his shoulder, he removed the hook from my throat, turning toward his brother. As he fell backwards with a shocked look, he fell over the banister of the porch and hit his head on a rock. Lying on the ground, blood ran from his head freely. It didn't take a doctor, to see he was dead. Later, Matt said I screamed, but I don't remember it.

Matt grabbed me and held me in his arms without saying anything at first. Then letting me go, he told me, "I shouldn't have allowed him to be with you alone." Then walking over to his brother's body, he told him, "Robby said you were no good. I guess he was right. Now I won't have to pay off anymore of your victims."

Not saying anything more, Matt walked over to the barn and got a shovel. Even then, he didn't ask for help but drug his brother's body off behind the barn. As I watched, I shook harder than I could ever remember shaking. I wasn't sure if it had been a nightmare or if it had really happened. All I knew was I couldn't stop shaking.

When he came back, I waited for him to say something. I told him, "I would've helped."

"He was my brother. He violated you as he has done others too often. With him being my brother, it was my duty to take care of the problem," he told me, as he took me into his arms.

"What do we do now?" I asked him.

"Let the ants eat him," Matt answered.

I knew no one around would have thought a rifle shot was anything to worry about. At the same time, no one would know or care if Matt came here or not. In the end, what was going to happen, the ants ate him. From that time on, we never discussed anything about Mark, other than he died an accidental death. I know Matt's action was out of fear of me being hurt and he still had a lot of resentment built up in him. I also know if he could have thought of any other way of handling the situation, he would have. I can honestly say I love him as no other could.

On March 1, 1906, we headed for San Francisco to visit with Harold for a few weeks. Our stay lasted a little longer than we had originally planned. It took a little effort to separate Matt from the grandchildren. I now wonder if I should have had a child by him. I tell myself as I'm thinking, *It's too late now*.

Looking at the calendar in Harold's kitchen and seeing what the date is, I asked Matt, "Do you realize what day it is?"

"No idea. The only thing I know is this little girl likes her Grandfather," he answered.

"All I know is you're the only one that can get her to stop crying," Harold's wife Betty tells Matt.

"Don't encourage him. She has two uncles waiting for us to come see them. That's not counting Robby," I told her with a smile.

"What is the date?" Matt finally asked.

"April 18," I answered him.

"I guess your Grandmother is trying to tell me something," Matt tells our little granddaughter Molly.

"Sounds like you're leaving," Harold said coming into the kitchen.

"Think so. You know how it is with wives," Matt answered.

"We've only been here three weeks longer than planned," I reminded him.

"I guess we had better take the first train out in the morning," Matt suggested.

"I'm sorry, but that will mean going in tonight," Betty said looking questioning at us.

"We can get a room," I offered as a suggestion.

"You don't have to worry about the two of us, we come from rugged stock," Matt added, handing Molly to her mother.

We had a quick bite, and Harold drove us up to the train station. With having got there so late at night we decided to sit up and wait for the train rather than getting a room. The night went by pretty fast with meeting that young man about our move coming west. I wondered if he realized there was something Matt didn't want him or anyone else to know. This is why he didn't say much about living in Northern California. Otherwise, in a condensed manner what he said was true. We now have three college graduated sons happily married and five grand children.

In writing this on a separate page, I will send it to the young man. I hope I remember to send it and that he gets it. I'm sure he'll appreciate it.

In another hand, there is another entry:

April 18, 1906 at 5:12 AM, San Francisco was to fall in ruins because of an earthquake.

This diary was found in mama's hands, five days after the earthquake hit. My father/stepfather was laying over her as if he was trying to protect her. I have no idea if mama loved Matt more than he did her, but they loved each other. If they had to go, it was best that they went together. Many will miss the two of them, but not as much as myself.

Having read this diary, I know what father did and that mama loved my real father. Not that I approve of what Matt did but he didn't really kill him, I also understand why. May God forgive him and take care of them.

I love them both,
Harold